COSMIC
ENCOUNTER

COSMIC ENCOUNTER

A. E. VAN VOGT

Carroll & Graf Publishers, Inc.
New York

All of the characters in this book are fictitious, and any resemblance to actual persons, living or dead, is purely coincidental.

Published by arrangement with Doubleday, a division of Bantam Doubleday Dell Publishing Group, Inc.

First Carroll & Graf edition 1990

Carroll & Graf Publishers, Inc.
260 Fifth Avenue
New York, NY 10001

ISBN: 0-88184-677-5

Manufactured in the United States of America

To Lydia, my beautiful wife

1

The falling object began to impinge on earth time and to be in an earth location.

Time: 1704 A.D.

Place: the sky above the Caribbean on one of those hot, sticky afternoons.

In the water below was a sailing craft with white sails full-set, reflecting a glaring sun. At first the vessel seemed a small, flickering dot on a dark, watery vastness. If it moved, if its breeze-filled sails were actually propelling it, that was not visible at any of the finitely few number of moments that the object was in process of falling from the outer edge of the atmosphere down to the waves.

With so many sun reflections flashing everywhere, the moisture content of the lower portion of that atmosphere was not at dew point anywhere along the line of fall. But on the sail craft men had sought the shade beneath the big sails on the side away from the hurtling thing from space. There they lay or sat, gasping and suffering from that heavy mix of heat and moisture. Thus, the falling space vessel was seen only by pirate seaman Figarty, a small, agile type with one of those rat faces, and like most rats not very bright.

For a semi-petrified period of about seven seconds,

Figarty watched the tumbling object. By the end of that
seven seconds an entire series of stimuli had run their
courses through his vicious little brain. The rapid feedback
between mid-brain and cerebral cortex, normally useful
even to a small mind, in this instance evoked progressively
fewer symbols. So swiftly thought ceased. The formless
blankness from the lower brain took over.

Simultaneously, the motor centers responded with what,
when all else failed, was the time-tried mechanism of
simple get-the-hell-away-and-start-screaming.

Outwardly, then, the visible action was: he turned from
the stern railing and started forward at running speed. In
any less blank mental condition, even he would have
realized the madness of that.

The deck of the pirate vessel was not in good condition.
In the course of weathering in sun and spray, multi-millions
of the tracheid cells that made up the planks had lost their
firmness. Even in a mild wind, the ocean waves washed
over the ship; and the tropical heat of daytime did the rest.
These two intense elements did their daily passion to wood
that should have been painted oftener. But—as Captain
Fletcher had remarked more than once in his driest voice,
"Who can get a pirate crew to do all the work that has to
be done on a ship?" As a consequence, the planks were
warped and even sprung in places.

Each twist in that wood and each pitted, dead tracheid
cell offered to passers-by a steady signal: Walk carefully,
particularly if barefooted. Here are killer splinters for the
unwary, and in addition a crushed toe for the hurried; and
for the genuinely impatient even if shod, a destroying slash
for those handsome boots.

In his mad run from the forward bow, Figarty was
lucky. Nothing broke. Nothing tore. He simply and fero-
ciously stubbed his toe. The pain was absolutely hideous;
but, as he would presently learn, it would go away.

Nevertheless, during those decisive minutes he gave an
almost miraculous performance of dancing about on his
left foot while clutching the right with first one hand and

then the other. As he did so, he uttered earthy oaths and simultaneously pointed (with one hand and then the other) at the falling object in the sky and yelled for an audience to come and see.

The mad squalling disrupted the peaceful progress of the vessel. The racket penetrated the remotest cabins. The first to arrive were several amazed crew members. They stared at the cursing, bouncing Figarty. First Mate Shradd rounded the nearest mast and stopped. Those always-narrowed dark eyes of his widened a little as he watched Figarty's gyrations and listened to his screaming, incomprehensible words. Like the others, he did not immediately notice that the little rat's flailing arms were trying to point a direction.

During those vital moments, the glittering object fell down and down, grew large, acquired a distinct oval shape, and then plunged into the ocean at the very edge of the horizon. At that distance, it was instantly hard to see. And, when it swiftly sank beneath the waves, it became rapidly invisible.

Thereupon, at almost the exact instant that the ship's lean captain strode onto the scene, the first mate's eyes narrowed to slits. With a curse, he leaped forward and grabbed Figarty. "What'd you see? What're you sayin', you fool?"

At the instant of being grabbed, Figarty ceased his yelling and his scrabbling. And so the words of the first mate projected clear and loud on the hot, sticky afternoon air. They struck the large group of men that had gathered by this time; and they must have had a false implication. A tremor of anxiety was evoked from every man there. They twisted. They turned. They looked uneasy. It was the anxiety that can come swiftly to a pirate crew, each of whom knew his fate if he were ever caught.

Naturally, nothing was in view, and that was unfortunate —for Figarty. These were violent men. For a minute, now, they had felt threatened. No thinkers, they; so they had no way of dealing with their feelings, as evoked by that extreme threat, except by expressing them.

Captain Fletcher's gaze glided over the faces in front of him with a swift knowing look. Every face under its beard or hair fuzz showed a reaction: in some the flush of rage, in others a pallor, and still others seemed to have swelled out or contracted in a twisted way. The awareness in Fletcher was that it would take a while for so much deadly emotion to subside.

Even as he had that realization, a big brute of a man, known only as Big Head Evans, gave Figarty a kick. The words he spoke, as he lashed out with his foot, were the London gutter equivalent of "I'll-teach-you-to-play-a-trick."

What Big Head discovered in that instant, if he did not already know it—or had forgotten—was that it is not easy to corner a rat; or, if you have him cornered, to make contact with him. Figarty did that swift, evasive motion. The kick caught him a glancing blow on the baggy part of the trousers only on his right leg. And it affected him because he was inside the trousers. No pain. But the trousers were flung about three feet, and Figarty along with them, screaming every millimeter of the way.

The wiry little man landed like a clawing, squealing animal. Even before he struck the deck, his legs were flailing, and his body ducking and twisting. And as he hit, he moved. Another man, whose blood vessels stood out on his face like purple cords, made a grab at him. Missed . . . Figarty was already gone, darting, twisting, screeching.

Other men tried to catch him, or shove him; and what might have happened with so many suddenly against one was a deadly, unsolved question. Except at that moment there was a baritone voice saying something. It was the voice of the captain.

According to the historical records of the pirates of that period, Captain Nathan Fletcher was a gentleman gone bad. Fletcher had a different view of cause and destiny. A thoroughly alienated male, he sometimes permitted his men to murder an offending crew member, and sometimes he didn't.

At the moment, he had a strictly practical reason for

interfering. He was puzzled. Something had happened; and since, unknown to the crew, the pirate vessel was lying in wait for a specific British craft, he wanted very much to find out what Figarty thought he had seen.

He was a trained orator. His voice at full roar could overwhelm a huge audience; and he had used it for that purpose many times when he was in England trying to fit into the endless madnesses of being politically in and then being politically out.

What he roared was, "Leave him alone. I want to question him."

Both meanings reached into minds that were almost always in a fog. The first sentence was a "don't." By itself, it slowed men who had spent a lifetime either obeying orders or resisting them. In this instance, each recipient went through the tortuous process of automatic obedience to a commander, whose commands he had agreed to accept. But then, when that had delayed his reaction, each individual crew member separately realized that a rat was being protected from justice. That was intolerable, so—to hell with commanders.

By itself, the order to cease and desist would not have protected Figarty. But it did bring that momentary halt in the automatic behavior of several score men. As a result, the second sentence had time to go all the way through a million neural channels to where it made contact with the tiny area where a minute portion of reason still resided.

The combination of two sentences had saved Figarty's life, as Captain Fletcher intended they should. He understood simple minds. He also understood that no one there *intended* murder. Each crew member merely had a violence charge built up inside him. Expressing it would have involved raining blows, or kicking, or maybe slashing angrily with a knife. Nothing that of itself would have killed. But human flesh—so Fletcher had observed before—could not survive a combination of disablings.

To make it look official, the captain took the rat man down to his cabin, and there drew out of him a misty story

about an object falling from the sky. Fletcher was an
educated man, and had heard of falling meteorites. So that
was how he interpreted the superstitious account of the
ignorant, illiterate creature who stood on the carpet in front
of his desk.

First Mate Shradd had come down to the captain's cabin
by formal invitation, loudly spoken so that everybody
could hear. He sat now glowering at the wretched little
guy. "You're not gonna tell that tale up there, are you?"
He jerked his thumb, pointed with it up toward the deck.

Fletcher believed that the pirate officer did not like him.
He suspected that the first mate was jealous of him, and
would like to be captain. Shradd could read and write, and
on occasion pronounced words and spoke sentences with
meticulous grammatical accuracy. So the man had been
subjected to education. Yet for the most part he spoke in a
slovenly, colloquial fashion.

In the three years that they had sailed together, Shradd
had not let drop a hint of his true past. Where had he
learned sailing and navigation? He volunteered no information, and had once told the bosun's mate to mind his
own g.d. business. He killed easily. He struck quickly. He
had a rough but comradely way with the men. His actions
and his manner somehow placed him on their side. Watching that, it had more than once occurred to Captain Fletcher
that, in a personal crisis, the crew would trust Shradd and
not himself.

For a gentleman pirate, such matters were of minor concern, to be considered but dismissed with a shrug and with
a steely philosophy that accepted violence and gambles,
and hated only conformity.

The mate's words, nevertheless, gave pause to the simple solution for Figarty that the captain had in mind. His
idea was that they, all three, go up, call the men together,
and tell them about meteorites. Thus, as was always best—it
seemed to him—they would dispose of the matter with a
truth.

Yet now, ridiculously (sort of), he half-accepted that

Shradd did have the best and most detailed awareness of what the crew would, or would not, stand for.

Another reality made him hesitate. Unless immediate decisions were required in an emergency, or unless he already had a policy on something, he *always* listened courteously to the views of the ship's officers or even to those of the men. So, now, it was no problem for him to defer utilizing the simplicity of truth on Figarty's behalf.

Instead, he turned those intensely blue eyes of his toward the first mate, and asked, "What do you recommend, Mr. Shradd?"

Shradd was one of a dozen large men aboard. Sitting there, he shrugged his massive shoulders and made a dismissing movement with his head. "They'll be over their scare by this time," he said. "Just say Cooty here went crazy from the heat for a minute. They'll understand that. They're almost crazy from it themselves."

The man in the ruffled shirt and beautiful red velvet jacket, who sat behind the heavy desk, allowed a frown to crease his handsome face. Then he said, "Hmmm!" in a favoring tone.

What attracted him to the explanation was the equally simple possibility that it was, in fact, the reality of the whole incident. Mentally, silently, Fletcher chastised himself. Still on the trusting side, he thought. Still, when he was unwary, taking people at their face value.

As he came to that ninety per cent (at least) acceptance of the first mate's suggestion, there was a wordless sound of protest from Cooty Figarty.

The two officers turned as of one accord and glared at the wiry little man. "You don't like that idea?" asked Captain Fletcher softly.

"I saw it. It fell out of the sky. It was all gleaming metal and glass. And big."

The total madness of that brought decision. The rat had clearly been out of his mind. "Look, fellow," said Fletcher with finality, "we're trying to save your life. Remember what happened to my cabin boy. We told him to stop sassing the crew, and he wouldn't; and so one night somebody threw him overboard. My advice: let First Mate and me go up on deck with you, and I'll tell them what Mr. Shradd suggested. And that's the story. Understand!''

All the rest of that afternoon, Figarty was the butt of coarse jokes. At first he was silent. Then he began showing his teeth in a snarl. Finally he uttered threats that included such chillers as, ''Don't ever turn your back to me. Some night I'll slip a knife into it!'' These statements gradually damped the ardor of his tormentors.

And there wasn't any doubt or question. Despite the grim give and take, his own life was no longer in immediate danger.

On this note, the hot afternoon slowly waned. And night spread over a sea that shifted in color reflection from blue white to blue dark, and then to dark with slashes of foamy silver as far as the eye could see.

2

Swiftly, now, the human noises of the ship died away. In the hold, men abandoned the dice game and sought their sleep quarters. A few heavy snorers presently made what sounds still intimated the presence of living beings.

The vessel continued to creak its way through the darkness. About midnight Fletcher, who was still at his work, came on deck and took a reading from the tiller's compass. Then for a while he stood at the railing, gazing down at the water. It was an expert's gaze; he made an estimate of the ship's speed.

Returning to his cabin, he performed that peculiar navigator's feat of drawing the vessel's course and probable position by dead reckoning.

. . . Yesterday at noon, ship was here—his feather marked the location on the map he had spread out. . . . In twelve hours ship has traveled at an average of eleven knots north plus five degrees west. So now ship would normally be here—he marked the spot. Wind has veered gradually, and is now blowing ten degrees more easterly.

He calculated what that would have done, added another seven degrees for an east-veering current, and then made his guess, drew his line in the draft board, projecting the ship's course and location forward to the moment of dawn.

By such dead reckoning he would guide his vessel, first, to a rendezvous with their next prey, and then all the way to England. There they would, as a group, dispose of the cargo seized from several captured ships. And there he, as an individual, would secretly collect the bounty of ten thousand guineas. That was over and above the five thousand he had collected in advance.

For Fletcher it was a grim but satisfying prospect. With fifteen thousand guineas collected all unknown to the rest of the crew, added to certain other sums, he might very well return to England—or at least to Europe.

He preferred France. But that might be difficult, with the other Churchill's army in Europe fighting for England the War of the Spanish Succession.

Maybe Italy. Naples.

He stood there with that pleasant possibility flitting past his mind's eye in the form of a number of images of pleasure; at first the mental pictures soothed him. Then— the first frown.

Suddenly it almost seemed as if he were actually remembering something that had already happened, so vivid and detailed were some of the fantasies. His eyes narrowed, and there came a distinct sense of confusion.

What disturbed him was a developing memory of having already lived out his whole life in Naples, Italy. Now that the duties of the day, and its distractions, were out of the way, images of a life of pleasure, with names and faces of men and women he had associated with—a hundred men, at least, and several dozen women, and the whole busy, fantastic Neapolitan existence, *at least thirty-five years of it,* floated before his mind's senses in an almost endless series of pictures and sounds, smells and tastes, and snatches of ten thousand conversations—an incredible mélange. And, of course, utterly impossible. Because here he was on this blasted ship.

Finally exhausted by everything, he went to bed. Presently, he was dreaming of a certain dark-haired beauty of sunny Italy who—according to his recollection—he would not meet for about eight years.

All too quickly, the secure night—when pirates are as safe as they will ever be—yielded to dawn and blue sky that grew brighter with each passing minute. Somewhere in there, when, with all sails set, the sleek *Orinda* was plowing through a choppy, early morning sea, when the coming of the sun was already a great glitter in the clouds of the eastern sky, and the sea smell was brought pungently into everybody's nostrils by a strong breeze from the west, behind them—at that moment, the third mate, whose watch it was, let out a screech of alarm.

Captain Fletcher, coming hastily out onto the deck, was not too surprised to see what the finger of the alarm crier was pointing at. Sailing toward them from almost dead ahead was their victim.

Everyone awake, breakfast in their stomachs, and at stations. No laggards now. No rebels, no resistance to commands from officers.

Around the ship, out there on the restless water, and up in the sky, the world was brightening but misty. The pirate vessel, with its British flag fluttering, drove through a choppy sea. High in the crow's-nest, the lookout peered at the misty universe, seeking to maintain contact with their prey.

The tense minutes took their toll of seamen and officers alike. Strained faces peered in every direction visible to each glazed pair of eyes. It was the timeless fear. They wanted to make sure that they were alone with their intended victim.

Fletcher, who had returned below deck, taking Shradd with him, said to that individual: "The way of it, Mr. Shradd, was supposed to be that when the escorting man-o war has taken the *Red Princess* within twenty-five miles of port, it will turn back. After all"—he smiled his grim smile—"it has other duties, other ships to protect; and besides Marlborough's brother is chief of Her Majesty's Navy, and his is a gentle, trusting nature. Unlike the captain-general, he assumes that his subordinates give instructions based on good sense and unrelenting loyalty; and besides everybody knows that pirate vessels do not venture near naval stations."

He paused, studying the heavy face in front of him as it showed in the light from the two portholes. The first mate's eyes were slitted rather than merely narrowed. His wet lips were separated. His uneven teeth glinted inside them, like something bright seen through a small opening. It was not a pretty sight, for he was not a pretty man. But the entire effect was of a man thinking with intense attention to the details of a plan.

Finally: "I have to admit, Captain, I don't have your political connections that enable you to send messages to spies in the admiralty—"

"—With bribes!" interjected Fletcher. "Don't forget that money often buys not only the purity of a woman but the integrity of a chief clerk."

Shradd continued, "But I think this time we're taking a grave risk. It is too close."

"We are committed, sir!" said Fletcher, with finality. "It's a good ship, I'm told. I think you will like the result."

To everyone's relief, including Shradd's, the chase and capture were routine for the heavily armed *Orinda*.

Soon thereafter cargo was being hastily transferred, the women were brought aboard and given their choice of death by drowning or violation. Fletcher didn't really care which choice the heiress made. If she agreed to rape, then some time before it was time to return the female contingent to the *Red Princess*, an accident would be managed. And it would be her that the accident happened to.

As it turned out, not too surprisingly in view of what he had vaguely heard about her . . . she chose death. And so—

Lady Patricia Hemistan stood with frozen face as the cable was fastened around one ankle and the other end tied to a piece of heavy chain. Her lips moved.

Captain Fletcher could not restrain himself. "I presume you are praying to God, miss."

She did not reply. Her cheeks were dead white. It occurred to the man that she was possibly in too great a state of shock to have heard. It was important to his purpose that he appear to give every woman a choice. There were a few perceptive and suspicious people aboard. They would be puzzled if he were too hasty in getting rid of her; and, since he didn't intend to share a penny of the death money, and was already convinced that she would not change her mind, he continued with his argument.

"If, like me," he said, "you doubt the existence of a hereafter, I strongly urge you to choose the way of the flesh."

Something of that must have penetrated. The girl said, without turning her head, "I believe in God."

There was a frankness about her, as she uttered the words, a purity, that unexpectedly aroused desire in him. He thought: After all, she could appear to die of an accident . . . later. His lips parted, and his eyes blinked with a gray-blue hunger.

"Miss," he said huskily, "your youthful beauty—you are too young to die. I promise you. Only the mate and I and one other shall violate you—"

A groan of protest went up from the crew.

The lean, tense man made a cutting gesture with one hand and arm, as if he would slice the sound away. By the time it had died down, there was a tiny color in the girl's cheeks. "Spare me your brand of mercy," she said, "and get on with this assassination."

For the first time a faint smile twisted the tanned, handsome face. "This is not an assassination, miss. This is murder."

He was about to make a casual dismissing gesture,
when, amazingly, he realized he was hesitating. An old,
an almost forgotten emotion was stirring deep inside him:
compassion, consideration, courtesy.

The awareness of his madness was all he, with his
enormous motivation to villainy, needed. "Throw her overboard!" he commanded. Harshly.

3

The Caribbean, an extension of the Atlantic Ocean, gains its sea status from the manner in which the West Indies separate it from the vaster waters to the north and east. The sea itself consists of two deep basins and a connecting submarine plateau.

At no point is this plateau more than six thousand feet deep, a reality of which those aboard the Transit-Craft were extremely appreciative; for it was into the water above the plateau that their ship fell out of control. By zero moment—the instant of contact with the sea, out of control and at a cruelly dangerous velocity—they had of course transformed from vulnerable flesh to the virtually invulnerable energy state necessary for ultra-light-speed transit travel. That was their only possible protection against a free-fall impact.

And so, as entities, they survived. And, because their ship could withstand the pressure of a six-thousand-foot depth of water (but not much more) *it* also survived. Naturally, since the Transit elements were neutronium variants, the buoyancy provided by its hollow interior served no surface purpose. Down it went into the depths, almost as if it were a solid object. But not quite solid, fortunately. It did slow; and it actually came to rest on the bottom without an impact. It did settle into the sand, but it stopped after going down only a few yards. And there it sat.

Inside the ship were rooms that were not rooms at all by 1704 A.D. standards. Thin, metal streamers hung down from high ceilings almost to the floor of each room. The effect was . . . feathery.

Intricate designs. Like lacework. The light danced through the threads of colored metal, making a design, and creating a sense of space and energy that was unhuman but beautiful.

Time passed. Something in the ship was aware of the night that came far above these silent depths. And then of the dawn. A little later that same perception observed the girl being thrown overboard. It offered the dead body a subtle connection; and the body accepted. As a consequence it was drawn rapidly down into the frightful distances of the ocean and a position beside the dead ship.

Her arrival was like a signal. Inside the vessel for the first time amid that framework of light and shadow, something moved. A sparkling, luminescent something that seemed to flow among the thickly bunched metal threads, as if it needed them to hold onto. Like a man climbing down a narrow ladder from a height, the glittering beingness shimmered through the several rooms and came to a stop in the largest at the transparency which separated the interior from the ocean bottom outside.

It looked out. It saw—a woman's body.

The body did not float. It strained against the metal line that held one ankle to a piece of heavy chain. The impression was of someone still alive reaching toward the distant waves above with her right arm and hand upraised, and the other caught in a torn fold of what had been an ankle-length gown.

Thus restrained, it turned in a slow undercurrent, and presented first the full face and bare breasts and part of the upper waist of a young woman. Then, still turning in that aimless fashion, a profile view. Seen from the side, she looked younger, little more than a girl. Eighteen. Nineteen.

There was a pause during which an unhuman type of communication took place between the energy thing at the window and another entity elsewhere in the vessel. A few moments later, the girl's body began to move as if a much stronger current guided it. The body disappeared from the sight of the view window, and it moved up and along the side of the ship, and into a water lock.

Carefully, carefully, the dead girl was eased to the small Transit-Grid which the vessel carried as mandatory equipment. As carefully, it was put *through* the grid.

What emerged from the orifice at the other end was not exactly the original Lady Patricia Hemistan. But it was a fairly good approximation. It had most of her memories. It looked very much like her. And, most important, she believed that she was Lady Patricia.

Awakening was not painful. The girl lay for a while with her eyes closed, remaining very quiet, and thinking that if she didn't move, nobody would notice her.

The nobodies she had in mind were the pirates.

In drowning, she had taken a single, gulping breath (of water), and was instantly gone. Or so it seemed. There was actually no memory in her of dying; what she had done in breathing the water straight into her lungs was the best way.

Since death had been dealt her so swiftly, she had no awareness that death was, in fact, what had occurred. And so she was actually slightly confused, and thought that she was aboard the pirate vessel again.

Presently, she peeked. Then she hastily shut her eyes again.

Puzzlement came. *What* was it she had seen?

The streamers! . . . Metallic, silvery, threadlike strands— the afterimage of them was there in her mind. Once more she opened her eyes, and this time kept them open.

She gazed up and out at . . . fantasia.

First discovery: she was lying, not on a bed, but on a soft substance, which seemed to be a part of the floor, or perhaps even was the floor.

From that low-down condition, she was able to see—
second discovery—that the delicate, silklike, shining metal
threads did not hang all the way to the floor. There was a
gap of perhaps eighteen inches.

Eyes wide open, Patricia lay there soberly considering
the incredibleness of all that had happened. . . . I was
thrown overboard, and then I must have been rescued.

But she had to admit to herself that what she was seeing
didn't look like the interior of a pirate vessel, or of any
other place that she had ever been in.

By an hour later, when she had seen the ocean bottom
through thick glass, and when she had crawled through a
dozen great rooms, each with the same masses of metal-
like streamers, and found no living creatures whatsoever,
and nothing to eat, she had become extremely anxious.

4

And that second day also ran its course; and night fell again on a glittering sea.

In that great, dark ocean, there now transpired an improbable event.

The water roiled, and a small craft emerged from below.

There were actually several improbabilities in that sudden appearance. One was, of course, the nature of the object. It was made of metal, yet did not gleam. It seemed light, and therefore must be hollow inside. It was completely enclosed, which suggested that a vessel could be sealed against intake of water, and could come up from a depth. But what was especially improbable was the way it came up. It flouted the laws of buoyancy.

A hollow torpedo, surfacing from a great distance below, would normally come at a speed that would send it bouncing high into the air. How high? That would depend on the depth from which it had leaped.

This torpedo-shaped craft split through the top of a wave. Came up about half its length. Then fell back with a sloshing sound. Wobbled for moments only on the moving water. Then steadied. It became enormously stable. It performed, then, as if it had the metacenter equivalent of a

large, well-balanced ship. Yet it was only as large as an
oversized rowboat.

What it did, it headed toward the pirate ship.

In that moonless night, the sailing vessel was not easy to
see. Its dark hull was almost invisible against the black
water. And the white sails, still full-set, made a pattern
that blended harmoniously with the darkened, cloudy horizon and the white of a choppy sea.

In water, nothing that moves is soundless. Thus, there
were splashing noises, and the slap of the waves against a
hard, smooth substance. Yet the decisive factor was that
whatever was the driving force of the little craft, *it* made
no sound.

When the torpedo surfaced, it was less than half a mile
from the pirate vessel. Approximately three minutes later,
it had gone through the process of accelerating in water to
a velocity that was nearly seventy miles per hour at its
peak, and then decelerating and swerving alongside the
sailing ship and matching speed with it.

As this improbable feat was accomplished, the upper
half of the torpedo shape split in two, lengthwise. Each
side of the split rolled downward and disappeared into a
perfectly fitted slot.

Abruptly, the craft looked a little bit like a long, rather
narrow, open boat. Without oars.

A little bit like that only. Among the numerous differ-
ences was that there were symmetrical bulges along the
bottom. Built into one of these bulges was an oval cavity
large enough for a man to sit in.

In that indentation sat a boy.

The water wrapped itself around the pirate ship, embrac-
ing it with strong, wet fingers, hands, and arms, so to say,
that pushed, and shoved, and tugged, and strained. It was
a tremendous, never-ceasing hold-back effort against the
colossal pull of the sails far above. Moment after moment,
the sails won that battle, and the ship moved steadily
forward.

The boy stood up. He stood in the darkness, apparently

balancing himself without trouble on the bottom of his little boat. Some of the wind that was whipping and snapping through the canvas caught part of a wave and sprayed him with cool air and water that wet his hair and glistened on his small, white face.

He seemed unconcerned. He stood there, and he looked up evaluatively at the high—for him—bow of the large vessel that was creaking its way with such determination through the night.

All the sounds from aboard came down and out to him with startling clearness. Men yelling. The clatter of pans in the galley. The footsteps of a man walking toward him on the deck above.

The possibility that the sentry would glance over the side did not seem to disturb the boy. He seemed to sense that after dark the untamed spirits aboard this ship relaxed what there was of discipline. Day was the danger time for a pirate. Night brought long hours of security. The watch above was routine, unconcerned, and not alert. The man, whoever he was, did not see the strange boat that held so steady in the shaking waters below. And he was not aware of the boy who now did an incredible climbing job right up the smooth, wet side.

Below him, behind him, the "row" boat performed an operation even more improbable than what had already transpired. The two sliding sections, which had separated a few minutes before while the boy was still aboard, now—when he was not—emerged automatically from their slots, and slid together soundlessly. The unoccupied craft began to sink—automatically. In seconds it was awash. It disappeared into the night-black waters without as much as a glimmer of reflected light. One instant it was still visible. The next it was gone.

Down in one of the holds, where a dice game was in full roar, Softy Jones had a thought. He picked up what was left of the coins in front of him, and said, "I'll be back."

"Where you goin'?"

"Oh, I feel stuffed up. I gotta have a breath of fresh air. I'll be back."

He thought it was his own impulse; and no one wondered how it came about that Softy, for the first time—for the *very* first time—could bring himself to depart for even one minute from dice or cards. Gambling had been Softy's road to ruin. Except for his uncontrollable impulse to bet on anything and everything, and except for a long career of cover-up lying, he had no vices.

He didn't take advantage of captured women. In an attack, it had long ago been established that he would do deck and sail duties, or man the tiller. There was no record of Softy ever killing or maiming anyone.

He went on deck now, unremarked by men whose sensitivity to danger did not include noticing character violations. You were who you looked to be. If you were a leopard you could change your spots, and so long as your face was recognizably yours, *nothing* that you did that was different caused even a ripple of awareness.

Arrived on deck, Softy headed straight to where the boy was. And there, just before the intended capture by the only safe pirate aboard, boy perceived man.

. . . Looked first at the shape and then through the substance: saw in the second state an amazing contraption of tubes and sacs of liquid held together by long strands of flexible cords and an even finer network of internal electrical communication, which flowed to and from a central mass in the head to smaller centers throughout the three-dimensional structure. Noted that there were numerous centers in the head and body, each of which had some monitoring function, and that the entire intricacy was supported by a bony frame and was contained inside a thin but unbroken outer skin.

Boy observed on another level of perception that the man was not aware of his interior physical self; that he did, he thought, and he felt without considering how these things came about.

Softy, seeing the boy in the dark, seemed to know

exactly what to do. He lurched forward past a stay, ducked under a taut rope, and grabbed. His motions and his intent were singly and severally totally convincing (to himself).

He was a thin, medium tall man, toughened by years at sea; and so as he established with his fingers what he had already seen in the light from a lantern that hung behind a sail that this was a boy, he was confident of his own capability in the situation.

A bare edge of superstition touched him; just enough to bring the thought that this was the cabin boy who had been thrown overboard. But he was actually a semi-educated man, and so he dismissed that swiftly. The thought remained as a faint anxiety, and as a consideration in helping him decide to make no outcry, for fear that if the murderers discovered that there *was* a boy, they wouldn't wait to identify him but would act immediately against.

Another fleeting influence on Softy was the memory of the ultra-anger of the crew members the previous afternoon.

Thus motivated, he silently urged his captive forward. And his impression of what happened was that he half-dragged, half-led, the kid down to the captain's cabin. And the fact the boy made no sound either was not significant to Softy Jones.

Captain Fletcher was surprised by what he saw when he opened his cabin door. But he listened with a progressively more thoughtful expression on his face to Softy's story about how "on seein' the kid on deck, I grabbed 'un and dragged 'un up here." As soon as the man completed his account, Fletcher reached forward, took hold of the boy's arm himself, and sent Softy to the first mate's cabin with instructions to "ask Mr. Shradd to step into the captain's quarters."

Minutes later the two men gazed together at what Fletcher had been looking at alone by the light of his fine bronze lamps. They saw a boy in a velvet suit. He was small but sturdy-looking. He had dark hair and dark eyes in a round white face; and he told them in educated English that he had been cabin boy aboard a ship that had gone down several days before after striking a hidden reef.

Looking at the lad as he talked, Captain Fletcher had no sense of any falseness. But because he was thorough in all things, he asked the necessary questions: Name . . . Billy Todd; ship . . . *Black Falcon;* out of what port . . . London.

It was an ordinary story of a simple shipwreck, with intense confusion in the darkness; and with boats being lowered by frightened men who didn't wait for the command to abandon ship.

Considering the source of the story—a boy of fifteen— Fletcher accepted it as true.

Aloud, genially, he said, "Well, lad, it looks like you're in luck. I have need of a cabin boy. And so if you'll sign the indenture, you can serve out the balance of your term aboard our happy little vessel. I should advise you that we engage in a variety of activities that may take us out of these waters for a time, but we shall eventually return."

First Mate was gesturing violently; but Fletcher ignored the big man and his motions with their negative implications. In fact, later, after Billy had solemnly agreed to the bargain, and after Fletcher had personally taken him below and introduced him to the men (and told them Softy's story), he drew the first mate aside and murmured, "We can always throw him overboard, Mr. Shradd."

The red, intense face and the gimlet eyes rejected his words. The first mate said through his teeth, "If we're ever captured, he'll be a witness."

Fletcher laughed his grittiest laugh. "So will any acceptable type who is willing to turn crown's witness. When that moment comes, it'll be half the crew and half the officers; only the captain will not be allowed to squeal. So you see, my own neck is always in total jeopardy. Yours will be subject to whatever swindling you can manage at the time."

As Fletcher well knew, his words were not true. British law executed *all* persons involved in a murder, even though only one of a group had actually committed the murder.

But Fletcher had observed that all of these alienated people lived in an inner universe of illusion, secret hopes, and schemes. At some level they were aware of the remorselessness of the law, and so in a crisis they fought like devils; but on another level was an almost conscious desire not to know the facts.

"They'll never take me alive!" was Shradd's reply, now.

But the big man's attention—his captain saw—was diverted; the argument evidently real enough to him. Seeing a good moment, Fletcher said quickly, "Better get to bed. We are early risers tomorrow, and have a long day's flight ahead of us."

By the light of his beautiful lamps, he saw with relief that the big fellow's basic rage and suspicion seemed, indeed, to have temporarily abated. Shradd grunted something, and then went out and along the narrow corridor to his own cabin. Fletcher shut his door and returned lovingly to his task of dead reckoning the *Orinda*'s route for the next day . . . toward far England.

Swiftly now, the human noises of the ship died away. In the hold, men abandoned the dice game and sought their sleep quarters. A few heavy snorers presently made the only sounds that suggested the presence of living beings.

Captain Fletcher was one of the sleepers, adding his genteel, occasional snore to the medley from the crew's quarters.

While he slept, a significant event occurred. The boy came up confidently from below, and seemed not surprised to find both the helmsman and the watch dozing, each on his own portion of the deck, well separated.

Ouickly, the boy used rope available for the purpose, and lashed the helm to a steady course. As quickly, he hurried to the large hatch that covered the hold. From his pocket, he drew out a small metal object that gleamed in his fingers. In moments he had attached the little item to the iron ring by which—usually—two men lifted the hatch.

There was a small glow of intense white light. The hatch raised itself effortlessly.

To the boy's left there was now a sound, a scraping effect. Moments later, a dark metal structure, dripping water, reared up over the railing, settled on the deck. It rested there several moments, almost as if it were getting its bearings. And then it lifted once more, and this time swung over, and down, through the open hatch, and out of sight into the hold.

During a period of approximately ten minutes, seven additional dark metal structures, each differently shaped from the others—none very large—was transported by the same, apparently effortless means from the night waters, up over the railing, across to the hatch, and down into the hold.

As the eighth object disappeared into the darkness below, the boy lowered himself down through the opening. After he, also, had vanished, there were light flashes below, and vague sounds, as if many objects were sliding back and forth. In fact, he was manipulating the cargo and his own machines, so that the latter were presently hidden under boxes and canvas.

The concealment task completed, the boy emerged again on deck. He closed the hatch. He unlashed the helm. Then he walked back across the deck and down the steps that led to the crew's quarters. On the deck behind him, first the helmsman, and then the watch, awakened and hastily scrambled back to their respective duties.

5

A cabin boy sleeps in an upper bunk of the forecastle with the crew. He undresses in the small front portion of his bed, because that way he can get more easily out of his pants. Having stripped to his underwear, he slides deeper into the bunk. The farther back he lies the less chance there is of falling out while tossing in his sleep. So long as he is awake, he lies there carefully, consciously restraining himself from sitting up involuntarily; for that is a sure way to a smash on the head.

The boy from the sea, whose 1704 A.D. name was Billy Todd, dutifully undressed, and as carefully as any of the other upper-bunk occupants had done earlier, settled himself into the narrow space provided. He lay there, then, troubled, and for the first time feeling vulnerable.

He was human; he would have to sleep.

Until this moment he had used tiny instruments as extensions of his conscious mind. They were tuned to his thought while he was awake. Each contained an amplifier which depended on proximity to him in its first stage. While close up, it could catch the faint thought patterns which he had learned to formulate and project. Feedback expanded the pattern, and made possible subtle variations of ideas and awarenesses.

Once amplification started, he could pick up the thoughts of people as far away as a hundred feet, which, on a ship this size, was about as far as one needed.

That was the real purpose of that particular device: mind reading. The fact that a person unaccustomed to thought transference could also have certain brain centers manipulated (to some extent) was incidental. In the boy's own era that ability of the mechanism was used to control animals.

In its way, a pirate crew qualified as, at least, animalistic. And so, during the intense moments on deck, he had taken the preliminary precaution of activating the sleep centers of every person on board. And, on returning to the crew's quarters, he had triggered the wakefulness centers of the two men doing duty on deck. But had left everyone else asleep.

Unfortunately, most of his protective instruments could not be left on while he slept. That was his problem now. The reason was that the sleeping brain sends forth random instructions, and cannot be trusted to issue sensible commands.

There was, of course, some protection. Two devices would guard him while he slept. One was set to awaken him if anyone approached him in a threatening way. The other would discharge an anesthetic gas at the attacker.

It was, he decided, the best he could do. With a sigh, for he was not happy with such limited protection, he realized he had no other recourse. It was absolutely vital that he go to a location where a factory was available.

—England, early eighteenth century, here I come. I sincerely hope I have correctly recalled that foundry and other large metal-handling facilities exist in this era . . .

He lay for a while listening to the snores of the noisy crew members, and the breathing of the quiet ones; sensing the motion of the ship—which was the easiest perception of all, for the vessel creaked, and swayed, and wallowed, and every other few minutes seemed as if it would tear itself apart, except that, abruptly, all the sounds and the strainings would cease, and it would go forward

once more almost silent—and it was a strange feeling to
realize that a single space-time convulsion had brought
him and his Transit-Craft and its precious cargo down to
this remote location in the time stream.

But it was the time that now existed. He might have to
live here from now on. His one other hope was that he
could repair the spaceship, and go somewhere outside of
the portion of space that had been affected by the time
fallback.

. . . It was as the very first faint light of dawn seeped
in among the sleeping men, that Figarty did his rat thing.
Without of course noticing the dynamics of the condition,
he had, as the result of his experience of the day before,
been drained of most of his tiny component of inner
emotional strength.

At some later time in history, the impulse that now ruled
him would be called the kleptomaniac syndrome. Whenever he had had such a compulsion in his own past, the
wildness of it frightened even him. He wanted to grab
everything, and somehow get it inside him to the empty
spot. As a boy he had once actually run along a London
street, and snatched, and snatched, and snatched. Adult-
hood had brought control of a kind, and cunning. He still
had to grab; but he could wait.

He had felt the emptiness all evening; and so of course
his bright eyes had observed avidly that the new cabin boy
was well dressed. An instant corollary suggested itself: the
boy probably had a few small but valuable possessions.

During the night Figarty awakened repeatedly. Each
time the greed was almost unbearable. The craving grew—
and grew. But reason told him that he had to have *some*
light so that he could see a *little* bit. Finally, here it was,
the first hint of the coming day.

Silent as a thief who has ill-spent many hours perfecting
the stealthy approach, he was across the room, and up
beside the boy in a few well-rehearsed movements. In
what now transpired the boy was quite accidentally a
victim of bad luck. First of all, the threat from Figarty was

not personal; the rat had no thought of harming the kid physically. As a result, the warning device merely gave its preliminary signal. It was a sort of tentative mental nudge which—had the boy been awake—would have attracted his attention to the possibility that a problem was developing.

Unfortunately, he was in the Stage Four, delta-wave sleep, to which human beings are naturally subject for a portion of each ninety-minute cycle of their sleep time. It would have required some equivalent of a mental battering ram to nudge him out of that sleep.

Dutifully, as Figarty came close enough for personal contact, the warning device triggered the discharge of the protective anesthetic gas.

The rat man felt what seemed to be a sudden quick breath of air against one side of his face. But he was holding his breath. That had become a part of his system years ago, ever since in a moment of predatory eagerness he had breathed on the face of a prospective victim, and awakened him. Since that disaster he had practiced diligently, and had learned to retain a huge inhalation of oxygen for almost two minutes.

In slightly more than thirty seconds now, he probed under the little pillow pad, fumbled through the pockets of the neatly folded boy's suit, searched for hidden pockets—ripped, slashed, grabbed—and was gone. It took him nearly twelve seconds to return to his own bunk with the fruits of his thievery, because he walked—in case somebody had awakened. . . . Crew members were always walking up on deck to relieve themselves. Nobody so much as opened their eyes to observe a walker.

Figarty still couldn't see what he had; it was too dark. But already he was disappointed. His take consisted of a number of surprisingly small objects, exactly fifteen of them. What was disappointing was that in the process of filching the items, his knowing fingers in each instance established that what he had was not a gold or a silver coin.

It was as he settled into his bunk, already gloomy from his instant analysis, that Figarty grabbed his first slow breath. And of course he immediately got his initial share of the anesthetic, which was in process of becoming diluted with the interior air of the forecastle.

The dosage released was not intended to harm; merely to incapacitate. It was designed to dissolve quickly in the blood stream of its victims, and then to undergo a chemical transformation, and act as an awakener.

That was thirty or so minutes later. As at a signal, everybody in the forecastle, including the boy, snapped awake. Each man had his own reason, then, for getting dressed, and going up, and out, and around. During those noisy minutes and those confusions, a startled cabin boy discovered that his worst fears had been realized. Hurriedly, he dressed, still hoping that, by getting close to first one, then another, and so on, the thought device in the thief's pocket would be triggered, and he would spot the villain.

But it was too late. During those decisive minutes, Figarty, on deck, skimmed through his spoils. Mentally, then, he dismissed them as children's junk of some obscure type. And he tossed them over the side.

By that time Captain Fletcher was yelling for his cabin boy. "Billy," he roared, "bring my breakfast!"

A subdued ex-super-boy was presently doing exactly that mundane task.

6

At that moment, when, with all sails set, the *Orinda* was moving through a choppy, early morning sea, and when the coming of the sun was already a great glitter in the clouds of the eastern sky—at that moment, the third mate, whose watch it was, let out a screech of alarm.

It was such a piercing yell, with so much terror in it, that even Billy Todd, who was made of better biological stuff than anyone else aboard, felt the chill of it go through him. He ran with the others. And he stood. And he held onto the railing. And he stared with them at the fantastic thing that was visible on the horizon.

A ship!

The vessel was at the very rim of the horizon, and it did not seem to be moving. It was the sailing ship, with every sail bloated with wind, that was heading toward the still distant . . . giant. And that was the reality that brought the first alarm. Its size. Its length.

It was such a ship as Billy had seen in accounts of the early space wars. A Lantellan battleship, he identified. . . . It must have been caught in the same time collapse as his own, smaller Transit-Craft, but was, of course, from an earlier period. Late twenty-fifth century was his tentative recollection.

He turned, anxious and disturbed, searching. With relief, he saw that Captain Fletcher was only a few feet
away, gazing with eyes as wide and amazed as anyone's.
Billy ran over to him, ninety per cent convinced that he
would never be able to persuade anyone; but a hundred per
cent certain that he must try. He tugged at the captain's
sleeve.

"Take down your sails!" he urged. "Maybe they won't
see us, since we have no large metal for their detectors to
notice."

Fletcher turned, in spite of himself, as that shrill voice
came up at him, commanding and demanding in a way that
was almost as startling as the enormous ship out there a
few miles away.

"Hey!" he said, "look who's giving orders."

Billy Todd, from the eighty-third century, minus all
those marvelous gadgets that could have helped him in the
crisis that was developing, was desperate. "They mustn't
see us," he said. "They're robots. They have no mercy on
human beings. Get your sails down. It—"

He stopped. His gaze had been partly pointed past
Fletcher. So to speak, from the corner of his eyes he was
watching the great battleship from space, which was capable of operating in water with the same ease as it normally
did in air or out in the airless vacuum between planets or
stars. Now, as he finished speaking his warning, he saw
that it was too late.

It was a moment of many things happening simultaneously. The sun, which had been peeping over the tossing
waters to the east, was suddenly up above the horizon by
at least an inch. As a consequence, suddenly, a million
green and white flares danced up from the water and
sparkled in every direction. The breeze, already spanking,
chose that instant to quicken. It sent long streamers of
spray up into their faces, wet, and cool, and delightful.

And a man yelled hoarsely, "They're sending a boarding party. They've seen us."

They were indeed. They had indeed.

What had sounded that very morning on the Lantellan ship was not an alarm; it was an alert.

Nodo paused in his purification exercises. First, he clarified for himself that the alert commanded A to M classifications to take up action stations. Being an N (of the N to Z group) he was required to scan the vessel's memory core and acquaint himself with location in space, condition of ship, and probable cause of the warning. Thus he would have Minimum Advance Recognition.

. . . What bothered him was a memory of having in some previous "time" experienced this voyage without, of course, such an incident as was now transpiring—

(Since the strange memory instantly threatened his performance capability, he closed off that circuit.)

Nodo did his scan and promptly felt what in a Lantellan was an analogy to astonished interest. The ship, may its brain continue to understand truth, was sinking into the atmosphere of the planet Tellus. Since Lantella was at war with the Tellurian Federation in this year, 2494, of our lord, the Universal Mind, that should normally have produced a general alarm and battle stations for all categories.

Nodo waited, feeling the while especially wound-up in his lower solidities, an area of himself which he had not yet purified this morning. Hastily, he resumed the purification routine. When the ritual maintenance program was completed, and he was fit again, he tuned once more into the core, and was pleasantly stimulated to observe that the ship had come down into a body of water.

We've made surface . . .

The Lantellan battleship had no commander, as such, and no chief engineer. Each individual aboard worshiped the same Universal Mind, and had direct communication, and always did the right thing, as who wouldn't.

No laggards, no sinners, no one alienated, each individual keeping himself fit so that he could serve the blessed center of all things; his limitations allowed for, no excessive demands ever made; everyone on call in rotation, in

groups, in alphabetical order. There were temporary leaders, yes; but only because the nearer the eyes and ears to a
situation the quicker the response could be; and someone
was assigned (in rotation) to oversee what the response
was, depending on whatever was happening right now.
. . . "Men, go there! Men, do this!" And they did. And
the Universal Mind merely watched, and tried to understand from a distance what the problem was, and might
even offer advice but no interference. Unless something
seemed wrong.

That was the way it had always been. And that was the
way they started to do it now. But—but—

No Universal Mind. Nothing to be connected to.

But, but, but—

Small pause. Then a voice said: "This is Captain-by-
rotation Darkel. I herewith assume command of this vessel
for my term. All hands, attention! Whatever has happened
has temporarily disconnected us from our Beloved. This
will no doubt rectify in due course. Until then, everyone is
reminded that individual activity is possible, and that such
individual behavior can be just as dedicated, and it might
be well for everyone to bear in mind that what has happened may be a Test for all of us. Take heed. Do the right
thing. Follow your current lead man, whoever he might be
at any given moment. Accept your humble lot, knowing
that if you do you are a king."

The voice continued: "I now inform you that our chief
engineer-by-rotation reports that we have come down in a
tropical sea, and that within the range of our instruments
there is visible an extremely tiny sail vessel. Boarding
Party Number One will accordingly launch an N-Unit,
with authority to board and take all necessary actions."

"Hey!" thought Nodo. "Boarding Unit N, that's me.
I'm the commander-by-rotation."

He forthwith acknowledged the instruction, and in turn
contacted the approximately 100 Ns who would accompany him.

"While you are performing this task," said Captain-by-rotation Darkel, "the engineering department will determine our situation. Certain instruments appear to be signaling in an unusual way."

Moments later, the magnetic-powered N-Unit, with its personnel, was airborne and flying over a brilliant green sea with the sun almost directly behind them.

7

There came a moment, as Fletcher watched, that his eyes began to play him tricks. He had brief impressions that he could see open sky between the tossing water and the craft that had been launched from the remote monster ship. The big vessel was a little closer, but it was still partly hidden behind the horizon even to his unsuspecting gaze. (What he did not suspect was how much there was that he could not see—yet.)

The famous pirate captain stood there under the high, wide Caribbean sky, breathing hard. Into his lungs came one gulping breathful of damp air after another, and with each gulp a feeling that no one can ever know who has not himself experienced it.

It was a feeling of total helplessness. His inner conviction: there was nothing that common sense, or bravery, or anything at all of the eighteenth century could do against the mighty vessel from which the smaller attack ship was coming. (Automatically because of what Billy had said, he assumed it was an attack that was about to be made.)

Helplessness . . . and worse. The presence of the giant vessel violated his reasons for being an evil man. Its mere existence, with all that that existence implied of an entirely different, infinitely stronger reality than anything he had

turned against, made nothing of his bitter rebellion against
the politics and politicians who had won the favor of the
Crown as against those, like himself, who had lost it.

Thinking of Billy, he turned to look for the boy—and
almost bumped into Shradd. The big man was pale.
"Cap'n," he mumbled, "that's a bird out there. Biggest
one I ever saw—but a bird!"

The first mate was visibly in a distracted state. His eyes
had a staring look. His lips continued to move, as if he
were still mumbling, though no sound came forth now.

Seeing the big man in that unstrung condition was instantly good for Fletcher. Somehow, he was able to brace
himself. He reached over and up, and clapped one of the
great shoulders. "Mr. Shradd," he said in his heartiest
tone, "birds have wings, and I don't see any such on
that—"

His voice dwindled into silence. Because at that precise
instant his keen gaze, reaching forth, saw that the impossible was indeed occurring. No birds, no wings—true. But
abruptly there was no doubt. The approaching craft had by
this time covered half the distance from the horizon, and it
was blue sky between it and the water. The thing was, in
fact, floating through the air.

The strange feeling in his head became a confusion.
Because it was impossible. They lived in a world in which
every movement of a sentient creature required an effort.
Birds were paper-light entities that flew with highly developed flight muscles by an enormous expenditure of energy, and the use of large amounts of oxygen, at the same
time maintaining a rigid skeletal support against the stress
of air resistance. Each flying moment depended on feath-
ers that provided an insulating coat of great efficiency
against cold air. Men walked with bodies braced against
gravity by a bony structure and attached bundles of con-
tractile fibers, which moved in relation to each other at
each step. These multi-millions of muscles were separately
sheathed in connective tissue, nourished by blood vessels,
and subject to communication from a complex of nerves.

To move faster than a human being could walk or run, men rode horses. Such equines were similarly structured but had an even more powerful skeletal frame. Or men traveled inside carriages drawn by horses using an even greater expenditure of energy. Only on water had man long ago discovered a method of transport over distance that transcended muscle power. There, able-bodied flunkies possessed of sturdy skeletons and masses of oxygenated muscles contained inside a solid sheath of skin scrambled precariously over a latticework of stiff wooden poles and logs, fastened sheets of canvas, and thus harnessed the first outside force. It was the first use of magic: the taming of the marvelous wind.

Fletcher's confusion did not include precisely that reasoning, but it had that background. And so he came to a purpose:

—We could tilt the cannon up a bit, and shoot it down. . . . Maybe it would sink. The fleeting hope, the feeling that we'll-fight-to-prevent-them-from-getting-aboard caused him to swing around once more. Almost at once he saw Billy. He called out: "Hey, kid, think we ought to fire at them?"

The super-boy shook his head. "Sir," he said, "they seem to be in some kind of trouble—the big ship, I mean. So I get the feeling they want information. Let me talk to them. But don't do anything unless I yell!"

Fletcher was almost his sardonic self again. "And if you yell, what then? Do we attack with cutlasses, knives, and pistols?"

"Well"—doubtfully—"I guess that would be pretty useless. But something! We can't just give in."

Something!

Standing there, staring out over the water, aware of the great sails above making their cracking sounds still straining to move the ship, Fletcher did have an ironic thought. During these four long years of piracy the greatest fear had been always that one day a ship of the Royal Navy would engage them, and at the end of the losing battle tough

seamen would board the pirate vessel and either seize or
kill those aboard. At which time, for the survivors, there
would be the swift trials by a naval court, and men and
officers alike hanged from the yardarm.

. . . What will these strange beings do to a pirate crew
when they do their boarding action?

The approaching craft was so close now that he could
see something of how strange these beings were. . . .
Their method was logical. The mechanical . . . bird . . .
came down level with the deck, and the bronze-bright
creatures who were gathered at the point of contact vaulted
over the railing and onto the deck of the *Orinda*.

Fletcher had ordered his men to stand well back. And so
there they all were, looking very disturbed, and watching—as
fifty armored men—that's what they looked like—came
aboard.

Nodo, who was one of the fifty, commented to his
brothers that ''there is no resistance, so let me attempt
communication.''

His comment was, of course, not audible to the group of
humans since it was broadcast on a narrow radio band.
Fletcher stood with a faint, strained smile on his face, and
said, ''All right, Billy, you do the talking.''

Nodo did not argue with the truth of existence. He said,
''Until a short time ago, I was a part of the Universal
Mind, which knows everything. I and my brothers are to it
as sons to a father. We seek to discover what has happened
to disconnect us.''

The boy looked up at the bronze creature, and said,
''What you call the Universal Mind is a giant computer
located on a huge spaceship. It was originally in orbit
around Tellus, but something went wrong, and it went off
on its own. Thereafter, it and all it controlled were enemies of the human race. Yet man originally created it,
originally programmed into it all the knowledge known at
that time, which was a lot.''

The boy and the robot stood facing each other midway
between the two groups, the pirates crowded against one

railing, ready to retreat to the rear of the sail ship, and the robots gathered on the deck where they had come aboard, well forward.

Nodo said with dignity, "The origin of the Universal Mind is a mystery known only to the Universal Mind. It is wrong of you to place false information into my receptors about my father's origin. I shall accordingly erase what you have said."

"You will get no help from your father where you now are," said Billy. "This is the year 1704 A.D., which is more than seven hundred years before your time. In order to understand and deal with what that has done to you, you will need my help. But if you want help from me, you will have to do as I say."

"I have my instructions," said Nodo quietly. "We plan no harm to anyone aboard at the moment, but we do intend to mark them. So, stand aside, boy! You have given us the information we seek, but now we must complete our mission and depart."

Billy turned to Fletcher. "Tell your men not to resist what these robots want to do. In fact—" He swung about and faced Nodo again. "How about the men," he said, "coming forward, one at a time, and being marked?"

"Figarty," commanded Fletcher, "you first."

The rat man tried to sink down out of sight among the bigger men around him. But the voices of the boy and of the robot yelling at each other had been loud and clear, even above the splashing and the creaking and the slapping of the sails in the wind. So, it was a bad moment for the Figartys of the world. Savage men were shaking inside with the threat of what being marked might mean; and right now they wanted most mightily to see it done first to someone else. And of all those someone elses Figarty was the best choice that Fletcher could have made.

Strong hands grabbed his collar, lifted him up, and shoved him away. He came wobbling forth from the group and, once out in the open, seemed to realize there was no escape. As he staggered to his doom, he mumbled over and over, ''What they gonna do? What they gonna do?''

The boy turned him until his back was to the robots. Whereupon, one of the robots raised what looked like a pistol and pointed it at Figarty's back, high on the shoulder. Then, apparently the job done, he lowered the gun. If he had fired it during the pointing, nothing showed. Figarty, who had been bracing, was nudged by the boy. ''All right, that's it. You're finished.'' He pointed to the lee side forward. ''Go there.''

Figarty scrabbled over to the indicated position, and seemed to be well enough so that the other men, when named in turn by Fletcher, went forward for their marking. Still, it was—Fletcher could see—touch and go. Veins stood out on the angrier men's faces. Eyes were narrowed with hate and rage. Something must have held them, the strangeness of it all, perhaps—a ship that could fly, men in armor, yet somehow not looking quite like men. Clearly, some of the lame-brains aboard had received a wordless message from the events. The message was: Be careful! There's power here! . . . Even though they were not tied with ropes, they obeyed instructions; but Fletcher saw behind several pairs of narrowed eyes the beginning of cunning, the wrong thoughts visibly forming. These same men, having been marked, walked off muttering imprecations. Shradd was one of the narrow-eyed, and as he joined the marked group, he cursed the loudest of all. . . . That so-and-so, thought Fletcher, grimly. He's trying to curry favor—

The degrading procedure ran its slow course. Each pirate, in turn, stumbled forward to his purgatory, taking time to move. Fletcher, who had his own urgencies and never quite lost his head in a crisis, used that time to conduct a tense, though intermittent, interrogation of Billy, beginning with:

''Billy, what's happening? Who are these people? Where did they come from?''

The boy sighed at the questions. And the story he told in

reply was interrupted at least once a minute. An additional disadvantage: it was not a story that could have much meaning even to an educated pirate captain of the early eighteenth century. Yet he and his men were seeing with their own eyes the Lantellan battleship, the obvious non-men who had boarded their sail vessel; and so Fletcher automatically, almost unnoticingly, stretched his mind to encompass the impossible answers he was receiving.

. . . The impossible answers:

Until now all of time had been like a continuous strip, continuously in existence, and contactable by proper technology. Meaning, everybody was alive at every minute of his life, stretching all the way from the beginning of the universe to at least the eighty-third century A.D.—from which time Billy had been precipitated.

Suddenly, everything in the multi-billions of years since time began telescoped. And settled out at 1704 A.D.

Instantly, everybody in the other portions of that colossal span of eternity was dead forever, no longer contactable by any method.

Confronted by such an explanation, Fletcher was out of his depth. But he was still able to ask practical questions like: "When they point that small black pistol at our backs, nothing seems to happen. What are they doing?"

Once more, Billy was unhappy. He sensed that he was in the presence of an intelligent man who was not up to that explanation either.

. . . A sensor embedded in the shoulder muscles of a human being theoretically could be an irritation to him. The sensor the Lantellans were injecting was a gas that was also an anesthetic. Its speed of entry was so great it penetrated the skin, leaving only a small redness to indicate that anything was happening or had happened. To counteract the process each individual would have to be cut open by a needle or a knife—very accurately. If done skillfully, that would allow the gas to escape. It was the boy's unhappy conviction that on a pirate vessel no one

would submit to so severe an operation when, in truth,
they felt nothing and would see nothing.

All this entirely aside from the difficulty of trying to
persuade an early eighteenth-century human being that a
gaseous insert invisible to the naked eye was now sending
out a signal minute by minute, locating him in space.
Locating him exactly to detector instruments that would
eventually be thousands of miles away.

It was difficult, but Billy tried his best. Mere seconds
went by, and then—

It was Fletcher's turn for "marking"; and so he was
tense, and with just enough fear to send hate flashing
through him against Shradd, who was trying to take advantage of this dangerous situation. Or so it seemed.

The boy touched his hand. "It's done," he said. "They're
leaving."

"Huh!" said Fletcher, startled. He had felt nothing at
all.

The realization relieved *him*. But as he joined his men,
he saw that the real lame-brains had found each other.
They were clustered together, and they were muttering the
sounds of the alienated from the London gutter, each
individual among them loaded audibly with stupid impulses, irrational evaluations, and downright insanity.

No sensible person has ever figured out what to do with
a real lame-brain. There the idiot stands under an early
morning Caribbean sky—all nine of him, in this instance.
The reason he's a lame-brain is because he cannot add
simple facts together logically. In his head the world doesn't
come together as it is.

Why not just let the Lantellans leave the ship?—which
they were now starting to do. But, no, a lame-brain doesn't
think like that.

Two things happened, following quickly one on another.

Billy Todd, who had been well to the fore during the
entire invasion, turned and called out to Fletcher: "They
want me to come along."

He was apparently simply giving information. For, having spoken, he went forward briskly, and 'one of the robots lifted him onto the deck of the airship.

That was the first happening; and it distracted Fletcher. His feeling: he ought to do something. His momentary confusion probably made possible the second happening. It was just possible that otherwise he might have tried to use his authority to control the men.

As the last dozen Lantellans were milling, waiting their turn to clamber back on their airship, the lame-brains' moment came. The curses spoken were a forewarning in their tone. But the words were not easy to interpret for their direct meaning.

"Rough 'em up!" Something like that. "Gi' 'em what for!" And other madness.

8

The battle—if that was what it was—began with that most sensible of all tactics: a surprise attack. If there was a signal, Fletcher didn't hear it or see it. Common agreement and equality in stupidity seemed to be the uniting factors.

Nine rough-dressed louts. Bearded. Black scarfs tied around their heads. Teeth showing. One of the nine lunged, and the others lunged after him. Significantly, Shradd brought up the rear. It was significant to Fletcher because the big fellow was an exceptionally brave man, and often led boarding parties, pistol in his left hand, gleaming cutlass in his right, and knife clenched between his teeth. Thus armed, and with his large mustache, he was a ferocious-looking figure.

To Fletcher, the fact that Shradd brought up the rear was one more piece of evidence that this was a calculated move on his part. Playing it cautious, but being out there with the most villainous of the rascals aboard.

Within instants after that first lunge, the whole group was bearing down on the enemy at a dead run. The distance they had to cover was only twenty feet—because of where Billy had directed the marked men to go. . . . That realization suddenly flashed through Fletcher's mind.

Billy! Of course. The boy had wanted the crew to be able to attack in case there was violence from the robots.

For bare moments that gave Fletcher hope. His feeling had been: since the robots were simply going away, what the nine were doing was a disaster. But if the boy had believed that they might, just might, be able to do battle with these men of bronze, then perhaps all was not lost.

In their own fashion, the nine had a good plan. Within the frame of the basic foolishness of attacking *at all,* what they tried to do was, under the circumstances, a kind of good sense. They came up to where the robots were just beginning to be aware that something had gone amiss. The metal men were turning, in their heads a warning from Nodo. Nodo standing on the deck of the airship, supervising the re-embarkment of "his" boarding unit, saw what was happening and barked orders. His commands were not audible to the human beings, but, of course, he was "heard" inside every robot head.

Heard moments too late by Nast. Two pirates grabbed him, seemed to be braced for the hard metal they had to get a grip on . . . and threw him overboard. Two other men grabbed a second bronze monster and started to throw him over the side, also. And a third duo of human beings reached for a third robot—

That was it. They were not able to complete the action. Because from the deck of the airship, brilliant beams of light sprang from the foreheads of several robots. The light was coherent, each beam a narrow band of brightness, actually visible in the morning sun, which was now at least a foot above the horizon. The beams touched the attackers only, the four men who had also grabbed two of the robots.

All four of the men fell. At once. Like dead or paralyzed creatures. Or rather, like people who have suddenly become dead weights, every muscle · totally limp and unresisting.

It was not a moment for detailed thought. A thorough

analysis of the situation, or of what had happened, was not possible.

"Get down!" yelled Fletcher. He himself dived out of sight behind the upjut of wood which supported the bridge. Seconds later a dozen men had followed him there. After a little, Fletcher raised himself and peered cautiously at the scene of action.

Swift relief. The robots were all back on their airship, and it was sinking down toward the water; presumably, the intention was to rescue the Lantellan who had been doused in the ocean. Although it was not possible to see the rescue from where Fletcher remained cautiously concealed, the robot in the water was apparently lifted out; for after only a few minutes the airship was visible a hundred feet away, and receding rapidly. It raised itself higher and higher, and was presently a remote craft moving through the air like a bird but without wings.

As it drew farther away, the men came out of hiding; and Fletcher issued the order that veered the *Orinda* off the course that would have taken it close to the colossal ship sitting there on the horizon, and sent it at an angle, actually closer to the direction of the wind.

Thus, they missed seeing the dilemma of the giant spaceship, and never clearly understood why it didn't immediately follow them to where they were going: London.

. . . Coming through the gaseous shell of earth, the Lantellan battleship—like the Transit-Craft before it—had reacted to the atmosphere in an abnormal way. The less sophisticated equipment of the big ship was slower to sense that anything was wrong. But even if it had interpreted correctly what was happening, it had no corrective system. As it was, it had to strike something as solid as water before needles moved uncertainly, not knowing for sure what was wrong but detecting an unusual condition.

Unusual it was. Metal from a future time was in contact with the water of 1704 A.D. In a small way, by deduction, the robots were able later to reason out what must have happened. Undistilled water boils at 100 degrees Centigrade at sea level. Which was exactly where they now were: sea level. Compressed, and cooled, it turns into, not just one kind, but several kinds of ice.

The contact between the metal of the spaceship of the twenty-fifth century and water of 1704 A.D. produced a beautiful visual phenomenon—and a chemical madness. Within seconds, crystals of ice formed on the metal that was under the water. Within minutes, so intense was the reaction, the ice extended more than a hundred feet below the surface.

The metal walls themselves, which, of course, consisted of antigravity lift patterns, altered. In a rough fashion they fitted themselves to the different time, and they did so without shattering.

But they forgot what they had been "taught." They ceased to be anti-gravity.

A chemical reaction is automatic. The atoms and molecules do not, unless "trained," choose what the reaction shall be. They go through their motions, and end up in whatever stability is required by their structure.

And so, after minutes only, just another sea vessel sat there, sunk forever at the bottom of a planetary atmosphere.

In that warm Caribbean sea, normal responses resumed. The ice, which had probably cooled to 30,000 or 40,000 degrees Centigrade below zero, began to melt.

When Nodo's boarding unit left the mother ship, he saw the ice and reported back: "We seem to have come down on the only ice pack that's visible. Better try to break free."

Captain-by-rotation Darkel and the chief engineer-by-rotation, a robot named Frot, made a simple decision about that. They would use the forward thrust engines—and, in effect, drive themselves right out of the ice.

The part about using the thrust engines was no problem. They were nuclear-powered; and that was a source of energy that altered only slowly with the passage of time. To them seven hundred years was as nothing. Even after ten thousand years they would have functioned as if no time had gone by.

"Apply forward thrust!" commanded Darkal.

"Fire engines one to a hundred!" Frot ordered his aides.

As that colossal power was applied, the ship leaned forward. Literally tilted slightly. The island of ice, in which it was encased, tilted also. That was all. No other movement occurred.

There was a long pause while, first, the engines were shut off, and then, while Darkel and Frot, as leaders, tried to understand what was wrong. Suddenly, their exterior wall scanners brought the awareness that they were not just in an ice field. They *were* the ice field.

On earth the Lantellan craft, with all its equipment and its great engines, and its 30,000 Lantellan robots, weighed about 120,000 tons, and the ice island about 1,500,000 tons. So they were not, as a group, going anywhere until the ice thawed.

It *was* melting. With every warm wave movement. And with the breezes that swept across the green-blue water. And from the direct rays of a tropical sun; which would soon be higher in the sky and much hotter. Accordingly, the great spaceship in its cage of ice sat on a relatively calm sea, with water stretching to every horizon; and only two objects visible as far as the eye could see: the sail ship and the boarding unit commanded by Nodo.

The ice that held the ship was cold, cold as no ice on earth had been before; and it would take a while to thaw.

Time would have to pass. During that time—what?

What good use could anyone make of the time gained?

9

It was over.

The incredible! The impossible!

Fletcher stood on the deck of his wooden ship. A wind blew into his face. His lips felt dry. His eyes watered. As through a mist, he looked after the receding metal "bird." And then, blinking hard, he stared down at the four ruffians who sprawled limply on the hot wood.

Already it was hard to remember in any meaningful way that they had been "shot" by what looked like rays of lethal light.

There was something else struggling in his mind. A thought. A feeling. What it amounted to was a faraway awareness that a decision would have to be made here.

Vaguely: . . . We should tell somebody about all this. Tell whom?

It was his very first moment of realizing that he might have a role to play in the madness that had descended on the planet. But, of course, it was far too soon for him to realize that all the basic decisions would eventually have to come from him.

Now, merely asking the question—tell whom?—made ridiculous the idea that it was up to him to do anything.

There was actually another factor. It was a truth that he

consciously even now did not admit: the reality that he
was, at heart, a loyal Englishman. He believed in his
groin, or somewhere, that England was the center of the
universe. He accepted that England should be protected
from its enemies.

He was kneeling on the deck by the time those fleeting
images had come and gone. Kneeling beside the twisted
body of a ruffian known as Nat Arkion. (To an educated
man like Fletcher, the name held echoes of the early
occupation of Britain by the ancient Romans.) Nat had an
outthrust jaw, and he was quick with a knife or saber. That
chunky jaw, and the face above and behind it, was burned
a deep brown by the tropical sun. Even in stillness it had a
mean look to it. Life in the streets of London had done
unpleasant things to the boy that had become this man. But
Nat had been paying back everybody he could stick his
knife into for a long time now. And perhaps the debt was
the other way around.

Fletcher picked up one inert wrist, and was surprised to
feel a pulse. . . . Not dead! Well, I'll be!

It took a minute or so to establish that the other three
creature-men also had heartbeats.

He stood up. And for the first time, so intent had he
been, he grew conscious that the crew members were dead
silent, and not moving. Their eyes, murky brown or steely
blue, watched him sullenly. They were either frozen in
some emotion, or were waiting—for what was not clear.

Fletcher said, "They're alive!" He raised his voice,
added: "Some of you bullies carry them to their bunks!"

No one moved.

Fifty men, give or take a few, stood there under the
Caribbean sky in a solid pack of male depravity. The wind
wiggled uncombed locks of hair on dozens of heads. The
almost hundred eyes remained staring at Fletcher.

Once again came the feeling: They're waiting!

That brought a reaction thought, slightly startled:. . .
Did I say that wrong?

After mere seconds, it occurred to Fletcher, hopefully,

that at a time like this he should perhaps handle the men more diplomatically.

And so, he said smoothiy, "Mr. Shradd, will you see to it that these injured men are taken to their bunks, where I can give them proper medical attention?"

What Shradd did was to name names. And it was the men, thus selected, who awkwardly came forward. And awkwardly, two to each limp body, they grabbed and tugged.

Whereupon, having got the rescue under way, Shradd walked heavily over to Fletcher and said in a low voice, "Better watch it, sir! They blame you."

So that was it! Fletcher was instantly in his sardonic state. It was astonishing, but he kept forgetting that these men were *all* lame-brains. Even Shradd had acted *as if* what had happened was an opportunity for personal advancement.

He said sarcastically, "What do they think I should have done?—prevent a boarding!"

"They don't ask themselves questions like that, Cap'n."

It was at once an obvious truth. And a slightly shaken Fletcher was about to turn away without additional comment, except his gaze happened to stray toward the rescue operation.

At that precise moment, one of the bodies was dropped. The injured man had been lifted. His head and shoulder—which were supposedly supported by a man named Drayton—slipped free. It fell a foot and a half. The head landed first with a sickening thud.

Fletcher cringed.

He saw that Drayton didn't seem to be aware that anything unusual had happened. The man was in the act of taking a dirty rag out of his pocket. Into this he blew his nose stentoriously.

Meanwhile, the other man continued to drag the limp body. The head bounced and thudded on the uneven deck. Moments later, Drayton grabbed again at the shoulders. And this time, when he lifted, he held on.

A swift, shuddering scan of the other casualties apprised
Fletcher that they were not much better off. Each of the
injured bullies was being partly lifted, partly dragged,
carelessly bumped against every protruding edge, bashed
into solid objects like doors and posts, and dropped three
or four times a cruel distance of as much as two feet.

Yet, as he was presently able to verify, they all still had
pulses when they finally sprawled, each in his narrow
bunk.

As he stared down at the unconscious men, an odd
thought touched Fletcher's awareness: Wonder what the
light did when it went inside their heads?

He was a man who normally noticed his own stream of
consciousness. But the unusualness of that idea, as it
moved so softly through his own head, did not catch his
attention.

The enormous involvement of the moment held him.
His immediate surroundings reached first to his nose—

It was nearly a year since he had been in the men's
quarters. And already it seemed too soon to be back. The
bunks, the unconscious men in four of them, and the
onlookers behind and beside him stank of sweat, of unwashed clothes, and old leather. A damp over-odor of
decay permeated everything.

Grimacing, but sardonic as always during his medical
moments, Fletcher took out his clean white handkerchief.
He spat into it several times. And with the thus wetted thin
linen cloth, he wiped the face of Nat the knifer. Then,
with more saliva, he did the same for Big Dingy—a
beetle-browed brute of a man. Dib Clutterbuck, short but
muscular, with a face that bore some resemblance to a
shark's, was next. And, finally, he used the now grimy
handkerchief on Will Spire. Will had a twisted mind. But
he occasionally put forth a word or two of black humor.
His jokes had in their time even evoked a pained smile
from Nathan Fletcher.

Having done so much of nothing, Fletcher ended up
facing the door. And saw with a tiny relief that a mere

handful of brawny hearties stood at the exit. Ordinarily,
their presence in any number would not have been a
problem. But he was remembering Shradd's words: *"They
blame you!"*

He had an ironic thought. It was a grim enough experience that a pirate captain was straining to reason out how
he might ward off a mutiny. But his worry was even more
ridiculous: How was he going to get out of this narrow
room? That is, without getting a knife driven into his back!

His unhappy decision: Better not try to leave.

Yet.

But now—what to do for these jingle brains!

The four unluckies kept right on breathing, slowly but
steadily. The trouble was, as captain he was expected to be
the all-knowing medical officer. And he actually had a
book on the subject that he had read intermittently, and
had shaken his head over. But he could dress a wound. He
could bleed a sick man. And he had the equipment for
giving enemas. But he had never given one, and didn't
intend to start now.

Because he was baffled, he suddenly recalled his earlier
thought. Except it was different now. . . . The light inside
their heads—it's watching me.

What!

He caught himself with an effort. Smiled grimly. And
had the absolutely mad idea pass through his mind that the
four men were aware of him. And then, even as he had
that Irish addle in his head, the four men had a thought in
theirs, which they projected at him.

They said in unison, "Don't worry, Cap'n. No'un's
gonna muzzle you this minute. So whyn't you jump ship
in London like you gotta mind to, collect the topping man
stuff for what you did to the girl, and that'll be the way out
for ya.

"An' don't worry 'bout us. We'll wake in about an
hour—"

Near Fletcher, a rough voice said, "Whyn't you just let
'em sleep it off, Cap'n?"

His brain was—what? He didn't know—spinning. It was reaction, but mostly amazement at himself. At such a time as this—was the self-chastising feeling—to have his mind flapping loose in his head was all he needed.

So, when the voice spoke to him, he turned more or less blankly. Mostly more. And noticed automatically that the speaker was one of the three frosty faces aboard the *Orinda*—Sol Tyke, a crewman who had in his awful fashion helped carry the bodies.

The first observation that a man who had had smallpox was among the tougher types on ship brought awareness that Sol was not the only one. One of the other frosty faces had also joined in the attack against the metal men. Was it possible the disease made a man angrier? He'd have imagined it the other way around. That is, that it would have scared him silly.

It was actually a good moment. The spoken advice of Sol. The wildness of his own thoughts. . . . All added up to a positive feeling. Fletcher was somewhat but not entirely astonished to hear himself say in a loud, carrying voice, "They'll be all right. They'll waken in about an hour."

He made a dismissing gesture. "All right, let's clear out of here! Give your pals a chance to breathe."

Afterward, Fletcher conducted a silent argument with himself. It was all about how predicting an event only an hour away had approximately sixty minutes of security in it.

Then what?

10

The morning sagged by. During those numerous minutes the sailng ship was a white epitome of grace and motion on the surface of a vast ocean. Nobody did anything. Nobody asked any questions.

What bothered Fletcher—again—during those minutes was that, once more, he had a distinct recollection of having done all this before. But without the Lantellans and without Billy.

To have been or not to have been, that was the question. . . . The Shakespearean paraphrase mildly amused him. And, of course, it was impossible. Yet it was in all ways the most vivid dream he had ever had.

Once more, he allowed the memory to jog through his mind. It was all there. The girl—in deep shock. . . . We threw her overboard. She drowned. I went to England, and collected the balance due me, and then went off and lived in Italy the rest of my life—

What an incredible fantasy! Because here he was. A pirate captain. Still in his early thirties. If he had a future most of it was still ahead of him. He realized there was a little more hope in him. He was taking slightly deeper breaths, as if, now that the sun had climbed higher into the vast sky, there was a future. The greatest relief, of course—he had to admit it—had come with the disappearance of the Lantellan battleship. It had slowly but with finality sunk below the horizon to the west and the north.

As he sat there on the deck, the beautiful wind kept blowing on his back, kept filling the sails, kept driving the ship farther and farther from the giant vessel. It was a hot wind, hot as only the Caribbean hell could be. Presumably, those aboard the alien vessel were Pursuing the *Orinda*. And so it was beginning to look as if his only immediate problem was Shradd's incipient mutiny.

There was a sound behind him. A clearing of someone's throat. "Uh, Cap'n."

Fletcher turned and stood up. All in one movement. Not too fast. But good enough.

Four grinning men stood at the head of the steps that led up from below.

The bullies! The quartet whom he had last seen unconscious in their bunks an hour ago—

His thought poised. *An hour ago!*

"Hey!" said Fletcher.

"At your service, Cap'n," said Will Spire, in a significant tone. "All four of us, sir."

Except with Shradd, the slender, beautifully dressed man who stood there on that small ship sailing over that remote sea had never been a man to avoid a confrontation. It took a tiny bit of inner bracing, and a conscious determination, to make that confrontation. But Fletcher did it.

"I thought you were Shradd's men," he said.

When none of the four answered immediately, Fletcher merely glanced from eye to eye. And waited.

It was Will Spire once more who replied. "Mr. Shradd, sir, has our respect. There's a good man in there somewhere. But he's not up to handling this situation, Cap'n."

"And you are?" Pointedly.

The silence was longer this time. But again Fletcher waited. This time it was Dib Clutterbuck—stupid, vicious Dib—who answered, who said, "Cap'n, we've been wrong what we'uns been doin'. Not wrong all the way, y'understand.

Bein' a pirate in this day'n'age is just part of the whole low-level game. But there's better ways, sir, than killin' an' stealin', if you think about it.''

The concept of a pirate sailor thinking was too new for Fletcher to absorb easily. But something of the meaning came through. And it was so transcendent that a phrase from his early religious training came up all the way from where it had been buried these many years: "Purified in the light of the lord!"

Purification of *some* kind was what had happened to these four. That fantastic beam of light—Fletcher thought, awed. It drew itself inside their heads. That wasn't just my imagination. Once inside, besides rendering the men unconscious, it brightened all the darknesses of those damaged minds, seeking out every twisted memory, and every evil decision.

That was the appearance that he seemed to be confronting.

Bullies, murderers, and a hundred low pirate instincts. Could it be that such were merely outward manifestations of the madness of what life had done to them?

Even as he had that enormous thought, his second reaction began to come through: Don't get carried away. This is still the world where my land and fortune were forcibly taken from me. Still where, if we meet a British man-o'-war, we'll all be racked up on our necks.

But he stood a little straighter as he spoke again: actually felt hopeful in a different way, not just about himself, but about the whole world. He would continue going forward with his plans—no change there—but . . . "Gentlemen," he said courteously, "you have my good wishes. I shall take your remarks at face value, and act accordingly, and—"

A scream! From somewhere behind him! So loud, so terrified, that his unspoken words choked in his throat. It was such a hoarse caterwauling that Fletcher, literally, lurched about, almost falling. And then he had clutched the near railing. For long, deadly seconds, he crouched there and glared.

A wall of water. Out there to the southwest. Thirty. Fifty. Two hundred feet high. He kept revising each improbable dimension as his estimate of distance was modified by his experienced brain.

Naturally, he thought of the awesome thing as a tidal wave. He had heard of such cataclysms. He had never before seen one.

The utterly appalled feeling that came did not prevent him from abruptly yelling orders. To the steersman: "Turn the vessel north by east!" To the crew: "Get the sails down!" To the four former bullies, he said urgently, "We can talk later. Get down there and help!"

"Yes, sir. Yes, Cap'n."

The swift minutes raced by. The terrified men worked under the yelling voices of Fletcher and Shradd. No disobedience now—Fletcher noticed in a vague aside thought.

The huge pile of water swept past them little more than a mile away. It was beautiful to watch . . . if one could think of it like that—and Fletcher could. But the *Orinda* was whipped along by trailing tides that were less than the monster at the center by many multiples but they nonetheless had enough power to carry the vessel for a score of miles. And during the entire time the whole visible ocean was a sheet of moving foam.

Long before they were in the clear Shradd had joined Fletcher on the bridge and uttered a dark thought in a surprisingly threatening voice: "Something funny going on, if you ask me, ever since that kid came aboard."

Fletcher, wo had seated himself again, didn't get up. He had an instinct for crises; and a feeling of how fast a body movement should be in the presence of one. Sitting there, shrinking a little, and unhappy with himself for being that way, Fletcher had a recurrence of what was now an old feeling: that he had been getting ready for this struggle for power ever since Shradd was brought aboard his first ship by another ex-convict. That was three long murderous years ago.

He thought: I've got four men on my side that Shradd

doesn't know about. An interesting development. But that was for later. Now—

His only defensive action now: he drew his feet up under him. That done, he was ready to leap up if the threat continued. In its way, his failure to get to his feet was a hesitation not only of body but of mind. And he recognized it as such, and was reminded of that other, recent moment of hesitation. With the girl. The memory startled him anew. A man as tough and determined as he had, during those instants, become . . . unsettled, unwilling. Even an emotional appeal to her to give in. Suppose she had suddenly agreed—what a complicated situation that would have been, really. In fact, ridiculous. His whole future—it still seemed to him—had depended on the girl's being killed. And, of course, he had quickly braced up and carried through. But that earlier conflict interfered now with his usual clarity of mind to such an extent that he was only able to speak one word:

"So?" He did manage to say it in his best deliberate tone of voice.

"I spotted him right away as a wrong 'un," snarled Shradd.

"We were both puzzled," Fletcher responded.

"It was up to you to see to it that we took no chances with nobody," said Shradd, accusingly.

But—Fletcher couldn't help observing—the attack of his rival was with words, not action.

The reality was instantly so reassuring that he chose that as the moment to stand up. He moved quickly, true, but he tried to cover up by saying smoothly, "As you know, Mr. Shradd, we live in a world that is not yet perfect, and so we have strong emotions about that occasionally. I still remember as if it were yesterday when the Tory government seized my property. That was the moment I turned against the system. From then on, I was ready to play as dirty as they did." He smiled his grimmest smile. "And I have so played."

He put his left hand up and grasped a stay. At once, he

had a firm position for his body, and he was ready to draw
his sword, if necessary.

He said, "I think I am now ready to assassinate the men
responsible for my downfall. It is because of that purpose
in mind that I shall be leaving the *Orinda* in London."

He uttered the falsehood glibly. The truth was, the men
he hated were not vulnerable, if he knew them—and he
did. His enemies were sharp, tough, capable people. More
important, they had the protection of the state and the
military. Without that, they would have been murdered
long ago. And so, no, it was not for Nathan Fletcher, that
route.

But such murder intent was the sort of reason that would
have meaning for a vengeful type like Shradd. Even as he
had that awareness, Fletcher saw that he had achieved his
verbal victory. The big man's expression had changed.
Suddenly, there was ill-concealed glee in his heavy face.

Quietly, Fletcher recognized his victory. Later, he would
decide what he would really do in London.

11

She who looked like, and believed herself to be, Lady Patricia Hemistan, spent most of the "afternoon" lying down on the thick, velvet floor.

She was a little unstable in 1704 A.D. The molecules and atoms from the dead Patricia had been re-formed in a machine from the eighty-third century.

Not a perfect mix. Not a totally acceptable person. A human woman with—what?

People belong in their own era, not just psychically. They belong because they are physically part of an evolving universe in which every particle is in its proper location at any given time.

Suddenly, a shift—no! Suddenly, never. Something has to give, to alter faster than normal, but without shattering. It was that change that was taking place.

She didn't feel good. She was thirsty. She was hungry. Everything felt wrong inside her, as if she were on the verge of a fever.

Somebody should look after me. I'm not well . . .

But the machine had only known how to put her together the way people were in the eighty-third century. Physically, that would presently have a good effect. Mentally, because in her case no training went with it, the change would be slow in manifesting. But it would come. It would come.

The Transit-Craft had had its problem strictly with its engines. And they were off, of course, to be repaired. That was the hope of the beings who watched the scene inside the vessel and controlled the tiny, mobile twinkling points of sentient luminescence that clung to the silvery strands.

The living human bodies aboard—the crew—were in their encasements. Safe behind immensely protective walls. Automatically fed by nutrient solutions.

These beings watched the poor, trapped, thirsty, hungry girl, first, as she walked restlessly around looking for, principally, water. And then as she lay on the floor. At first she was on her side, with her head and face pointing toward the transparency through which she could watch the ocean floor. She seemed infinitely absorbed with what she saw there. And so they waited, and waited.

At long last, the position evidently became a tiring one to maintain. Wearily, with a heavy sigh, she turned her back on that fantastic sea scene.

Instantly, even as she turned, a luminescence floated down upon her shoulder.

It was like falling asleep. One moment you were there looking like, and believing you were, Lady Patricia Hemistan, utterly desperate now. The next—

An awareness of movement under her. That was Patricia's first sensation of returning consciousness. Her reaction was automatic; not a decision. She simply opened her eyes. But, of course, vision is not a simplicity. And there is a difference between awakening from normal sleep and from unconsciousness.

That difference manifested, first, in inability to focus. Brightness came in. Wherever she was, whatever she was looking at, was lighted by some equivalent of daytime. But, as with certain insects who merely detect light and not images, human eyes have a comparable primitive response under stress circumstances. The girl could see something. But it was a primitive reaction. The cameralike characteristics of the normal eye were not available in these early stages of her vision.

There came a moment, then, when she saw something. Abruptly, as the steady movement under her continued, a realization came: . . . I'm lying face down . . . The swift corollary: . . . I must be looking at the floor.

What was presently strange about that was that the "floor" was a glassy substance, but not—she discovered—slippery. She learned that when she brought her hands forward and braced them against the glass. Her palms didn't skid. In fact, there was firm contact. And she was able to raise up. And bring her knees under her. And so she lifted her body into a kneeling position.

And there she poised. Because the movement and the action had brought her high enough to realize that she was looking at the gunwale of a boat that was altogether about four feet high. And that the boat—far more sensational—was gliding over the surface of an ocean that (she presently discovered, as she came all the way up to full knee height) stretched to every horizon.

It was a surprisingly large boat: twenty-eight feet long by eight wide, with a portion of both the front and the rear covered. Her instant impression: the covered portions were accessible, and had safety features for her.

Abruptly, the speed at which the craft was traveling made her grab for the nearest side. She held on firmly while, once more, with great caution now, she examined her situation.

She had a sudden, wonderful realization: . . . I'm not thirsty any more. Or hungry. . . . She began to feel a lot more secure, with that awareness. Thus, since it *was* broad daylight, she saw presently that the prow was pointing in a generally easterly direction, with a northern slant. And that the craft was moving extremely rapidly without sails.

She was not qualified to comprehend a speed of nearly fifty miles per hour. But all that afternoon the boat skimmed along at that considerable velocity. And so she had time to discover that the rear covered section had a door that led

down to a little room with a large bed. And the covered
area up front had spigots and cupboards. There was a
glasslike container protruding from an odd mechanism.
She surmised its intent, and took hold, and pulled. It came
free easily. Whereupon, when she held it under one spigot
and pressed, water came out; which she drank. And when
she held it under another spigot a thick reddish liquid
squeezed out. With a tentative finger she brought a tiny
smear of the syrupy stuff to her tongue. A tart flavor, but
the basic reality was unmistakable.

Food!

The instant recognition, instead of bringing tears of joy,
seemed to have a calming effect. Feeling thus, she was
able to stare out over the limitless ocean horizon, and to
wander mentally through the five modes:

How did I get up to the surface? *Who* was I with? *What*
was that down there? Why am I in this boat? *Where* am I
being taken?

They were questions to which an extremely sharp mind—
and growing sharper—addressed itself. And realized there
was no instant answer available. But . . . the feel of
rapidly flowing sea wind, the shuddering motion of an
obviously expensive boat driven by magical power, the
glorious blue of the sky above, the limitless sea . . . all
told a tale of continuing survival. And it was not just
happening moment by moment, but intended to continue
hour after hour.

I am being looked after. She savored the emotional
meaning of that. And it tasted of truth. Somebody cared
for Lady Patricia Hemistan, drowned by purchase of a
pirate's murderous soul. The purchaser—the identification
of the culprit came utterly naturally—was her villainous
cousin.

She had in the past, occasionally, felt guilty about him.
As if somehow it was up to her to save him. Had even
thought: Poor Keith. What will become of him, once he
has spent all his father's inheritance money?—which he
was so rapidly doing. But she had nevertheless dismissed

his proposal of marriage, on the grounds, first, of consanguinity, and, second, with an airy: "You do not attract me in that way, sir."

With such memories and thoughts, and many hopes, she drank the water, and sipped the liquid food, and slept on the great bed.

Awake again!

It required a few moments to realize where she was not. The shudder and vibration of motion under her was the reminder. Eyes open, definitely remembering that the bed she was in was where it was, Patricia sat up; then stood up. It was a lazy movement, using only a portion of her strength. In the dark she fumbled for the door; slid it open.

Daytime! A clouded day. As she climbed the steps she saw that there was a special brightness in the clouds only a foot or so above the horizon ahead. The brightness suggested that the sun had just started its day. So it was early.

Because she was curious, and vaguely hopeful, she climbed farther up. And stretched, and craned for a quick look at the sea around her. The hope ended immediately. Still nothing but open ocean.

The act of looking that thoroughly had required full exposure of her body. Instantly, the sea breeze put its icy fingers on her. The girl gasped. Retreated down the steps, and under the coverlet, leaving the door open. She lay there, then, for a cozy minute or two, or maybe ten. Realization came of how cold it must have been outside during the night. Yet she remembered how evenly warm the temperature had been inside her sleeping quarters. . . . Could there be a fire burning in some hidden lower section of her little ship?

A passing thought ended that line of speculation: I'd better get up. They're counting on me, now that the boy has disappeared. . . .

It was a thought so completely without meaning that she noticed it. And finally twisted it into a special rationalization: They—her fellow passengers on the *Red Princess*—in some way depended on her escaping death. (The thought about the boy she couldn't fit in, so she forgot it as being irrelevant.)

She had crawled into the bed the previous night with all her clothes on. Now, somehow impelled to action, she sat up again. By means of the light from the stairwell she began stroking the creases out of her long dress with the palms of her hands. And suddenly noticed something.

There were lines drawn on what had seemed part of the flat, hard surface of the interior wall at the head of the bed. The lines took the shape of drawers. Three of them. So she bent over and fumbled.

Surprisingly, there were slots. She was able to insert her fingers and pull. Each drawer, in turn, opened. Inside were a variety of—what?

A peculiar thought came to her in connection with a rodlike object in the top drawer. As if the rod said, "Pick me up!"

The girl shook her head. It was a chiding gesture to herself for having such fantasies. Nonetheless, she lifted the small, gleaming object. And held it. Caressed it. Looked blankly at it from all angles. Wondered what it could possibly be used for. And finally put it back.

At the exact moment her fingers let go, the rod emitted a screaming sound.

Patricia jumped away. It was a half scramble that got her to her feet. She went hastily out on the deck, and along it. Behind her the screaming continued.

This is positively ridiculous! she thought.

The sound followed her the length of the vessel to the water and food spigots. It screamed during all the swift minutes that she stood there eating. And then went on screaming, as she walked slowly back and down to the open drawer.

One thought she had was that it was not doing anything harmful. Another, that an obviously mechanical sound is not alarming, really, except perhaps to a burglar. And there were no burglars around. Her third thought was that, in handling the thing, she must have turned on the sound.

So, tentatively, she picked up the rod. The sound stopped. Relieved, she laid the rod back in the drawer. As she drew her fingers away, it screamed. She grabbed it. The sound ceased.

Several experiments later, she had passed through the stages where she carried it continuously in one or another hand . . . to the point where she had it tucked into the intricate netting that covered her bosom.

That location seemed perfectly satisfactory to whatever delicate mechanism monitored the sound. Quiet prevailed.

But she had learned her lesson. She carefully closed all three drawers in her ''bedroom'' without touching another item.

Another long day.

A young woman alone on a power-driven vessel eventually sits down, or lies down, and waits. Patricia watched the clouds scud over the sky. Periodically, the sun came out, and those were the times she sat up and stared at the dancing light on the waves. There was always a wind blowing at—though she didn't think of it that way—the full fifty-mile-per-hour speed of the little vessel.

In a way, then, in the several days that went by, the lonely journey was an interesting event. The most interesting observation she made was that the craft was still headed in a northeasterly direction.

Toward north Europe? Toward England?

England it was.

So perfect was the ship's sense of direction that, presently, it headed toward the mouth of a river that, even in the misty light of early morning, she recognized as the Thames.

Her small vessel did a final, marvelous, directional thing. It brought her far up the river to a point where she recognized that she was near her London cousin's area of residence. And then, as she noticed an unoccupied wharf of the correct height—

The boat turned into it. And drew up parallel to the outjutting planks. Thereupon, it came to a stop.

There was actually the sound of its sides rubbing against the wooden platform, as it lay-to, idling.

Waiting.

It wants me to get off.

It was instantly such a ridiculous idea that Patricia chided herself. "My dear Mistress Hemistan, you've got to stop playing that childish game of talking to boats and little glistening sticks."

There were, in fact, good reasons for a young lady, alone, not leaving any secure place. Standing there on the deck of the gently rocking craft, she looked up and out at the immediate reasons. Her vessel was lying alongside a small wharf used by river boats. Just beyond the wooden platform was an embankment with steps leading up to a carriage road that paralleled the river.

The problem was: any London street.

The problem was that neither an unarmed man, nor a woman dressed like a lady, could, without protection, travel the streets of London in 1704 A.D., night or day. Every other man on foot was an opportunist criminal—if he but saw a possible victim.

At best, she would merely be assaulted every hundred feet. Her valuable clothing would be removed first. Somebody would pay money for it; however small the sum, it was treasure for the type of footpad who made a fearhaunted, fear-creating livelihood from such chance encounters. What abuse might be done to her body depended on the availability of temporary hideaways to which she could be dragged or carried, and probably also depended on the number of gentlemen riders who might be passing on horseback.

Troubling memories of numerous warnings about the dangers of a London street skittered through her awareness. And so, thinking thus, she parted her lips to murmur: "No, no, dear, wonderful little ship. I'm not leaving. Indeed, I would prefer that—"

The thought stopped.

"My God!" She spoke the half-prayer aloud in a stunned voice.

She was *on* the wharf, a full dozen feet from the water's edge. And the boat—

So swiftly did she spin around that she almost fell; so swiftly she was dizzy. But she was in time, then, to see that her home of many days and nights was gliding away. As she sagged there, dazed, it turned even more sharply away, and sped off.

In a manner of speaking she had no final view of it. Because tears blurred her vision. By the time she had wiped her eyes, and braced herself against the terrible sense of loss, and could see again, there was no sign of the little ship among the numerous other vessels that plied the great river.

She was actually more bewildered at first than scared. Because—how had she got ashore? She had heard of such things. A person blankly doing something without noticing. But this was the first time it had ever happened to her.

A buzzing sound interrupted that confused thought.

She jumped sideways. Almost fell. Looked wildly around. But the wharf and what she could see of the embankment were still deserted.

She was breathing hard. And so several moments went by before she realized: the buzzing sound was still there. Very close. Almost in her ear.

Abruptly—awareness.

The rod!

Even as she fumbled for it inside the netting at the top front of her dress, she thought: Really, who would imagine it to have two sounds?

First, that awful screaming noise. Now, the fainter, but insistent buzz.

She had the rod in her fingers by the time those thoughts had come and gone. What distracted her was that as she lifted the beautiful, smooth, six-inch, metallic extrusion out of her dress, the buzzing ceased.

That, it turned out, was the way it had to be. Only when

she held it in her fingers did the damnable little thing stop buzzing.

She finally had a reassuring thought about the little nuisance: It's my only weapon. I could hit somebody with it—

With that, she started up the steps that would take her up over the embankment to—

What it brought her up to was the carriage driveway. It also brought into view a scarecrow of an old man. He was standing about fifty feet away from her along the otherwise deserted road. The creature must have caught a movement out of the corner of one eye, for he turned and gaped at her. And then he made a horrendous sound of excitement: "Araaagh!"

Having made the raucous throat noise, he started toward her at an old man's speed.

Patricia kept her head and ran slantwise across the river road to the beginning of a street. There was brush at the corner. And, as she rounded that, *there* was a young man.

He had bright blue wicked eyes. And he showed his snaggled teeth in a delighted grin. And started forward.

She couldn't go back. And the young man barred the way forward. Behind her, the old man was making a vocal racket which sounded like guttersnipe words to the effect that she belonged to him.

The roughly dressed young man took the time to fling a violent retort at his elderly rival. And then—rushed toward her.

Exactly what happened next was not immediately understandable. But, suddenly, he stopped short. An awful look came into his unshaven face. His mouth fell open. His blue eyes glazed. He stood shuddering. And then he gave a long, agonized scream. And fell, writhing, to the ground.

Patricia was a hundred feet, at least, past him when a memory caught up with her. The rod had vibrated in her hand during those final moments of the young man's attack.

And it vibrated like that for twenty-seven additional men

of all sizes, arrayed in as many different varieties of poor male attire. After the third attack she was no longer running. She accepted.

I'm still being protected. That rod forced me to take it along. . . .

After leaving Patricia, the small vessel that had transported her across earth's second-largest ocean moved upriver to an abandoned wharf. Presently, it slid quietly into a small, dilapidated quay.

The following day it was still there. And the next day. And a week later. On the seventh day, two eight-year-old boys wandered onto the quay. And for a while they were aboard the little super-ship. Naturally, they tugged and pried at the end doors. And probably established by their instant willingness to break and enter what was not theirs that within a few years they, also, would begin a footpad career. At the moment, what was inside the locked sections was not for little boys. The metal held against their sporadic and ill-considered attempts at entry.

Finally, tiring of the nothingness of the situation, they departed. But that night the craft backed out of its no-longer-safe harbor, and sped farther upstream. Some time before dawn it located another backwater of the great London docking system. Glided in. And stopped.

12

A specific destination in the port of London was not easy to come by at night. The *Orinda* had its waiting wharf. But where in the darkness was it?

By arriving at the mouth of the Thames shortly after dusk, Captain Fletcher allowed himself a long autumn night to edge along, and calculate, and make forays to the right bank. First Mate Shradd, who knew his port, was the arbiter and the repeated negator: "No. Not here. Go farther. Another mile, my guess."

How much is a mile on a darkened river at night, for a ship going against stream, its sails distracted by cross winds?

In spite of the impossibility, there came a moment when, by the early light of dawn, they could see their destination. And they were able to edge in. It was not yet a time when the voracious trading merchants of England were subject to strict surveillance. So, once into shore, and lying-to, they had no problem, and no need for secrecy.

Shortly after sunup, the buyers came to look at the loot: the tobacco, and the wool, the stolen bricks, the hard woods from Central America, certain furs, and the odd-shaped metal objects (scrap it was called in the transaction) that the boy had brought aboard.

There were thirty-eight bidders for the spoils. It was a motley crew, a mix of English and Scot, Limey and Irish, Dutch and Jew, several Swedes, and three Chinks. The languages spoken were principally a variety of bastard or broken English, and that commercial tongue of the long north seacoast, Low German.

The man who brought up wagons and hauled away Billy Todd's machines was a swarthy type of indeterminate national origin—probably Jewish. But the name on his wagon was

Julius MacDonald, Dealer

Fletcher had a simple practical solution to the gibberish. When the jabber got too fast for him, he would grab the jabberer, and point, and yell, "This?" Meaning; "Do you want this?" And when he got a nod, he would add, "How much?"

They were probably suspected of being pirates, and that got them a measure of respect, and also, however, an attitude of you'd-better-sell-this-stuff-cheap-or-you'll-be-sorry.

These were undercurrents, and had some influence. But in the final issue cash spoke the only language that had meaning.

When the deed was done, when shabby hirelings began loading the pirated goods onto wagons, as the cursing grew loud, and then diminished, Fletcher remembered what Billy Todd had said: that there was no place in the time universe now but 1704 A.D. For the few moments that his mind had expanded to encompass the incredible universe that idea depicted . . . something happened inside his head.

Until that moment, until that concept was presented, he had always taken it for granted that his own daily life *was* the only time that existed—second by second. Suddenly, even contemplating such a limitation brought a feeling of shock.

He looked at the people around him—the buyers as well

as their aides and his own sleazy crew—and he thought,
shocked: This riffraff! *dese shlingels*—the Low German
term seemed only too apt—was where the human race
would now begin again.

His feeling: we'll never make it a second time.

After all the outsiders were gone, Fletcher was pleasantly surprised to find that he had cash in hand more than
his original estimate of what it might amount to. Since
there must be no suspicion, he had counted the money
with the help of Shradd and three crew members who
could add large sums.

Having done that very decisive task, they divided the
take into shares, and handed it out share by share. Each
anxious individual made his mark that it was received.
And then, off he went, given two weeks' leave of absence,
and glad to go. To each individual, it meant finding his
particular doxy or an abandoned family to live with again
for a while, and to enjoy—if that were the right word. It
was actually often a time of bitter recrimination from the
wives, and a tearful demand for extra money so that she
and "the little 'uns" could survive between voyages.

Fletcher made a point of speaking to several men. So
that when each in his turn of the four former bullies was
handed his portion he was able to speak to them much as
he already had to some of the others. In their case, the
dialogue was surprisingly similar for each man.

Fletcher: "You feeling all right now?"

Ex-bully: "Fair good, sir."

Fletcher: "Got a wife out there somewhere?"

Ex-bully: "A 'sponsible man could call 'er that, sir."

Fletcher: "If we needed you in a hurry, what are the
chances of getting your help quickly?"

Ex-bully: "This 'un'll climb aboard the first carriage,
sir, an' come arippin'."

So it went, with Shradd sitting right there, scowling.

Shradd and four men were planning to stay aboard. If
they ventured forth, it would be two men at a time, and

Shradd by himself. But there would either be three or four men on ship at all times.

With Shradd's permission, Captain Fletcher would sleep aboard that second night, also. It was understood that he would depart permanently early in the morning for an unstated destination.

When it had grown dark, he invited Shradd to have dinner with him at a nearby inn. The two men sat in an alcove, and ate, and watched a couple of lissome girls sing and dance on a small stage. The girls presently exchanged significant glances with the men, and for an offer of small bits of silver—a couple of shillings each—agreed to rendezvous later that evening.

It was 1704 A.D., a time that still was without mercy on women who had no fixed income. The coercion of poverty would ensure that they would indeed keep the tryst. And so, Shradd and Fletcher chatted a little, drank a little; perhaps, in Fletcher's case, a little too much, for at one point he spoke rather freely of his past.

"My mistake," he said, "was being attracted by the concept of free competition and Whig liberalism. I was labeled a turncoat, and by questionable means, which were nonetheless legal, was divested of my inheritance. When this happened, I became so filled with hatred that for the first time the deed of murder was possible to me. Suddenly, I could strike, and slash, casually, as I tried by devious means, and self-justification, to get back the share of the world of which I had been deprived."

Shradd said, "You were a Tory who converted to Whig, sir, as I understand you. So my view is that you were actually lucky that somebody didn't swindle a sentence of hanged-drawn-and-quartered on you, a destiny"—the first mate concluded—"that is still being meted out to unlucky businessman-type Whigs, who are accused of trying to destroy the perfect world created by Tory wisdom and generosity."

"I was indeed lucky," agreed Fletcher quickly. "A

friend in high places warned me, and I slipped out of my quarters one night just ahead of an arrest order—''

. . . Later, after the girls had come, and gone, and he was alone on deck, Fletcher wondered if his evening of calculated camaraderie with Shradd would buy what he hoped he had paid for. Simply, and starkly, he wanted the *Orinda* to be there still when he came back. That was just in case things went wrong, or there were other negative developments.

If that should become necessary, what would he do about getting back his command? It was a problem he would confront when, and if, it arose . . . he told himself.

I should go to bed. . . . It was a truth, but he didn't move. Abruptly, once more, he realized the problem. As an Englishman, he felt, of all things, loyalty to England. And so, again, his feeling was that he ought to warn somebody about the Lantellan battleship.

Warn whom? Merely asking the question brought an ironic smile to that lean face with its determined blue eyes. Whom, indeed?

With that, realizing what had been bothering him for many weeks now, he sensed a change inside him. And, just like that, he crinkled his nose, aware of an awful stench. He thought, appalled, what, what? The confusion lasted seconds only. Suddenly, he recognized what it was: the time-honored perfume of a London wharf.

Incredibly, his self-absorption had deadened his senses. The smell had actually been there all day and evening, and for centuries before that. It was something he had never really thought about before; but, now, he was curious. He tilted his head into the soft breeze that blew from the river and sniffed. Hmmm, interesting. The vile odor seemed to be a mixture of the wet damp wood of the docks themselves and of decaying garbage.

Fletcher grimaced. And he was turning away—starting to turn away—when a distant brightness in the sky drew his gaze.

He poised. Then slowly faced back as before. Straight ahead, toward the sea, the night horizon was lit up.

A fire?

Even as he stood there, staring, the brilliant thing came closer, grew brighter.

A frown. What a fire! What a fantastic fire! His startled impression: an entire portion of the city was burning.

Even as he had the thought, the blazing thing came closer; and it was a ship coming up the Thames.

A huge ship! The terrible feeling of shock had already come. It was the Lantellan battleship.

B-but—how could it be? . . . For God's sake, the river wasn't that deep. And there were all those bridges.

Shuddering, he pictured London Bridge itself thrust down and aside by the monster, the river bed dredged, and the mud and the rock shoved up to form new riverbanks by the sheer power of the enormous forces that drove the mighty vessel.

Vaguely, Fletcher realized that he had backed away from the railing. It was a completely instinctive move, with basic fear moving him. The thoughts under the cringing feeling were: They marked us. They can locate us. They'll send somebody. . . .

His evasive movements continued, second after second: First, to his cabin, softly, so as not to awaken anyone. Second—and swiftly now because he was in an enclosed place, and that seemed the wrong place to be—he grabbed up his leather case with his belongings packed in it. Third, back on deck, and off the vessel. The entire departure required minutes only.

He trudged along the wharf, and up from the banks, away from that brightness which now seemed to suffuse the whole sky behind him. Soon, though all too slowly, he was heading up a sleazy street, a brave man scared stiff and in an awful hurry.

13

Climbing a back stairway into the palace residence of the English Queen and her Consort in 1704 A.D. has, at best, very faint scientific aspects. The most likely science: psychology. Of course, the law of gravity is, so to speak, a scientific factor in such an action. Indeed, from the beginning of life on earth *any* movement up required much more muscle and organic output than did movement down or level. And many a creature, animal as well as human, has experienced a developing apathy of purpose as the hill turned out to be higher than the matching motivation for climbing it. Each creature was thereby reminded of a natural phenomenon of the universe—of, in short, a scientific fact.

Fletcher had a small bit of that reluctance as he ascended the "secret" stairway. And, since he had a score of doubts about the wisdom of coming here at all, and was already weary from his long walk, quickly now came an ever greater negative reaction.

He slowed, then stopped. Psychologically, it was a complex moment. A mental something had brought him all the way from where the pirate ship was docked to this dangerous location three quarters of the way up a dark stairway. Suddenly, he needed an additional mental impetus.

What had brought him this far was a genuine decision. Even he recognized reluctantly that he was going far indeed out of his way in order to tell what he knew.

What made it a decision was his feeling that he owed these people a debt. It wasn't just a feeling about England. He was finally going to pay in comparable coin what he owed.

As he poised there, muffled sounds came through to him from that upper level of the palace toward which he had been heading. It was long after midnight, but people were audibly moving around.

For a tired walker, it was a welcome signal. Fletcher deduced immediately that the arrival of the Lantellan battleship was the cause of the activity. And, of course, that was why he had turned aside from his original escape plan. The feeling: I really should not abandon my former cardplaying companions without giving them the information I have.

By this route he had come on occasion to the palace as part of the entourage of Anne before she was Queen. Those were the final days of the reign of William III (alone after the death of his co-monarch Mary II). It was also a time when there was an outward camaraderie between Anne's group and William's government people. But that was before the schemers decided that William had not long to live. Whereupon, those same ambitious ones made arrangements for disposing of certain intimates of the future royal couple, like Fletcher.

Hearing the sounds from that familiar place brought surging energy again. Up he went, two steps at a time now. Came to the door. Reached into his pocket. And carefully brought out from it the years-ago-written elegant invitation card that had brought him many safe entrances into this very private residence.

Clutching the card, he knocked.

The uniformed guard who opened the door looked just a little bit startled as he saw the to-him stranger who stood on the threshold outside. But he evidently recognized the type of card which Fletcher extended toward him. The man was young, new, and definitely not known to the famous pirate captain. But it was also obvious that the velvet clothing and the courteous manner of the visitor were also recognizable characteristics. For the youthful guard stepped back, and Fletcher stepped forward.

Fletcher said, "Will you inform His Excellency, Prince Consort George, that my visit relates to the great enemy ship which has appeared in London harbor."

The man backed away, taking Fletcher's card with him. And the tall, slender, wiry, elegant man had time to consider the extent of the risk he was incurring. The Prince Consort was head of the admiralty in close association with another George—George Churchill, brother of the Duke of Marlborough. Churchill ran the Navy. Prince George supervised his running of it for his wife, the Queen.

A brave man, this Danish Prince, considered goodhearted but dull-witted by the brilliant Englishmen who had access to the royal couple. Yet, surely, he would know his former card-table companion Nathan Fletcher had escaped the Tory net and had become a pirate. And surely he would be wary of any face-to-face meeting with such a deteriorated person, except that he came in the presence of a military protective detachment.

The analysis was not quite correct, but close enough. The great, carved door opened, and the men in officers' uniforms who came through it on the double trotted with drawn swords over to Fletcher and took up positions around him.

The pirate commander noted that the five were, respectively, a captain and four lieutenants. It was the captain who faced Fletcher and said in a formal tone, "Your sword, sir."

Fletcher removed it slowly from its scabbard and, holding the pointed end, handed it over. He watched as the officer carried the gleaming blade to a sideboard twenty feet away and laid it on the flat surface. Whereupon, the beautifully uniformed officer walked stiffly to the door by which he and his companions had entered, stepped through, and was gone for about a minute.

When he re-entered, it was as a second person. Preceding him was a plump individual in fine velvet clothing. For Fletcher, who had known this new arrival, it was, of course, instant recognition. And he, thereupon, bowed respectfully. Straightened. Waited. And observed.

One of the things he couldn't help but notice was that the man had gained weight. Seeing that, he was not able to restrain himself. He said in Low German, *"Yeeat, du muss nich zou fail ayten. Dout wa nich ziyah gout foh die. Voutt saycht Momka Anne? N'vo best du?"* (George, you must not eat so much. That is not good for you. What says Lady Anne? And how are you?)

"Nate," the Prince replied in English, "you shouldn't have come here." The puffy face was concerned rather than antagonistic. "I've had unpleasant reports that have gradually made me regret the assistance I gave you."

(It was he who had sent private word to Fletcher that the Tories were after him, thus enabling him to escape. And that was the debt Fletcher had come to pay.)

"My duty," continued the Prince in a severe tone, "is clearly to place you under arrest. Can you give me a reason why I shouldn't?"

Fletcher said earnestly, "Your Highness, that great ship out there in the Thames is operated by strange, mechanical men, and is big enough and strong enough to destroy all the navies of Europe, by itself. The Queen must be moved inland. The enemy ship has problems, and those aboard it are evidently limited in number. So they must be forced to come out of their invincible vessel, after careful test attacks with the largest cannon. The whole world is in danger."

There was a long pause. The overdressed fat man stood there; and it was a bad moment because Fletcher suddenly wondered if, perhaps, there were in truth dim wits inside that rather long jowly head, so dim that they would not be able to grasp the meaning of what he had said.

Another, more personal thought came. Farfetched. Dangerous to broach to a dull-minded person. But the awareness must be somewhere inside the Prince Consort's head, as it was in Fletcher's, and as it had to be in that of every living person on earth.

Fletcher said it in Low German, urgently: "We've lived all this before, George. And, as I recall, you died in 1708 of the cough you've always had. The story, as I remember it from my previous living of this life, is, you began to spit blood, and after that you were a goner."

The silence continued. Then, abruptly, in English: "Wait here!"

The Prince Consort, thereupon, walked to the great door. Went through. And, after nearly a minute, came back with a woman.

The officers guarding Fletcher saluted. She made an acknowledging gesture, and then waved them away. Then she came over and stood in front of Fletcher. There were tears in her eyes.

"Nate," she said, "I've been crying since August. I'm ashamed of myself. I used to say I could always smile to hide my tears. But that's no longer true. As we know, George has a lung problem. And he has just told me what you said about his dying—something that I also suddenly remembered—if that's the right word—back there in August. Nate, the whole palace is crazy with memories that can't be—memories of the future." She broke off. "What day, Nate, what month, do you remember for my dear George's passing?"

"I was in Italy, Your Majesty, when I heard. And I lived to the age of seventy-eight, according to my memory of the future. But, of course, it was a great shock when the news came through. And I don't even know if I ever knew the day. But it was fall, late in October."

"The twenty-eighth," said Queen Anne—and burst into tears. Prince George came forward, and took her hand. To Fletcher, he whispered: "She's right. Everybody's comparing notes. And remembering things that can't be. Yet, now, here you are with the same ideas. And what's this ship?"

It was an encouraging moment. Because with it came a sudden insight. Somehow, this dull-witted princeling had kept his Queen-wife away from most of the sly whisperers, and, until recently, compassionately balanced between Whig and Tory. He had kept her brave and seldom misled.

The comparison that had flashed was her dismal destiny after his passing. She had become confused—as Fletcher saw it—and progressively hardhearted; an egotistical woman, taken in by schemers, and, as a consequence, had betrayed her armies, her best friends, her allies, and finally died (after six years), a lost soul, if ever there was one.

If she was savoring all that in her inner vision of the future, no wonder the tears and the anguish could neither cease nor diminish.

"I fled to Italy after my disgrace," said Fletcher. The lie, since he had enough memories to prove that he knew the Italian scene, came smoothly from his tongue. "From there," he continued, "I watched the English news."

The story was his attempt to negate, for these few minutes, whatever they might have heard of his pirate career. And it didn't—it seemed to Fletcher—sound too bad.

The Queen, he saw, had paused in her weeping as he spoke. Her bright, misty eyes stared at him. Without turning, she said, "George, we know he didn't speak Italian before. Can he speak it now? If he can, it would surely establish something."

The Prince Consort chimed in bluntly, "Nate, can you speak Italian?"

The words had moved so rapidly to that meaning, Fletcher was taken aback. "All these weeks," he said in a wondering tone, "that possibility never crossed my mind. But I think so." Tentatively, he ventured, *"Buona sera, signora e signor. Godo di vederla. Mi ascolta un momento. Ho parecchie cosi da derle."* (Good evening, madam and sir. I am glad to see you. Listen to me for a moment. I have several things to tell you.) He broke off. "It seems to be no problem, Your Majesty. The words come easy. But, please, listen. With what I have seen, I deduce that the future can be changed. There is a great science available from this ship, and from another one—if we can but make use of it and them, which will cure such ordinary ailments as that which dear George suffers from. And, of course, your own subsequent illness came from your grief over the death of your beloved. You see that truth as part of your view of the future, do you not?"

His answer was a sound.

The stair door, through which he had come only minutes before, opened abruptly.

Several well-dressed men came in.

The arrival of the newcomers was swift, and there were just enough of them to be confusing. Fletcher observed a flicker of faces, bodies, cloaks, long hair, movements. They all seemed like strangers. And that was, moments later, stunning. In all these four years of hell, it had never occurred to him that he would not instantly recognize the Earl of Oxford, his deadly enemy.

His thought poised. Because—just a minute. One moment, please. Robert Harley didn't get his first earldom until 1711 A.D.

It was a startling realization. A perfect example of the very type of memory mix that was confusing so many people.

Whatever the reason, Robert Harley saw him first. At the instant of recognition, the powerful Tory leader actually uttered a piercing cry. And then came the words: "My God, the pirate! Catch him! Kill him!"

It was too dramatic. More important, the men who accompanied him, and the officer-guards of the Queen and her Consort, did not immediately realize who the person was that was thus identified.

Fletcher had time to notice that the face of his enemy had grown puffier with the years—young though he still was. And had seen also, that it was indeed the future Earl of Oxford and Mortimer, the great British Secretary of State.

At the moment of confrontation, everybody was startled. Literally, they all retreated. And that retreat, though it had slowed, was still continuing. And it was that automatic action of withdrawing that now gave Fletcher his opportunity. Tough, calm, at ease in an emergency, he also withdrew. Backed all the way over to the table on which his sword had been deposited. And there he stopped.

Standing there, he said, "Robert, I came to warn Her Majesty about the great, dangerous ship in the harbor, and about an enormous disaster which has befallen the entire universe. Perhaps you can tell us if you, also, have a memory of having lived out your whole life. And if you, therefore, remember—if that's the right word—the date of the death of poor George here, and—"

The second loud cry from Harley cut him off. This time the sound contained the words, "Kill him!" yelled in a savage tone of command.

The killing part probably could have been done to a less alert, less agile man. But the soldiers and officers in that glittering room were a few years, at least, away from the last time they had been involved in battle action. During those moments of their slow reaction, Fletcher snatched his sword and leaped.

The direction he leaped brought him at a dead run and a skidding stop beside Harley. With steely fingers, he grasped the beautifully clothed left arm. And pressed that fine sword point against the body beside the arm.

"Mr. Harley," he said softly, "you didn't answer my question."

There was a long, shocked silence. Fletcher had time for a strange thought, indeed.

The thought: This is not a true moment in British history. . . . Historians of the period of Queen Anne would search in vain for an incident involving the Queen herself, one of her most important ministers, and a pirate captain, all of whom were somehow together in a very private chamber of a royal palace, with the pirate threatening to kill none other than the great Robert Harley.

Neither Fletcher nor the other people present had ever heard the concept of alternate worlds. So they each had the task of facing the sudden crisis without clearly grasping that in the natural course of events no such incident had ever taken place.

A confusion? Not really. At least, not enough to prevent what would have been normal then from manifesting now. Normally.

Brave men in an emergency do not hold back from action more than seconds. And these were all men required, if for no other reason, by their oaths of allegiance and by their rank and station to be ceaselessly courageous.

Robert Harley could not cringe—even though he might be run through. The captain and the four lieutenants had to attack. The men with Harley must unsheathe their swords and jump to his defense. To the death, if necessary.

Even the Queen would later be judged by the extent of her self-possession in the crisis that had so suddenly confronted every person in that elegant room. And, of course, she was the ultimate power, the final authority. According to her subsequent history, what she did at this moment fitted her character.

This was the woman who so hated war and violence that she, finally, simply, ordered her armies back from Europe, abrogated all England's commitments to her European allies, discharged the great General John Churchill—who fought so skillfully—and spent her final years in a peaceful England. And then, to the relief of her entourage of frustrated violent men, passed away.

Queen Anne's voice came abruptly loud and clear into the silence that had settled after Fletcher spoke. "Stop!" she said.

Everybody stayed where he was. It was certainly a form of stopping. Yet Fletcher had the impression that each of the men around him, in his fashion, was poised in his personal mid-action.

"Nathan Fletcher," the woman went on in a high-pitched voice, "I appoint you commanding general of the armed forces to deal with the invading enemy."

There was a relaxing of tension as those words were uttered. These were, after all, Englishmen of wit and brain, accustomed to power. Somebody laughed. Even the future Earl of Oxford seemed to regain his composure.

"Your Majesty," he said softly, "no one is above English law, certainly not a pirate converted into a general."

In those words was not a single awareness that it was his sly action that had driven a man to total desperation; forced him to take arms against his countrymen's ships, and brought him into disrepute. In all these centuries of struggle for human rights, no one had yet come to such consciousness of human motivation. Even in England the law accepted no reasons; and on the Continent, of course, all law favored only the nobility. Without qualification.

Fletcher was sheathing his sword. "Your Majesty," he said in a deliberate tone, "I think I should be allowed to remain a general only long enough for me to get down those stairs. I have delivered my message to you and the Prince Consort. Let British brains and courage follow through on the basis of what I have told. But you, ma'am, must go inland immediately. Tonight. Now."

There was a pause. Then the womanly face, which had lost its tearful aspect during those brief minutes, relaxed into acceptance of his solution.

"Thank you, Nate, it was brave of you to come here. I decree that you shall remain a general until dawn tomorrow." Sharply. "Hear that, Mr. Harley!"

The great man bowed. "Your Majesty," he murmured.

Fletcher wasted no time. He walked rapidly around the group of noblemen. Opened the door through which they had come so precipitously. Went through it. Closed it behind him.

And, because he had no confidence in any promise of a Tory in relation to a Whig, headed down the steps three and four at a time.

14

A great reality had already been noticed by the highly trained minds that could understand it. There were no ripples. No, so to speak, aftershocks.

The colossal collapse of forty million years. And then—instantly—steady-state forward progression. Second by second, moment by moment, the quiet hours passed. A miracle? It almost seemed so.

There were, as a result, persons on the earth of 1704 A.D.—in the Transit-Craft and aboard the Lantellan battleship—who could, and did, consider the implications.

"We may deduce," one of the luminescent beings communicated, "that time is not an energy of itself. It is rather a reflection of energy transformations. A particle moves from one location in space to another location; and the consequent movement is a silent time phenomenon. The meaning of 'silent' in such a context would parallel the meaning of shadow in relation to a beam of light. An interposed object casts its shadow. An interposed energy transformation has its silence, which is time."

"What," asked another luminescence, "practical application does your observation suggest to you?"

On board the Lantellan battleship, the chief scientist-by-rotation replied to a similar question: "A shadow is a reduction of light in a shaped area. A time silence is an orderly reduction of explosive-level charge by a process of spacing the transformation of energy. Apparently, now that steady-state has returned, we can space out the adjustment transformations that will be taking place. In other words, we *can* survive in this time era."

On both vessels, the analysis was extremely relieving to all personnel. Life, electronic and organic, would go on for all intruders from another era, and for the inhabitants of that era.

Since the human beings of this period of history were not capable of even imagining that non-survival might have been an outcome, they never had any hope, anyway. There were, of course, individuals—like Nathan Fletcher—who had already had a tiny inkling of what had happened. But even for them anything more would take a while.

It was not the kind of problem that, on this particular, bright morning, engaged the mental gears of a certain handsome male passenger on a stagecoach bound for a south England destination. The passenger—Fletcher—was, however, definitely not in a normal frame of mind. Sitting there opposite a couple of stodgy middle-aged females, and beside their plump spouses, he had had a new thought.

It was a thought that derived from his observation of the palace people the evening before. A realization so improbable that it barely touched the edge of his mind. But even that tiny contact left a pain behind. Like a bee that alights on a sensitive portion of skin, and is brushed off before it can more than insert its stinger. Yet the mere fact that it has been there at all with such an intent has a shock effect.

Could I have been wrong? . . . The impossible question. Real men of the early eighteenth century never—but *never*—doubted their hard decisions. To them the world was what it was; and they had merely come to understand that reality, and had learned to act accordingly.

Fletcher grew curious after the first, startled reaction to the new idea. Thus recovered, he was able to examine the concept in more of its dimensions.

Civilization had been slowly evolving. In that evolvement the big problem had been maintenance of order among masses of individuals, each of whom needed food to survive. How to grow that food, how to distribute it, was a problem that, in this intermediate stage of history—as he now realized it to be, having seen later stages—had not yet been solved. No one was guilty. The problem transcended all the techniques that could be devised in this middle period. People who resisted the available system merely created additional problems. The real solution was technical, requiring new methods not yet available.

Seeing Queen Anne the previous night, and seeing Robert Harley, had brought awareness. Harley's intense jealousy of Fletcher's close, personal association with the future royal family—the man had plotted with the intent of total destruction of his younger rival. And, in effect, had succeeded. But . . .

The truth is, I was trying to push into a higher nothingness. And when I was ousted by another pusher, I got viciously angry. . . .

A woman was sobbing. Fletcher was drawn out of his mentalization, and realized that a minor drama had evidently transpired inside the coach while he was preoccupied. It took a moment, then. Required a startled backward look. At which he discovered that he had registered the matter at a remote edge of his awareness.

There had been an argument between two of the stodgy characters. The woman bringing up an earlier feeling, the man—her husband—suddenly shamed by her reiteration in public, speaking to her sharply.

It was sharp, indeed. The words were: "Shut up, you stupid woman!"

That was when the tears burst forth. Whereupon, the man, noticing that, as he put it, "Look, now you've disturbed this fine gentleman!" added, apologetically, "This past few weeks, sir, my wife has fair taken leave of her senses. She feels that she lived all this once before, and she remembers the future going on until her death seventeen years from now." He added indignantly, "She has me marked for an earlier demise. I'm to go in three years."

Captain Nathan Fletcher, pirate captain extraordinary, who suffered from a similar affliction of future memory, said to the dumpy female, "Madam, when did you first have this feeling?"

It took a little while. But presently it was evident that she was thinking, and that his courteous question had been good for her. She stopped crying. And her answer came finally in a thoughtful tone: "I remember it as if it just happened. It was August—" She named a date.

Fletcher had his own moment of confusion. August was correct. And since, as captain, he kept a daily log, obviously, he ought to have noticed the date. But he hadn't. Or rather, it was a time of murder and stress. And so that detail had flashed by unnoticed. At sea, in a way, the days were timeless. Dates tended to merge one into another.

Interesting—Fletcher thought. In the palace, the top people were bright enough to notice, and puzzle. Here, just a few steps down the social ladder, one person who noticed was viciously negated. And, of course, on the pirate ship, the "memories" must have evoked instant internal rejection. Because nobody—not even the redoubtable first mate, Shradd—had shown any sign of inner turmoil.

"She's always had a lot of imagination," the husband was explaining. "So everybody gets some crazy idea going

through his mind. You don't pay no attention. Hell!
—begging your pardon, ladies—you'd go out of your wits
if you let things run wild through your head.''

With such attitudes extant, it was not a conversation
with a future. So Fletcher sank back in his seat and
contemplated a wildness on another level. Really—he
thought—the political maneuvering of the strongly egotistical males involved in the British government four years
ago had had nothing to do with the real problems of the
country. And for him, for his goals then, one word covered it: stupidity.

I was forced out of a situation I should never have been
in, to begin with. . . .

It was quite a thought for Nathan Fletcher, gentleman
murderer, pirate, thief; and—as he recognized wryly—a
little late for simple reform. At this advanced stage of his
career, he dared make not one change in his plans. How to
survive his idiocy—that was his principal task.

And so, with courteous murmurings to his fellow passengers, and the coachman, he climbed off at a small
village hostelry (called Temple Inn), rented quarters,
and after eating a late lunch, walked rapidly along a
country road toward the Hemistan estate a mile or so
out of town.

There were no problems. The new squire, when confronted, promptly paid the balance due. And then stood on
his late cousin's porch and silently watched the pirate
captain walk off into the afternoon brightness. In a small
way the Hemistan heir had considered not paying the final
sum. But it was actually simpler to pay, he reasoned. That
way there would be no living person with a grudge. Everybody would have his personal reasons for silence and
secrecy. As for violence, it would require him to hire
several bullies who, not being gentlemen, could not be
depended on. Particularly was this true because there would
be more than one.

Besides—the new heir thought smugly—I have a pretty

good idea that our fancy, soft-spoken pirate will be visiting his mother and sister during the next day or so just fifty miles from here. During that time, I can change my mind, should I so choose—

It did not at that moment, standing there, occur to him that events would swiftly impel him to choose exactly that.

15

Early that evening, Fletcher boarded the night coach for Cadman Village. Shortly before 3 A.M. he climbed off at the Cadman Inn. After registering, and after the innkeeper had sleepily shown him to his room and then shuffled off to his own bedroom, the new boarder eased out the window (he had a ground floor accommodation by request), and set forth on the final leg of his journey.

The night was cool, but he walked rapidly. He felt relaxed mentally, because he "remembered" having made this journey successfully in his "memory" of the future. At that time, also, he had come first to Cadman Inn, for a simple reason: the innkeeper was new to the area, and would not know the people from the surrounding villages. Not by sight, anyway.

The feel of the road—which was his route the early part of his walk—the moonless night sky above, not too many thoughts. The over five-mile journey obviously required over an hour. Yet the time passed rapidly. And, presently, taking no chances—as "before"—he left the road and started across the semi-swampland. And still it was easy for him who knew this area from his childhood and youth. Thus he was not totally alert at the moment of the attack.

Whoever it was had better night vision than Fletcher. For he leaped like someone who could see his victim.

A faint sound! That was all Fletcher heard. A small rustling sound of brush thrust aside, then a soft padding noise on the ground. The next instant incredibly powerful arms grabbed his whole body. The impression was of a large manlike form shorter than the tall, slender Englishman, but as thickly built as a small horse, pressing at him, against him, around him.

Fletcher was seized in mid-step. His arms were entrapped by the great, cablelike arms of his attacker. It was virtually total surprise. His reaction: shock and astonishment, but not fear. More important, his body, though slender, was tough. And his endurance had never in his pirate career been forced to its limit. Tireless was the word for the muscles of Captain Nathan Fletcher.

The battle that now began in the darkness was a combination of mass and surprise against wiry toughness. Part of the surprise was the slow realization by the victim that this was an attack by an unarmed man, whose weapons were his powerful hands.

Who? What? Why?

There was no time to imagine answers in advance. No time for more than the faintest beginning of the irony of a sea pirate being attacked by a land pirate.

As he now attempted his first jerk away, and braced for his first effort to free his arms, Fletcher made an electrifying discovery. His assailant was naked.

Fletcher was struggling now, breathing hard; and aware of the equally hard breathing of his attacker. But because he had learned to fight without mercy, and because his hands were forcibly held low down, his defense matched the merciless intent of the big fellow. The unexpected, again. A great open mouth reached for his throat—and at that exact instant, he grabbed for the naked man's genitals. Wrenched them with all his strength.

What he suffered in that exchange was a bloody tooth slash across his throat. But the other there in the night grunted hideously with pain. Grunted. Let go. And struck Fletcher with the side of a hand that was as hard as a piece of wood.

The pirate captain gasped. And in his turn let go and staggered back. But it was victory. Because, being free of those binding arms, he had time to draw his sword and make one hard thrust, heart high and heart side.

Fletcher knew by the feel of the blade in the big fellow's body, and by the way that body shuddered and stood absolutely still, that he had made the kill. . . .

There was a light burning behind the curtains and the blinds of the bedroom window that had always been his sister's. On this window Fletcher knocked with a rat-tat-tat rat-tat-tat that had, in earlier days, been a signal between them. As a youth, forbidden by his mother to go out, young Nathan would come to his sister's window in the early morning hours and rap with his knuckles. Whereupon, she would slip to the back door, unbolt it, and let him in.

At getting-up time on such occasions, his mother found him asleep in his bed, and fondly called him sleepyhead. If the widow suspected that she had the makings of a rascal on her hands, it didn't show in her tolerance of his reluctance to rise for breakfast.

After the knock, now, there was silence. And then, the blinds and curtains were thrust aside. On the other side of the pane appeared a startled female face. Fletcher pressed his own face close to the glass. After several long moments of peering, the young, dark-haired woman gestured with one hand, pointing toward the kitchen door.

Moments later, she had let him in, and stiffly accepted his brotherly embrace. That stiff response was also reflected in the conversation which presently began behind the closed doors of her bedroom.

"There are strange goings-on," said his sister.

They were both sitting, she in a long, white robe; he completely clothed, still.

"To what do you refer?" Fletcher asked.

"Yesterday, in the swamp, a body of a man was found

half-eaten.'' In the light from the flickering candle, she stared at him suspiciously. ''When did you arrive in this area?''

Fletcher described, accurately, the details of his coming. But as he spoke he was thinking that, according to his ''memory'' of the future, it was fifty years since he had originally made this final visit to his sister and mother, before proceeding to a haven in Italy.

As he ''recalled'' it, his sister's prospects for obtaining a husband had been ruined by his disgrace. And there had been tears shed by both women at the immense social diminishment they had suffered. So his return ''then,'' because of filial and fraternal sentiments, had produced mixed reactions and regrets on all sides.

Nothing of that—yet.

Because, as he finished his account, she said, ''Then you had nothing to do with that half-eaten body?''

''My dear sister,'' said Fletcher, dryly, ''despite the severe reversal in my fortunes, I have never been hungry for human flesh.''

She seemed not to hear. She went on, ''All around the body they found strange animal footprints nearly four feet in length. What monstrous creature could have paws like that?''

Fletcher's mind abruptly flicked back to the naked man he had killed. His eyes widened. Could there be a connection? After a moment's thought, he decided it was impossible. The size of his assailant's body had been impressive. But it was unlikely that he had feet forty-eight inches long.

He saw that his sister's intense blue eyes were again regarding him, unsmiling. ''Have you been practicing your religion, Nathan?'' asked the young lady in the white, filmy robe.

''My dear Marion,'' he replied in his friendliest voice, ''that is between me and my God.''

''I have heard rumors,'' she said, ''unknown to our dear mother''—she added hastily—''that in London your God was a deck of cards, a bottle of whiskey, a rapist's opportunism, and an orator's lies spoken on behalf of vile men since cast out of the government. When they were dismissed, you disappeared. That was four years ago. Where have you been hiding since then?''

. . . He had been advised that it would be unwise to contact his family. Any attempt to do so might be regarded by his enemies as proof that they could hurt him by damaging the two women—

"It so happens," said Fletcher, glibly, now, "that one of my card-playing friends was a shipping owner. So that when in my time of distress he offered me the opportunity to be captain of a commercial vessel, I accepted the position. And have been at sea ever since."

"I presume," his sister said sweetly, "your skill in navigation derived from the days when you sailed a sea of liquor from one warm female body to another."

"I discovered in myself," said Fletcher truthfully, "a quick ability to learn under pressure, a certain boldness, whereby I used the knowledge of others and meanwhile put on a good front."

He paused, shuddering as he remembered his first days as commander of the stolen ship that preceded the *Orinda*. He was still considering that recollection, when Marion said, "I am sure it's sleep time for you. You know where your room is. In the morning, I'll prepare Mother before you get up. And"—she finished—"we can then talk about more pleasant matters."

16

From a distance Keith Hemistan watched the carriage drive off the main road and into the Hemistan grounds. There was interfering shrubbery; so he caught glimpses only, as the shining black vehicle with its four horses and coachman moved at trotting speed toward the large house.

He was not expecting visitors. Not now, only one day after Nathan Fletcher had come for the death money, and departed. But the carriage and horses resembled equipment possessed by a relative in London.

So, after a brief hesitation, the new squire postponed his plan to go to the stables and go riding. Instead, he made his way down a shallow hill, through some brush at the side of the house. Thus he emerged upon an unanticipated scene.

A dozen servants were gathered around a woman and a man, both of whom had evidently descended from the carriage. Keith recognized the man first. It *was* the cousin from London. Nevertheless, he went forward, scowling. These servants of Patricia's—he thought critically. Really, there will have to be severe words spoken about the place of the help. . . . Their place was *not* on the front porch and front driveway when visitors arrived.

He was almost upon the group now. And at this point

several servants, both men and women, saw him simultaneously. They drew aside.

"I say—" began Keith Hemistan, in his most severe tone. "What the devil—"

He stopped.

What seemed like a stone fell down into the pit of his stomach. It was the blood rushing there from his head and extremities. It was fear.

The woman visitor, who had been hidden behind the sizable bodies of, principally, the male help, was—as the men moved aside—exposed to view. It was a young, slender woman. And she turned at the sound of his intruding voice. That was when he recognized an impossible person: the Lady Patricia Hemistan.

With the blood temporarily drained from his brain, the man could only stand. And stare. And be numb.

While he stood there, she spoke in a clear, resonant, determined voice: "Cousin, I know you for what you are and for what you did. For such a crime there can be no forgiveness, no extenuating circumstances. Ever."

The stocky man in the gray riding habit seemed, and was, uncertain. That thickening face, portending future jowls, and the faint red lines which eventually would look purplish and swollen, if he lived so long, seemed to swell that very instant.

(The blood was rushing back into his head.)

"I want you," said the Lady Patricia Hemistan, "to remove yourself from this property, and forever stay out of my sight and presence. Take your baggage and be off within the hour. Temple"—to the butler—"have him assisted in packing."

"Very well, madam."

The problem that Keith Hemistan had in that moment was not a lack of basic male chauvinism. Along with other young, well-born Englishmen of his era, that he had in sufficient measure. What brought a flinching inside him was a fear the nobility of the time held greater than the fear of death: the fear of poverty.

Ten thousand guineas he had paid only yesterday to Nathan Fletcher—the balance due on fifteen thousand. The entire sum represented approximately ninety per cent of what was left of his inheritance from his profligate father, who had died less than two years before.

A tremor went through the man's body. It was a hot hate, the kind that a desperately threatened man can feel when, suddenly, he sees himself deprived of everything he owns. No thought of guilt. No shame. No sense of what a terrible thing he had done, had tried to do, to this slender, pretty, young woman in planning to deprive her of her life.

Only hatred. Against Nathan Fletcher.

. . . Maybe I can still get it back. Maybe he stayed over another day with his mother. Maybe—

There was no time to delay. It was late afternoon. Soon, people would be going home, and even police activities would be put over until the following morning. And so he braced himself, as macho males can. To Temple he said, "Have my belongings sent to the Village Inn!"

It was not Temple who replied to that. It was the male relative from London, a man of thirty with a strong body, and with eyes that were icy and unfriendly. He said, "Don't worry, Keith, your possessions will be sent. Just leave rapidly before I have you whipped off the premises."

The final words were actually flung after him. He was leaving, walking rapidly. In Keith Hemistan's nostrils was the smell of English countryside in the late fall, with its peace and with its silence, except for the thud of his feet, the pounding of his heart, the thunder of the disaster that rolled through his head.

He was not a tall man, nor a small one. But he was close enough to the ground so that he should not have been stumbling and in imminent danger of falling. Yet he was in exactly that danger.

In this second stage of his emotional reaction, there was again a great drainage of blood from the extremities, including the head, into the abdomen. But now the feeling he had was a false sense of emptiness in the pit of his stomach, where, in fact, the blood had settled. His eyes, partly drained of blood, also, had a glazed look to them. And very little vision.

Yet enough of cunning remained in him. He deduced that no countermanding orders had gone out as yet. So he strode to his original destination. Arrived at the stable, he affected sufficient calm to give his usual directions. Thereby, presently, he was astride his favorite horse, and off to the authorities in Bonnen Town. And so, later—

A red-faced Englishman, standing, talking to a red-faced Englishman, sitting. Two Englishmen of their time, one lower upper class, the other lower middle class, each putting on his most law-abiding manner.

More confident, more vindictive with each word by which he spoke his prepared story, mostly lies—but it sounded reasonable— Keith Hemistan went on grimly, "Seems she recognized the rascal. Met him years ago a few times when she visited a cousin. Went riding at that village. Little town of Wentworth. Saw Nathan Fletcher. Now, here's the good luck in this thing. I happened to ride down there yesterday, and I saw him also. I made inquiries. People said he hadn't been there in years. So it's a secret visit to his mother and sister, as well it might be. If he's still there you can have the fellow arrested, and brought over for the Lady Patricia to identify."

"Aha!" nodded the burly individual with satisfaction. "I'll take the coach down there that leaves at five, and speak to the authorities—whom I know well. We can surround the house, and snare this pirate captain during the night."

"I believe," urged Keith Hemistan, "you're wise to act that swiftly. Because I'm sure he's not planning to stay around very long." He finished: "I shall be waiting at the inn for your report."

As he walked away from that meeting, the would-be squire of Hemistan did not ask himself how his accusation might react against his own person. He had in a fleeting moment the kind of thought that he was now capable of, that the Lady Patricia, in ordering him off the property, had by that action established that she did not plan to file charges against her father's brother's son. He presumed, also, in that fleeting fashion, without considering the matter beyond his vindictiveness, that she would nevertheless be delighted to bring Fletcher to the hangman's noose.

On that issue, of course, she would be confronted with the request for identification before she had time to think. And surely she would not compromise herself by lying.

The one mystery that remained was how had she escaped her fate? Reports from the survivors of the *Red Princess* were unmistakable: the Lady Patricia had indeed been thrown overboard at the command of the pirate captain. Those reports, brought by a fast packet, had been forwarded to him by the British admiralty four whole days before Nathan Fletcher came by the previous afternoon to collect the balance due.

He must still have the money. I'll go there tomorrow after his arrest. I'll demand of those women that they let me go through his effects. They will not dare refuse. . . .

17

In the half light, as he entered, Fletcher saw that an oddly arrayed man was lying on one cot. The door behind him was closing. And so it became a quarter light, or even eighth light, filtering through the narrow, barred window.

He had had to bend that long body of his slightly to get into the dungeon. Now, he remained bent. And peered. And finally said, "Sir, you wear strange clothes."

The man made a reply. The words he spoke were familiar but twisted in a way not instantly clear. Fletcher, after several moments of letting the meaning go through his mind, said finally, "Rade, sprach, sprech, sage, speak, shpak langsam, slow—"

"I am an American," said the stranger. He spoke very slowly. "Where am I?"

Inside Fletcher's brain, the language spoken had settled into a frame. It became permanently recognizable to him as a Low German variation of a Low Dutch dialect.

So he answered aloud, sardonically, "You're in an English castle."

"One minute," the man continued, "I was airing over New York. Next second I fell. Tumbled to the ground. Air lift stopped working. Never happened before, and was supposed to be impossible. Fortunately, it was only a ten-foot drop.''

Having had that much opportunity to explain himself, he seemed suddenly to be able to have another thought. He asked in a puzzled tone: ''Where are we?'' In the partial light he made a jiggling movement with one hand and arm, indicating the bleak surroundings. ''What is this room we are in?''

''This is a prison,'' said Fletcher.

The older man rolled over and sat up on his cot. ''A what?'' he asked in a baffled tone. And added, ''Am I sick?''

There could have been a long pause at that point. But Fletcher was intent, himself. He still assumed it was a language difficulty. ''It's a jail,'' he said. He spelled the word, and finished, ''It's a place where criminals are kept, not sick people.''

If the explanation produced comprehension, it didn't show on the dimly seen face. And, besides—so it suddenly seemed to the Englishman—there were other, more important implications here. His quick mind had already darted over and around the minuscule information the other man had imparted. Startling stuff, it was. Fletcher hesitated, and then asked, ''What year is this?''

''Two thousand two hundred and forty-two.'' Puzzled tone. ''What else?''

What other, indeed, thought Fletcher, awed.

But he said nothing more immediately. Simply bent his way over to one of the other cots. Sat down on it. And sagged back against a damp stone wall. . . . Really, he was thinking, that boy and I—we're the only ones who understand what happened. And I don't understand it very well—

The actual process level of the event was probably more complex than the story which he now, slowly, elicited from his cell companion. But it had its coherence. While wearing an individual air lift suit, being wafted magnetically through the air over New York, this person was caught in a backlash of time collapse. Literally, a few strands of space-time fabric were pulled out of the era, and he along with it. His fall of ten feet just happened to be where he was in 1704 A.D.

His name was Abdul Jones. Following a period of bewilderment at the disappearance of a vast city, he had walked along a road to an inn. After eating, he presented the innkeeper with his Universal Credit Card in payment.

The outraged vendor demanded payment in cash from his uncomprehending customer. Not receiving it, he called the village constable. Abdul Jones was forthwith transported to this black hole and incarcerated therein.

A vagrant wonder came to Fletcher: how many people were plunged into oceans? How many fell thousands of feet? The details, for the most part, were lost forever. And besides, it wouldn't have been quite like that. These numerous individuals had, in fact, lived out their entire lives. So that each of them had a memory of a full life to confuse him even as he vainly struggled to survive in an abrupt reenactment of his existence.

"Well," said Fletcher, finally, aloud, after the tale was told, "perhaps we can get you out of here without too much trouble. During the next few hours we shall periodically try to attract the attention of our jailer. If and when he attends on us, I shall offer to pay the innkeeper twice the cost of your dinner. In return he will drop the charges against you. Then I shall give you some money. I want you to go to London to seek out there four men whose names I shall supply you. Tell them what happened to me—"

The words must have sounded hopeful. Because, after they were spoken, Mr. Abdul Jones belatedly came to a thought which was not about himself. He said, "May I ask, what is your name? And what are you doing in a place like this?"

The belatedness of the question undoubtedly proved something. Perhaps, it reflected the shock he had suffered. Or proved a more subtle reality about human nature of the twenty-third century. Could it be in that future there was no more crime? Fletcher did not inquire the details. He answered: "I was arrested in my home town, tried there, and condemned for piracy. And I am scheduled to be hanged in the morning in nearby Bonnen Town."

Did his hearer understand the meaning of those words? Did he actually absorb into his ears everything that Fletcher said? It seemed doubtful to the alert Englishman. Yet something of the truth of his own situation, or perhaps the possibility of the truth, apparently penetrated the confusion that, quite obviously, had overwhelmed this very ordinary man from an extraordinary time.

Because, suddenly, after Fletcher had spoken the terms of his fate, the man's eyes widened. "B-but—" he said then in a blank tone, "that must mean that Elora is dead."

It took additional questioning. But, presently, it was apparent that Elora was his wife. And she had been in their home, which was an apartment on the ninety-first floor of a skyscraper condominium complex.

With that thought—about his wife's death—Abdul Jones visibly shrank down. Literally curled up in his bunk, his face to the wall. If there was a live person in the cell with Fletcher after that, no clear evidence of it in terms of movement, or human sounds, was available.

18

Somebody at the door.

The sound had a shaking effect on Fletcher. Because he had lain down. And there was a small blankness in him, which he recognized for what it was: I must have dozed. . . . And if he had, indeed, slept, the timelessness of that state *could mean* that, outside, dawn was breaking.

Hanging time!

As he rolled over and sat up on the bunk, the chill of that penetrated even his frozen emotional state, all four years of it. Inner shock, outward darkness, as there came the sequential noises of the door being opened; it added up to delayed perception.

Somebody—a soldier, carrying a lantern, stood in the doorway. The whiteness of a woman's dress gleamed behind the man in uniform. And, bringing up the rear, was a dark, nattily dressed individual.

It was this third person who now pressed past the woman, and past the soldier. Entering the cell, he said . . . something —Fletcher didn't hear the words. He had recognized his visitor.

Robert Harley. His great, remorseless enemy.

Fletcher was still sitting as he had that awareness. Bent slightly forward as if he had intended to get up. He had no memory of such an intent.

Still sitting. Still blank. Yet certain automatic things were stirring in him. It was early eighteenth century. And masculinity was the first, the absolutely pre-eminent condition that a highborn male reacted with, the very instant that his wits began to manifest.

That came now to Fletcher. Came before he had a real thought, or any general awareness. Came before purpose.

"Well," he said aloud in his bravest voice, "to what do I owe the privilege of this visit?"

Having spoken, the dam in his mind broke. At once . . . several realizations. The most important: if, somehow, I can take advantage.

Just like that, the beginning of purpose. And hope.

It had to mean something. Harley coming here. For any reason.

With that great thought, Fletcher stood up. And, because other memories were finally surging, he spoke again. "I hope, sir, you took my warning seriously, and have borne the Queen out of danger."

"She's safe." Curtly. "At least, for the time being. That's what I want to talk to you about."

The hope was brighter. Fletcher stood there, nonetheless, with eyes narrowed and mind leaping in a dozen directions, including distrust every other leap. The mere fact that Harley had come to see him *at all* showed the enormous stress the man was experiencing. But—face it!—this was still the villainous future Earl of Oxford. Harley was here for the good of Harley, and, if Harley could avoid it, would not give anything in return.

So it's a deadly game . . .

With that awareness, suavely, Fletcher said, "I see that standing behind you is the lady of the castle. So why do not she and you and I and my cell mate here"—he mo-

tioned at Abdul Jones—"adjourn to some more appropri-
ate quarters, and discuss whatever it is you have in mind?"

In front of him the puffy face frowned. Harley said in a
surprised tone, "Why include your cell mate?"

The man from the twenty-third century had sat up earlier, and was now still slumping on the edge of his bunk.
And, of course, for Fletcher, Harley's objection merely
brought the reality of this whole incredible event into
sharper focus.

He said, "You'll see why after I tell you who he is and
where he's from."

The flickering light of the lantern, dim though it was,
revealed an expression of resistance on Harley's face. The
man's lips parted, but before he could speak, Fletcher
said flatly, "If he isn't included, there'll be no conversation."

There was an interruption. From behind Harley, Lady
Hemistan's voice came clear and firm: "After all, gentlemen, this is my home, and what is here is under my
jurisdiction. So, please, let me issue an invitation to all
three of you, to join me in my drawing room."

Harley turned toward the young woman, and bowed.
"You are most kind, Mistress Hemistan, and as so often
happens, it takes a woman to see the proper logic for a
situation such as this one. Indeed, this is your home. And
indeed, this prison, as has been the custom since many
centuries in the countryside, is in your cellar. Your authority prevails unless I choose to pre-empt, using the authority of Her Majesty; and I do not so choose. So—" He
faced about. He gestured at Fletcher and the other man.
"After you, Mr. Fletcher, after you, stranger—"

The "stranger," thus addressed, seemed dubious. But
Fletcher grasped his arm. "This way!" he said. With that,
he drew the man up from the cot, and started him toward
the door. Having done so, Fletcher suppressed any show
of his inner triumph and followed.

"After all"—Harley's voice came from the rear—"since

I have two companies of soldiers surrounding Hemistan
Castle, where inside these walls we have our conversation
is of no matter.''

The words, and the man's quiet confidence, did seem to
hold enough truth to dim somewhat Fletcher's soaring
conviction that freedom was only a few minutes, and a few
yards, away.

19

It was a night of magical things, for 1704 A.D.

A sleek, metal, cigar-shaped machine slid through the darkness close to the ground. It moved above a road, turning and twisting with it, but not touching. It had no wheels. No visible support.

Magic that understood the rules of matter and energy in relation to control of heavy objects near planetary bodies. Like a nineteenth-century explorer in Africa. Superior. Knowledgeable. And there were the villages of the natives. And here was the essentially nontechnological society.

Did anyone see the dully gleaming torpedolike craft? It didn't matter. At this remote distance from great London what poor country lout would dare stutter out a tale of such a sight even to himself?

Inside the machine's control room, Nodo said to Billy Todd: "I have been considering your statement that this pirate captain may be the key figure leading to the outcome of the great disaster to the universe. The logic of his connection continues to escape me. But, of course, we can locate him by our method, as you have suggested, and of course we shall use him for our purposes and not yours."

Billy looked at the dark figure of the robot and made a gesture to attract his attention. He said, "Nodo, something is wrong with you. Have you done your purification exercises long enough today?''

The expressionless "face" turned toward him, and the expressionless visual perceptors (which looked a little bit like eyes) stared down at the boy. The voice echoed his words, "Something is wrong with me?"

"You keep repeating the same sentences. When we were on board the battleship, you said to me, 'I have been considering your statement that this pirate captain may be the key figure . . .' And the rest of it exactly as you have spoken it three times since, including a few moments ago.''

"But it's true!" Nodo protested. "I have been considering it. The repetition merely indicates that there is no change in the consideration.''

Billy changed the subject. "Are we close?"

"Seven and three-quarter astral eighth units," was the reply.

Billy nodded. And agreed that that was close, indeed.

". . .The questions that are being asked," Harley was saying at that moment, "are, what do they want? What are they here for? Will they presently go back where they came from?"

"Sir," said Fletcher in his most courteous tone, "those are excellent questions under ordinary circumstances. But that is not the basis of the problem. These machine people have been precipitated here from a different period of time, and their machinery is for some reason not operative. Accordingly, they are now subject to the gravitational laws propounded by Sir Isaac Newton within the last two decades. So they are here to stay. Naturally, they plan conquest and control. But my information is that they probably must remain aboard their vessel and cannot venture far. Hence, my suggestion to the Queen and her Consort is that a scheme be devised whereby these intruders can be lured ashore, and an attack mounted against them there with enmassed cannon.''

"They have demanded," said Harley in a tense voice,

"that the Queen be surrendered to them as a hostage. So we may visualize a plan of conquest based on a system of captive heads of state. Therefore, they are not likely to risk a disembarkment until those goals are achieved."

There seemed to be nothing else to be said on that issue. Yet it had been a singularly straightforward discussion. True, there was no solution. But Fletcher was encouraged by the other man's openness to say, "And now, sir, I would like us to speak equally true things to each other in a more personal vein. I have a simple question to ask, and desire an equally simple direct answer."

If the great man who sat on the far side of that beautifully appointed room had a reaction to the words, it didn't show. His gaze was fixed on the floor. There was no indication from him that he was waiting for the additional words that Fletcher spoke next: "Was it brought to your attention, Mr. Harley, that I was being tried. And, if so, did you tell the Queen?"

Harley shifted, shrugged. "There is so much information comes into my office; and, as you may recall, you and I are political opponents. So, to be quite frank, I did not extend myself on your behalf. And, no, of course, I didn't tell the Queen."

It sounded to Fletcher as if he were saying that he had known of the trial, but had somehow made a point of not knowing.

Harley continued in an irritable tone: "Evidently, certain truths were either unknown to you, or you had forgotten, or you were just plain—let me put it bluntly—stupid. But I deduce that you did not take your appointment as commanding general seriously—"

He paused. And stared at Fletcher with those dark, sardonic eyes and an expression of what-an-idiot-you-turned-out-to-be.

Fletcher said slowly, "A general for one night, so that I might escape—"

The Earl finished the thought, cynically. "Such an appointment cannot be ignored, sir. It had to be recorded in the war department, and in Parliament. And, of course, when a man has been appointed a general he cannot be tried by an ordinary court but only by his peers or by some other high government agency. So there you are, Mr. Fletcher. I will so advise the local authorities, and you and I must forthwith ride off on the urgent business of a tottering government of a country whose Queen is actually considering surrendering herself to the monsters aboard that giant vessel, about which only you seem to have prior information."

He stood up. "Let us be on our way, Mr. Fletcher. This is business that cannot wait."

They had to go from upstairs to downstairs, but first along a corridor. The distance to be covered gave Fletcher time to become aware again of Lady Hemistan, walking slightly behind Harley and himself. He had an additional realization of how quietly she had sat, uttering not one word. And yet, her own experience, as yet undescribed, established her as someone who knew somewhat of these urgent matters.

So, now, halfway down the stairs, he paused. And he turned to gaze up at the slender woman. And he bowed. And said, "Ma'am, it is my belief that you, also, should accompany this expedition to save the British state."

If she intended an answer, it did not have time to take place.

There was a horrendous interruption: a wild pounding at the great front door. Such a shattering sound it was that Fletcher at once started down the steps at a dead run. Down the remainder of the stairway, and across the magnificent hall. Virtually without thought he took it for granted that, between the two of them in a time of danger, he must take the lead away from a mere civilian government leader like Harley.

Thus, it was he who peered first through some intricate glass artwork. He who unlatched the door. And flung it ponderously open.

A soldier in officer's uniform darted across the threshold

and raced over to Harley. "Your Excellency," he gasped, "a great metal bird is—is—" His voice failed him. And he pointed with speechless excitement back the way he had come.

By that time, Nathan Fletcher, who had already seen a metal bird, and was no longer terrified by the mere idea of such, had stepped outside. From that vantage point he observed that it was a much smaller bird than the one from which man-shaped metal creatures had boarded the *Orinda*.

This "bird" had come to rest on the patio, squashing about a dozen fancy garden bushes and one small tree. And out of it—at the exact moment that Fletcher's eyes grew accustomed to the darkness—stepped Billy Todd.

Moments after that Billy was inside the house. And it was quite an up feeling for Fletcher to be able to say to Harley and Patricia:

"The boy that I was telling you about, lady, sir—this is he."

20

In that great castle hallway candles cast a pale, flickering light upon a strange scene. Dozens of candles sputtered, each with its unique little flame (next to resinous wood, the first transportable light in human history) and which in all future time would be the measure of light energy. Candlepower! Such a primitive light source, yet a candle was chemically complex, and operated at the temperature of the solidification of platinum.

An entire group of tiny wax-fueled fires, product of animal fat, shone from atop a fancy candelabrum that hung down from a high wrought ceiling. Others were set in equally glittering glass holders attached to walls. In every wall, large mirrors picked up the light and sent it flashing back into the room.

Beautiful! But Fletcher had, for the first time in his life, the diminishing thought that candles (and oil lamps, the only other form of lighting that he knew) were a low-level augmentation of nature. The demeaned feeling: . . . I am standing here (and standing he was, very still) in an old-fashioned, countrified civilization.

As a residence of lesser British nobility, Hemistan Castle was an apex of its time and location. But in his state of heightened awareness, Fletcher perceived what it lacked, not what it had.

It was a glimpse only, and by comparison with a thought. A vision. Mostly, the fantasy he had so briefly, then, derived from what Abdul Jones had said. But there were also thoughts from Billy.

It was a vision of total beauty.

A mental picture—oh! Fantastic! What a castle might be like in the twenty-third century. Or in the eightieth century. Or during the Lantellan period.

Everything would be powered by machines. That was the first, obvious aspect. Lights would be as bright in mass as the tiny beams that, under a blazing sun, had literally glittered a pathway into the heads of the four bullies. There would be machinery for cooking, for cleaning, for guarding, for sleeping—pretty vague, that—and for transport, and—and—

The mental picture faded abruptly. And there he was still. And there the others were also.

Billy Todd and Fletcher nearest the door. Harley and the now silent officer at the foot of the stairs. And Patricia up half a dozen steps, with Abdul Jones unobtrusively behind her.

She it was, now, who moved first. She came all the way down. She stopped beside Harley. And said to Billy, "The person you will have to convince of the reality of the situation is this gentleman, who is a government leader."

The boy nodded as calmly as a man, came forward, and said, "I am here with one of the Lantellan landing modules. I am accompanied by Nodo, an individual whom you would consider a mechanical being. The landing craft has enough firepower to destroy ten thousand soldiers. Nodo insists that Captain Fletcher shall return with him and myself to London. Also, now that he has become aware of the woman, he insists that she come, too. And that man, also"—Billy pointed at Abdul Jones—"and, of course, yourself as a possible intermediary, if needed—"

As he heard those words, something else let go inside

Fletcher. The tight emptiness that had been in him ever since his capture had relaxed in a tiny degree, first, of course, with the arrival of Harley. But now, suddenly, it faded to a shadow of what it had been.

There was a wonderful thought in him. An amazed realization. On this night, not one but several rescuers had come, in effect, to save him. Suddenly, it was really for certain that death was not for him . . . yet. On the morrow the official hangman of Bonnenshire would wait in vain for his victim.

As he had that thought, with the immense relief it brought, he happened to glance up, and over. And saw that the Lady Patricia was watching him. Her expression was serious, but there was a significant something in her eyes.

She was at once aware of his awareness. She said sweetly, "Even I, Captain, would not have allowed it to happen."

It was not Fletcher's brightest moment. "Allowed what?" he asked. And then, belatedly, he realized: . . . She knew what I was thinking—

His memory flipped back again to the four roughnecks. Those bully boys had also taken the thoughts directly out of his mind.

His gaze fastened on hers. "You, too?" he said simply.

The pretty woman suddenly had a faraway expression in her eyes. "It's strange," she murmured. "It seems as if something happened to all of us out there. Even you understand it."

She continued after a moment, "Captain—or is it General?—Fletcher, you are evidently in a condition of reprieve. It could even be that you will never be penalized for your career as a pirate."

There was no answering comment that he could suitably make. Because her words spoke aloud the thought which he was allowing himself to have.

Lady Patricia seemed to accept his silence as permission

to proceed, for she continued: "You, accordingly, have a severe problem."

That was instantly baffling. "How do you mean?" Fletcher asked.

"You must purify your soul. Become a person of total integrity. No untruth or criminal thought must ever again cross your mind, or motivate your action."

Her eyes were bright, and she met his gaze as he stared at her in amazement. Finally: "Ma'am," he said slowly, "you apparently do not realize what purification would mean for a person such as I. At present I keep the vivid images of the dead and dying away from the forefront of my mind. Their piteous cries, their horror and dismay, the faces that showed fear or terror. What you are suggesting is that I must make my peace with those memories. That is impossible. If I offered the slightest inward amends to that part of my past, there would be an immediate rush of emotional disaster through my body. And I would fall dead at your feet, smoldering and, perhaps, even aflame from endless inner torment."

His description must have evoked a picture in her mind more . . . vivid . . . than she had anticipated. She shrank. Then, in a brave tone: "Perhaps, a dedication to good works in the future, leaving"— she concluded—"the past alone."

"I think," bowed Fletcher, ironically, "I had better introduce you to my sister, Marion. The two of you can discuss the details of how such matters might be dealt with. As for me, I dare not meddle with the matter in any way."

"Possibly, right now," she replied, "you should introduce me to this boy, who is standing by so courteously while we chatter to no purpose."

It didn't seem quite that purposeless. Her words had cast a small bit of light into a dark cellar of his mind. And he had taken one swift, shocked look. That was relieving.

And so, just like that, he was able to turn and say cheerfully, "Well, Billy, while this lady and I are discussing the disposition of my soul, you have told us that we are about to enter a new and unknown condition of imprisonment, which—to a man sentenced to hang in five or six hours—actually seems like a rescue.''

That feeling—of relief—lasted until he had his first look at Nodo as an identified robot when he climbed aboard. The instant sense of inhuman ''aliveness,'' and the conviction that came that there was no mercy for any human being in this darkly gleaming metal thing, was still with him moments later as he sank into one of the five seats at the rear of the craft.

He was aware of the others sitting down also, and then aware of a physical sensation. And realized that the ''bird'' had lifted away from the ground.

And that whatever the fate that awaited them, there was now no turning back by any method that he knew.

21

A kind of excitement. An actual body trembling . . . Nothing to do with good sense. Or safety.

A unique feeling: Fletcher was aware of being pressed back against his seat. And held there. It would have required a strong effort to lean forward.

A thought: My God, this must be what it's like to fly.

There was only vague awareness of his four companions. Of what they were doing. Of how they were responding to the fantastic event.

Abruptly, then, his free floating perception . . . focused. On Nodo.

Nodo sat in a chair in front of a curving window. It seemed an odd place for a window to be. Fletcher, who had a fine balancing of spatial relationships in his head, without ever knowing there was a special ability involved, could not recall having noticed such a glass from the outside of the "bird."

Through the curving transparency he could see a portion of Hemistan Castle and the Hemistan grounds. The entire scene was receding behind them rapidly—which was a strange window, indeed: looking forward yet picturing backward. Also, out there—back there—it was no longer dark. What was receding looked like what he remembered

from a journey through the Alps: standing on a cliff gazing
at a distant valley below as seen on a cloudy day.

Out of the corner of one eye, Fletcher was aware of
Abdul Jones—sitting opposite Patricia—stirring. A moment later the man spoke; and it was obvious that a
relational thought had passed through his mind.

He said, "You'll notice everything in that rear viewplate
looks different from what it would be in actual daylight."
Succinctly, then, the man pointed out that the base process
was infra-red photography. And that the rapidly receding
group of soldiers below, all staring upward, showed eyes
and lips as being extremely dark, and the faces light,
almost translucent. But that even though they were small
objects—getting smaller each passing moment—they re-
tained their shapes with a sharp clarity that was a
characteristic of infra-red. However, as the ever tinier
human shapes below continued to stay precisely silhouet-
ted, though they were now many miles away, that indicated computer image maintenance of the infra-red condition
to the twenty-third-century American.

"I figured," Abdul finished, "you wouldn't know about
things like that."

Indeed, Fletcher didn't. But what he did observe in his
acute fashion—Nathan Fletcher—was that Abdul Jones,
ordinary citizen of 2242 A.D. was beginning to assume a
mild leadership attitude. There was a change in tone of
voice that Fletcher recognized from his days near the seat
of government power: men newly appointed to positions of
authority beginning to "take over." I'll have to keep an
eye on this fellow! thought Fletcher.

Even as he took note of that initial warning signal, the
picture on the viewplate changed. It became a long sky
view.

"We're looking forward now, finally," said Abdul Jones
with quiet authority.

There they sat.

It was a small cabin with seats for five passengers. Why
exactly the right number of seats was not obvious. (Fletcher,

who was not aware of the possibility of structures that could fold exactly into the shape of a flat floor, did not look down, and so did not notice the tiny, meaningful lines that indicated the presence of several more possible seats.)

Nodo also sat. His seat was in front of the viewplate, below which was a spread of metallic glinting instrument board that went right down to the floor. On this lower section, many lights flickered. Nodo's act of sitting involved his metal, knobbed knees being almost as high as his black caricature of a human head. And the curved structure of him below his hips seemed to be fitted into a concave seat only inches above the floor. It would have been uncomfortable for Fletcher. It didn't seem to disturb Nodo.

During the entire flight, the Lantellan robot did not look around at his passengers. To Fletcher, who thought of such things, the metal man looked vulnerable. Except, it would be difficult to mount a useful attack with one's bare hands. In fact—Fletcher's guess—it would take a sledge hammer. There was none in sight, nor any equivalent heavy object.

The pressure that continued to hold him against the back of his seat once more drew his awareness. He had no comparable association for the sensation of steady acceleration except—vaguely—when sudden winds grabbed the sails—and everybody grabbed for something to hold onto. Nothing like this intense, persistent forcing of his body, so strong that he could actually feel himself sinking into the firm cushioning of the seat back.

Worse, and abruptly confusing, he was barely beginning to adjust to the invisible pressure when—a change. It was not instant. First, an impression of coasting. Then—a reversal.

Fortunately, he felt it coming. Felt *something*. And braced his feet against whatever it might be. On impulse, also, he reached with one arm across the aisle. Placed his muscular arm and hand high up against Patricia's shoulder. And, as the acceleration reversed, held her firmly, and held himself.

At his first touch, he felt her body stiffen. And then, almost at once, relax. After several moments she was obviously holding herself; so he let go and leaned back into his own seat. As he did so, Abdul Jones, the man from New York of the twenty-third century, bent over across the aisle and said to the youthful Lady Hemistan, "With your permission, I shall utilize advanced scientific equipment that I have available on my person to protect you during the difficult hours ahead."

The young woman answered that with a faint, almost enigmatic smile. And then she made what was easily the most sensational statement Fletcher had heard in a long time. She said, "We all have to make adjustments to the new condition, Mr. Jones. As for me, I have already, mentally, placed myself under the protection of Mr. Fletcher."

Abdul's gray-blue eyes widened with surprise. His face even twisted into a *moue*. He seemed to have difficulty swallowing. Then, with a visible effort, he recovered, and said, "At the moment of crisis, if you change your mind, I shall be available."

What struck Fletcher about the interchange was, of course, first, Lady Patricia's reply. But, second—stronger now— the earlier observation came back: that Abdul Jones had made—again—a leadership assertion. And this time, even more important, he had made a distinctly male attempt to take over a female.

That part was not disturbing. It was a little early for a choice to be made by anyone in this situation.

But what was disturbing was the implication that Abdul had something other than his bare hands to accomplish whatever he had in mind. Every word, and manner, of Mr. Jones's indicated that he possessed a hidden weapon of some kind. And that he was beginning to look over an unscientific age, and was sizing it up as something less.

Even as he had those awarenesses, Fletcher was shifting his own feet again. Once more, now, he stretched out his arm and hand across the aisle. This time he touched the small shoulder of the boy. To Billy, he said, "Why haven't they kllled us?"

Billy turned, and there was an expression of surprise on his face. "Why would they do that?"

"Because they are at war with human beings." He was abruptly, mildly, irritated. "Aren't they?"

"No, sir. They are at war with the Tellurian Federation."

It was a fine point, and, presumably, reflected robot logic. Nevertheless, after a moment Fletcher frowned. "I have the memory that you were terrified when you first saw them."

"When I first recognized them, I had only an instant recall of a situation that was far in the past from my time. It would be like your remembering that ancient Rome and ancient Carthage were enemies."

Billy paused. And Fletcher inclined his head, acknowledging the comparison.

Billy continued. "What really bothers me is that they're out of touch with their central computer. And they are now on self-responsibility. At this point that is strictly logical. But soon there will be defensive mechanisms triggered. Then they will settle into a more permanent self-protective condition, favoring their welfare at other people's expense."

"Oh!" Fletcher said. He was relieved. For four years it had been the now that counted with him. So he shrugged and said, "Very well, what's the plan now?"

Billy Todd said, "They want the machinery I put aboard your ship."

Fletcher parted his lips to say, "What machinery?"

Before he could say it, Billy continued. "I had to tell them about it. And the fact that they plan to use it for themselves is something we shall have to decide about later."

Fletcher was dimly remembering his surprise when the stuff was brought up from the hold. But truth was, he was not always on deck when goods were transferred from a captured merchant vessel.

Billy was speaking again: "Nodo will need you to locate the dealer who bought the machines."

Of that, Fletcher had no recollection whatsoever. He said irritably, "For God's sake, why didn't you tell me about the machines before you left the ship?"

"They had listening devices pointed at us," said Billy. "They would have heard. So I dared not at that time say a word."

"Well," said Fletcher, "all I can answer is that the information is written down in my log aboard the *Orinda*. However, Shradd intended to sail back to the West Indies after two weeks. So he's left long ago."

22

Dawn was a bright yellow fire in the east when Fletcher stepped gingerly down onto the deck of the *Orinda*. He did not look back, though there was a vague thought in his head that the "bird" might take off and leave him. Actually, truth was that wouldn't have been the worst fate in the world: to be out here again on the limitless sea, far from the unsettling events in distant England.

He could hear the lap of the water, and the straining of the sails; but during those first minutes not a movement was visible on the ship itself.

Surprisingly, he kept noticing small details. It was surprising because he had decided that he would need to be extremely alert to reactions from the lunkheads aboard; there was always some dim brain who, in his eagerness to impress the new captain—Shradd—might triumphantly snip off the life of the old one—without thinking.

. . . How could he think? He had nothing to think with—

The small details Fletcher noticed, in spite of himself: the deck looked more cluttered than he had ever permitted. His method of dealing with such: he'd made it clear that any personal effects he found on deck, he immediately tossed overboard. And he always had.

Evidently, old shoes, shirts, trousers, torn pieces of sail, unwashed tin dishes, and God-only-knew what some of the junk was, did not bother Shradd.

Fletcher had no time to dwell on the trivia. Because, abruptly, Shradd himself stepped out of a doorway, and came forward.

"Yes, sir? Yes, Cap'n?"

It was not the moment for a joyous reunion of pirate comrades. Fletcher said forthrightly, without preamble, "Mr. Shradd, I need the log in which I entered all the transactions of our last voyage. The name of one of the buyers is needed."

What he got was the entire listing in his own neat handwriting. And he got it quickly, without another word being spoken.

However, as Fletcher stood there, pretending to verify that what he had received was indeed what was wanted, he spoke his own personal purpose in a low voice: "Mr. Shradd, do you have aboard the following persons?" He thereupon named the four former bullies who had been shot by beams of light at the time of the robot invasion of the *Orinda*.

"Didn't show." Shradd was thoughtful. "Something strange about those men, sir, after they came to. I sent one of our bullies to look for 'em. Found only Arkion, n'he said he was gonna stay with the woman he'd had some kids by."

Shradd concluded with a shrug, "What happened musta scared hell outa him'n the others."

"Hmmm," acknowledged Fletcher.

"Whaddaya want 'em for?" Shradd apparently had a sudden suspicion. "What's up?" he demanded sharply.

Fletcher had to suppress a grim smile. How could he possibly tell a man like Shradd that he was thinking of having the beam of light discharged at *his own* head?

Smoothly, he spoke his prepared lies: About the four

being wanted by the metal people to see what the aftereffect of the light beams had been on human beings.

Actually, it was Nathan Fletcher who wanted to see what those effects were.

The report on Arkion promised well. And so the great thought that had come to him in the aircraft still made sense. After the light beam hit those men, they could read minds. And they changed dramatically for the better. If that could happen to four vicious nothings, the consequences for an educated man might just make a difference. He and his companions needed some thought, some possibility. As of now the appearance was that they were in a hopeless trap.

Standing there, he said urgently, "They traced me down, Mr. Shradd. And, unless you take evasive action, they can continue doing the same to you. Land at a safe harbor"—a small waterside village with no police or soldiers (such villages were on all of the larger islands)—"and scatter the men."

To that, a baffled Shradd replied: "Cap'n, what is goin' on?" He waved uncertainly. "Whole world's gone topsy."

Fletcher did not answer that. A sudden feeling had come that it was not wise to prolong this conversation. "Good-by, Mr. Shradd. And good luck." He turned and walked rapidly back to the "bird."

Aboard, he discovered that Billy had reminded Nodo about human needs. As a consequence, first Patricia—guided and guarded by Fletcher—went to the captain's bathroom. Then Harley and Abdul together were directed, respectively, to the captain's and the first mate's cabin bath facilities. Finally, Fletcher and Billy, silently observed by the familiar lurking, crouching, evasive male crew members of the *Orinda,* made their ablutions. And came up to the deck again.

Whereupon, Fletcher once more shook hands with Shradd, who said with a frown: "That girl looks familiar. Can't quite place her."

Fletcher said, "We're all prisoners. Pray for us."

"Do *what?*" said Shradd.

But Fletcher was already walking on after Billy. He boarded the aircraft and did not look back.

Minutes later, when they were airborne, Nodo turned to Billy, and said, "Is there any reason why, as a precaution, we should not destroy the pirate ship?"

"Let me think," said Billy.

Whereupon, he settled back in his seat. The answer seemed to satisfy Nodo, for he turned his head to its forward facing position. Presently, Billy leaned back toward Fletcher and said in a low voice, "I always think things over very carefully before I say anything to Nodo."

Fletcher could think of no suitable comment. He waited.

Billy went on in the same soft voice: "Already, the rotation system of duties devolving upon each individual in turn has ceased, though they still use the language."

The meaning was not clear, so this time he did speak; asked for a clarification. When it had been given, it brought a memory to Fletcher. "Well, I'll be damned." What he remembered was a tribe on the South American coast, where his pirate ship, putting into a small bay for fresh water, was the first visit of whites.

On going ashore, it developed that Fletcher was presumed to be the living embodiment of a natural stone formation from which the chief annually received the "message" that he was still the anointed one. Fletcher, who had learned a few words of the language from other coast Indians, played along with the ritual and personally affirmed the "king" as being the chosen of the god.

The fact that the robots had a machine as a substitute for a rock formation, and that the machine—now missing—had adjudicated rotation of all leadership positions, was a new thought but the same principle—it seemed to Fletcher.

He came out of his brief memory to realize that Billy, having "thought," was rendering his judgment. The brilliant boy said, "I advise against destruction of the ship, because we may later discover something else we need either of Captain Fletcher's or an article that may still be aboard.''

"Oh!" said Nodo. "Of course!"

What bothered Fletcher about the interchange was a feeling that control of an elemental force was being precariously maintained by someone—Billy—who himself had no clear understanding of all the possible repercussions.

23

During the air journey back to London, the only one of the three other adults aboard to show a reaction was Robert Harley. He had been silent, perhaps watchful, undoubtedly trying to understand. Now, sitting there, carefully taking account of the steady acceleration—so he had noticed *that*—the great man turned to Fletcher. And he did something positively sensational. He addressed his enemy by the title that Fletcher had lost when his land (to which the title was tied) was taken from him.

"Baron," said Harley, "are you seriously thinking of handing the machinery in question over to these metal monsters?"

It was a moment pregnant with personal implications. The use of the lost title was cunning. It suggested that there might be restitution and rehabilitation. In this case, the person addressed, Nathan Fletcher, the one-time Baron Wentworth—a title now possessed by someone else—simply sat briefly silent. His was not a response in any meaningful way. He was not even waiting for clarification, though he did continue to brace himself against the acceleration.

Harley went on grimly. "It is the duty of every loyal Englishman to refuse to collaborate with the Queen's enemies."

It was an argument that left space for no more than one response. And yet, after surveying the apparent absoluteness of it in one of his quicker mental scans, Fletcher leaned over and across. Touched Billy's shoulder. And having gotten the boy's attention—

"Billy," he said, "explain to Her Majesty's minister your motives in letting the Lantellan robots have the machinery from your Transit-Craft."

The boy's face, with his bright, intelligent eyes, pointed to Harley, then to Fletcher. "Sir—gentlemen," he said, "the repair depot in the battleship is sufficient for the purposes of bringing the equipment up to working order." He shook his head, sadly. "As soon as I saw London, it was apparent that nothing else, nothing here, could do the job."

He concluded, "We have to take the chance that later we shall be able to persuade them that it is logical to help us."

As a sophisticated, unredeemed adult, Fletcher had his unhappy thoughts at that moment about Billy being, after all, a trusting boy. But that was for later. At the moment, the kid from the eighty-third century had said exactly what Fletcher wanted him to. Blandly, the pirate captain turned toward Harley.

"Sir, what is your judgment?"

Harley was frowning. "Well," he admitted, "I have to say that I saw this boy dissuade the metal creature from destroying your pirate ship. And he did it with an extremely direct logic; so it all could work out." He nodded. "I suppose the first, most important consideration has to be the repair of the machinery."

The admission justified what Fletcher was doing. Yet, what bemused him about Harley's comment was the picture it provided him of the man's innermost being. The Secretary of State was accustomed to the uses of persuasive logic—something (Fletcher had to admit) he had personally neglected during his short political life. His forte then: sharp, insightful remarks, but never an attempt to convince anyone of anything.

It was called personal charm. And it had moved him up in London court circles until one of the persuasive types noticed him. From that instant, though he did not realize it immediately, his was a doomed career.

At that point in his thought, there was a movement from the girl. She turned and looked at him.

At once, Fletcher leaned forward. "I have a feeling from what you said . . . earlier"—he spoke in as low a voice as he felt would carry—"that I'm being offered a way back into the world of decent people."

"You're being offered more than that," said Patricia Hemistan in a tone of voice that almost (but not quite) reflected the totality of her eighty-third-century physical-mental condition. . . . The not quite part was due to her unknowingness about what had happened to her. "What I'm thinking is that because of our special experiences you may be the only man in this period of history with whom I might have a common understanding."

"You're offering yourself?" Fletcher asked, startled.

"Only if you change," was the reply.

"I don't know how—as I've explained."

She was turning away. She faced forward, and did not look at him.

The man repressed a smile. In her action he recognized the ritual now-it's-up-to-you in the manner of an imperious 1704 A.D. aristocratic lady. It was undoubtedly something she had seen other imperious ladies do to their men. It showed no awareness that the upper class male of her time was the ascendant being in the man-woman relationship by some geometric multiple. At court, until his downfall, Fletcher had been a philanderer on a scale that had startled even the old, successful roués. And it was undoubtedly the one thing about him that had offended Anne.

All ages of female were equally, and unknowingly, unable to resist him when he made his careful, understanding attack: The newly arrived (at court) eighteen-year-old virgins, the sophisticated mid-twenties to mid-thirties, and even the surprisingly nubile old ladies in their forties surrendered.

Against such a male, helpless was the applicable word for a twenty-year-old who, true, was motivated by many impulses of her eighty-third-century body, but, alas, still felt restricted by the entire female conditioning of her own era.

What happened: the man looked at her as she sat with her face averted. And into his mind flashed a—not outraged—but outrageous thought. It derived from the life-long automatic attitudes of the ascendant upper class male, but, of course, it related to their current situation.

Fletcher leaned forward across the aisle. What he said was spoken in the same low voice as before. His words were: "Miss Patricia, I have to ask a great favor of you. I would like to borrow the money from you to buy back that equipment when we land."

Those words instantly reached deep into Patricia's 1704 A.D. womanly passivity. And though there were vague resistant stirrings from the more powerful being that she would presently become . . . from that moment forth she was psychically under pressure.

"My situation," Fletcher continued, "is that the sheriff's office holds about twelve hundred pounds, which they took off my person at the time of my arrest. And, I presume, your cousin found where I had concealed in my mother's home the ten thousand guineas which he paid me."

At that point, the young woman tentatively picked up the purse in her lap. And Fletcher said, "I presume I could stand by while Nodo forcibly removes the machinery from the person who purchased them. But I should like to begin my return to total integrity by not being a party to such an act of violence. And I promise to pay the money back to you."

She flashed scornfully at that, "The word of a pirate!" (The victim was struggling. A little.)

"The word of a gentleman-to-be-again," said Fletcher. "They left me a few guineas but not enough."

There was a long pause. Then: "Sir," she said, without looking at him, "there is a certain irony that you should begin your rehabilitation at my expense, but—" Impulsively, she half-turned and thrust the purse at him. "Take what you need."

When, a minute later, he pushed the purse onto her lap, her fingers closed over it. But she did not look at him. Did not turn. And sat there gazing straight ahead. And spoke.

She said audibly, "I have placed myself under your protection, sir. Whatever is required from that, I will do."

And *that* instantly reached deep into the basic 1704 A.D. maleness of Captain Nathan Fletcher. It brought back with an odd finality the thought about what, among other things, he would have to do as a protector. . . . Definitely, the L-beam fired into his head.

In all these minutes, his keen mind, with its fighting experience, had in vain looked over the robot power and the virtual prison situation that they were in for a way of escape.

There was no other possibility that he could see.

24

Shortly before noon, the small—but not that small—
Lantellan craft settled onto a shabby street beside a junk
yard. Almost at once, literally within a minute after he
climbed out, Fletcher had reason to recall an old saying:
"Nothing ever really surprises a Londoner."

Here was a fantastic airship of the future. Probably
several hundred illiterate units of the human garbage that
festered as grimy a neighborhood as Fletcher had ever
shuddered at saw the "impossible bird" come down.

Were they scared? Were they awed? As Fletcher gingerly walked over the dried-out mud of the dingy street,
there were "araaghs" from a dozen cracked throats. When,
moments later, Nodo stepped out of the aircraft and followed the former pirate captain, by then there were at least
a hundred hoarse voices croaking their owner's—not exactly amazement, not from a Londoner—but at least it was
recognition that here was an odd one.

The sign on the rough, unpainted door of the junk yard
stated:

JULIUS MACDONALD
Buyer and Seller

Of the two persons inside, Fletcher recognized the more swarthy individual as the man behind the name. He was visibly a Scot in last "nomen" only. His eyes were a bluish black, and he had a Mediterranean cast of countenance. And when he spoke it was an expletive that could have been Low German, but had a twist to it—what might be called an accent—that made it possible for a man with Fletcher's cultivated linguistic ear to deduce that the words were Yiddish.

The words were not easy to understand for another reason. As he looked up and saw Fletcher, momentarily his expression was blank. Then came an eye-widening recognition. And then—

He burst into tears.

Just like that, even if no other identification had been available, he would have marked himself racially. All in an instant, he had adopted that best of all defensive actions of the Jews in a rigid Christian world.

. . . The crying Jews of the Middle Ages—

And as he cried, he talked in a mixture of English and Yiddish.

"I was a *mentsch on glik*—" (a man without luck) "when I bought your metal. Now, I'm just an *alter trombenik*—" (an old bum) "a *nishtikeit*—" (a nobody).

Fletcher said in Low German, "*Du hast de machinen billig gekuffin.*" (You have the machines cheap bought.)

The old man sobbed, "It was a *smeikel*—" (swindle) "The heating wouldn't melt them."

Thus, in an amazingly rapid dialogue, the unhappy story emerged. The engines had been returned to him because the material would not work in the best furnaces available to the buyer, who had extracted full repayment. And, by *Got* (God) Julius wanted his money also, with a substantial profit to compensate him for his mental anguish.

The immense irony would, of course, never be brought home to the secondhand dealer. That he had in his possession space drive engines from the eighty-third century, which, when repaired, were probably worth a trillion pounds—even for Fletcher that was a difficult concept. And, particularly, at the moment it was only a fleeting thought, because there was no time for anything else.

The older man's voicing of his discontent began so quickly, and the high-pitched bitterness he felt evidently involved total focusing of his attention on Fletcher, that he didn't notice Nodo immediately. Also, Nodo's "body" was partly hidden behind Fletcher's. And that undoubtedly helped delay Julius's recognition of a fact: that this was not merely an unexpected opportunity for good old hard-working Julius M. to confront a swindling seller of shoddy goods.

Whatever the reason, abruptly the high-pitched voice came to the middle of a word and stopped. What had happened, the blue-black eyes had flicked away from Fletcher. Immediately, they seemed to freeze.

From that instant on, not a word was spoken. Fletcher pointed toward the rear of the building, and Julius tottered outside, followed by Fletcher and Nodo. The sequence of events after that was based on a simple reality. In Fletcher's record, the amount shown beside the eight priceless metal items was eighty-two British pounds. Fletcher drew out his billfold and counted the exact amount into the outstretched palm. Then both men stood by and watched a phenomenon of weight-lifting by an unknown force.

The machinery moved through the air by entirely invisible means, and was thrust through an opening into the interior of the flying machine. When all eight structures were inside, the opening closed. Fletcher and Nodo re-entered the airship. Moments later, it floated up from the dirt street, out over the docks, and off over the water without so much as a murmur of resistance from the entrepreneur who had surrendered the equipment and asked no profit on the transaction.

There *were* sounds and action, belatedly. As the final act of the drama came to its close, the watchers on the sidelines reacted—violently. Suddenly, stones, sticks, hard pieces of dirt road were flying through the air. Presumably, because of the direction in which they were thrown, the emotional intent of the London gutter people was to hit the "bird."

If that was, in fact, the purpose, it failed. The aircraft's departure was too swift for such simplicities to make any impact either literally or figuratively.

"Now," said Nodo to Billy, "find out from the female where she last saw the boat that brought her to London."

Fletcher had leaned back in his seat. And was aware from the "feel" of the acceleration—or rather, the non-acceleration—that the aircraft was merely coasting along. And he could see in the viewplate that they were doing their coasting over the Thames. They were flying so low, in fact, that he kept catching glimpses of either river shore line at the edges of the screen.

Nodo's words caught him so unprepared that he actually went momentarily blank. And then worse, he heard a voice muttering, "What—what—you mean they get that also?" And then, shamed, realized it was his own voice. His first awareness after that was that the conversation between Billy and Patricia had concluded. And that Billy had already reported something to Nodo. To such an effect that the aircraft was turning sharply.

What transpired next was at another level of perception. Beyond the reality of a Fletcher or a Harley or—except in a puzzled, doubting way—Patricia. The two super-machines —the seeker and the sought—were presently close enough together to be aware of each other. The boat, half-hidden in the watery grass that grew tall on the water's edge where it had been waiting all these weeks, sensed an alien presence—above. From above, the aircraft sensors *felt* over all the traffic below, identifying and rejecting the simple materials of vessels of 1704 A.D.

It was not a problem for either robot brain. They knew each other as being different. Knew it at a distance.

Unerringly, the Lantellan machine settled toward its victim.

The sensitive little ship meanwhile backed out into the

Thames. Slithered in a churning turn, and prepared to fight.

At that point, through a tiny crystal that had been sent along in one of the cupboards came a message from the boy: "I'm aboard the airship. So don't resist. It will only hurt me and my friends."

The churning motion ceased. The boat came to a stop. Quietly, then, it maneuvered. And it was sliding again into its position at the concealed dock, when the aircraft, like an attacking hawk, settled down upon it.

Aboard the aircraft there was a sense of falling, and then a lurch. Fletcher heard a sound of metal scraping metal. The entire aircraft shuddered in a way that jumped his thought back to a time when the *Orinda* had scraped a rock. Something of the shock of that past incident came up and hit him in the pit of his stomach. Then—

They were in motion again. Climbing steadily. On the viewplate was a sky view. Yet the feel of the flight, once he recovered from the crunching in his stomach and other side effects, was different.

From the front seat, Billy explained, "It's too big to put inside. So he's got it hooked on with magnets to the bottom."

Fletcher parted his lips to express bewilderment. The words that remained, fortunately, unspoken were, "Got *what* hooked to the bottom?"

What saved him from speaking was that, finally, he was doing his first mental review of the sequence of events.

It was a bad moment. Because there was an awful realization. . . . The boat is captured. Now, they've got everything. ("They," of course, were the Lantellan robots.)

Just like that, automatically, it was for him the moment of decision.

Inside the cabin, Abdul was still sitting directly in front of Fletcher. Across the narrow aisle in three seats were the others. Billy up front. Patricia next—opposite Abdul. And Harley across from Fletcher.

They were still climbing as Fletcher in an even voice explained to Billy what he wanted.

Billy raised his voice and called, "Nodo, Captain Fletcher has a favor to ask you."

The head turned. The featureless black eyes stared at Fletcher. The lips parted, and from inside the mouth the voice box said, "We do not do favors for human beings."

"Perhaps," said Billy, "after you hear what he wants you may decide that it is logically to your advantage to do as he asks."

The eyes continued to focus on Fletcher. The voice said, "Very well, let him speak."

After Fletcher had explained, there was a pause. The internal machinery of thinking was clearly considering something for which it had no trained response. Finally: "Let me understand. You wish me to discharge an L-beam into your head with the expectation that you will be rendered unconscious but not killed. Is that correct?"

In the same even tone Fletcher explained the effect that he had observed in the four bullies of such a light beam. As he spoke he was aware of Patricia, off to one side, looking anxious and disturbed.

The girl leaned back. "Are you sure you should do this?"

"In my opinion," he replied, "it will do the task of inner purification which I cannot do for myself."

Actually, that part he was merely curious about. How a man with so much murder behind him could arrive at inner peace would be interesting to observe. His real purpose he had better not mention: attainment of a state of mind superior to his present helpless condition.

"B-but—" The girl was speaking again; she sounded distracted. "It's—it's . . . Perhaps, if you were to accept God into your heart again?"

That brought a grim smile to Fletcher's lips. God had a place in the heart of good Queen Anne, and apparently inside young Lady Hemistan God was still unquestioned. But anyone who had ever been connected with British politics understood that God was given a great deal of lip service but played no detectable role in actual government.

As a victim of godless government manipulation, Fletcher could never again—unless the light would do it for him— feel any moral conviction.

Even as that sardonic awareness permeated him, he realized that another thought was struggling to get up to the surface of his mind. Within instants after he noticed it, it came up from the darkness that had enveloped him at the moment that he realized what it was the aircraft had captured. He said, "Ma'am, I'd like to know what is this boat that transported you across the Atlantic? Also, I'd like—"

He stopped. And gazed beyond her.

Nodo was doing that mechanical head turn again. This time his eyes pointed at Billy. "What this man has said needs to be discussed with biophysicist-by-rotation Layed and biochemist-by-rotation Adla. The concept of such a character transformation from the L-beam is previously unknown to us, since, of course, we utilized such a limited method of control only because we had made the logical decision not to kill until we understood what had happened to our vessel. That does not apply here. So the answer is no."

"I should remind you," said Billy, "that the L-beam is close to being basic energy."

There was a pause. Nodo sat staring at Fletcher. Then: "I have been in communication with biophysicist-by-rotation Layed. He has reminded me that Billy Todd regards you as being somehow a key figure in what has happened. Therefore, it might be unwise to bring you aboard our keep in a conscious state. Therefore, he has instructed me to reverse my initial negative reaction, and to utilize the L-beam as requested. And deliver your unconscious body to him in his laboratory."

In the moments that followed those words Fletcher had time for the rueful thought that he had actually been relieved by Nodo's first reaction refusal.

It was one of those complicated moments that, in its

way, was too much for the responses of a human being.
Earlier, in making the request, he had braced himself.
Then, at Nodo's rejection, the internal reactions were those
of a person who has thereby been thrown off guard.

. . . Complexities of the autonomic nervous system
. . . decrease in muscular tone and body temperature, and
heavy discharge of adrenalin—all adding up to . . . shock.

The macho male thing, augmented by four years of the
conditioning of a pirate, came to his aid. So many experiences. And one basic observation over the years. The best
way to sidetrack fear: let yourself, force yourself, to be
slightly distracted.

Fletcher's method of diversion. In that awful moment,
as that metal hand came up, he said to Patricia, "I want to
tell you that I deeply regret what I did to you. I swear I
was enormously relieved when I discovered that you had
escaped. But I cannot imagine how, with an anchor tied to
you, you ever got to London—"

. . . *Got to London* . . . *Got to London* . . . He heard his
voice falter over those words, heard the echo of them as
from a distance. The metal hand was aiming at him one of
the instruments that Fletcher had seen so fleetingly at the
time of the robot boarding of the *Orinda*.

He had no additional impression. A dazzling brightness
flashed . . . over there in front of him.

He was momentarily aware then that he was leaning
over into a gray, formless, sightless something, and into—

Blackout.

25

Fletcher awakened to a sound.

By the dim light of the prison cell he saw that Abdul Jones was stirring on the cot across from him. Obviously, the older man, also, had heard something.

The shock of awakening so suddenly was still with Fletcher as he sat up. Also, there was a small time lapse during which he had no particular thought. During that lapse the realization came that somebody was fumbling at the outside of the cell door. Whatever was being used made a metallic sound.

He felt an instant qualm. Could it be morning?

Even as the blood drained from his cheeks, and the chill of fear hit him, he remembered the . . . earlier . . . moment when the opening of the door had produced the same belief that it was hanging time.

Good God! Fletcher thought, disgusted with himself, I'm going to have to—

The thought stopped.

An entirely different shock went through him.

. . . The memory of only moments ago being aboard an aircraft—

The memory was utterly vivid. And so totally true that

155

for many, many seconds the reality of being inside the prison was blotted from his consciousness.

Absolutely basic forces had created the anomaly. So the confusion of the two realities inside the man was momentarily close to an otherwise impossible breakthrough. Utterly basic! . . . For those few instants the incredibly rigid potent forces that maintained the illusion of life were actually affected.

Nature was that near to having its most fundamental secret penetrated by a human mind.

But, fortunately, this was an unscientific human being of 1704 A.D. Very sharp, in his way. But any man whose solution to a political defeat is to become a pirate has got detours in his head that leave no room for fundamental observations of life and the universe.

The danger of revelation ended as quickly as it had come.

Fletcher could now hear the sound as a steady manipulation of a key in a rusty lock. And that made sense now. So there he was, definitely in and of the prison cell, waiting to be hanged.

Also, he had his first dismissing thought that the aircraft and what went with it must have been a particularly vivid dream.

It is possible that the noise of an old iron door being unlocked can be described. The two men who were inside the ancient-style basement prison surely heard each clank, each clatter, the grating of the key in the first lock, and then the grating of the key in the second lock, and next a thud. The thud was when the door opener tugged at the heavy, twisted structure, and it jammed. But whoever it was, was persistent. Because after several more thuds there was a different grating sound. Whereupon, the door swung weightily open . . .

The person who stood in the dank corridor beyond the opening thus made was dressed in a woman's white gown. But the lantern she carried cast only a dim light. And so it took a goodly number of moments before Fletcher was able to make out the face above the dress.

He recognized it finally as the face of Lady Patricia Hemistan. In that dim light her mental and emotional state was not immediately detectable. And yet presently his impression was that it was a very strained-looking face.

She came forward into the doorway and stopped. Standing there, she spoke in a trembling voice. "Gentlemen, there's a giant beast outside. We've all been brought out of our beds in a state of terror."

The white robe shimmered in the dim light as she turned slightly. "Captain"—to Fletcher—"is it possible that with your experience you could—"

The final words were left unspoken. But they were unnecessary. Suddenly, this was real. It *had* been a dream. For here was the woman who had surely shared every moment with him. Here she was, indeed, and with an unrelated mission about . . . The meaning of her words had not stayed with him. Only the gist was in his head.

Something, some danger, had brought her to these depths of the castle, seeking help from a gentleman felon whom she evidently believed had enough violence in his soul to face the violence that was threatening outside.

Within seconds after that realization, because he was quick and accepted normal phenomena like dreams, all those courtesies and cunnings that had in the past been so habitual for him emerged from the psychic closets in his mind where he had stored them.

No plan yet. No exact purpose. But—

He spoke a reassuring word. He came off the bunk to his feet. He took several steps forward at exactly the correct, unthreatening pace. Gently, he took the lantern from her fingers.

"Show me the way," he said, "and then show me the danger!"

From behind him there was a voice sound from Abdul Jones. It was a puzzled bleat, as if somehow that individual had missed the implications of what was transpiring.

Fletcher hesitated. And then, though he had an immense reluctance to re-enter the cramped quarters *for any reason*—even thought of it as bad luck . . . went back. The far-future New Yorker was sitting up. But he had to be tugged to his feet, and drawn forward, and out. There was a moment, then, when something penetrated. And, thereafter, the man was definitely moving under his own direction . . .

The creature stood about ten feet tall at the shoulder. It was yellow in color and, though it was not easy to see in the darkness, with numerous red markings. Its body bulged in the lower portion, and it seemed to have a tail. Its jaws were three feet long and gleamed with white-pointed teeth. It kept opening and shutting that great mouth. Each closing produced a grinding sound.

(An expert from a later age would have recognized the monster as a member of the family of large lizards that had ranged the earth millions of years earlier. However, it resembled none of the well-known branches of that notorious group. . . . A strand of time energy had fallen momentarily into a distant period of earth's evolutionary history, and had flicked this unknown but formidable specimen up and up into the far future year of 1704 A.D.

Fletcher stood at the side of the large plate glass window in a high-ceilinged room. Stood there trying to make sure that he was out of sight of the creature, and trying to avoid any movement that would attract its attention. From that vantage position he stared out into the night past a clump of ornamental shrubbery at the improbable beast. Because of what had already happened, he deduced at once that it obviously was a victim of the same disaster that had brought the Lantellan battleship, and Billy, and Abdul Jones.

Also, there flitted through his memory his sister's report of footprints four feet long. . . . Could this creature have paws of that colossal size?

It was impossible in that cloud-filled darkness to determine the spread of those powerful legs. The beast seemed to crouch on its haunches—maybe that was how the four-foot-long footprint effect was achieved; it was actually a haunch print and footprint combined.

Fletcher seemed frozen there. But he was thinking, and cringing. Impossible, of course, to make a direct attack with anything smaller than a cannon. And, besides, a thought—fleeting, but it was spontaneous in his own head, and remained long enough so that he had to dismiss it consciously as being inapplicable here.

The thought: This could be the only creature of its kind remaining in a destroyed universe. Therefore, it should not be killed.

As if she had read his mind, Lady Hemistan said at that exact moment, "It seems wrong to kill so strange and wonderful a thing. Perhaps, we could trap it somehow. And save it."

With both of them having had the same life-conserving impulse—however brief his own savoring of it had been—from that instant forth, the awareness of such a purpose was never far from Fletcher's consciousness.

And, of course, being who he was, there presently came a return of his old sardonicism. He said politely, "Miss, at this time our problem is to save your property and ourselves from damage. Also, I should point out that *it* is quite safe from us. We have no visible means of destroying it, or, may I add, of saving it."

"I thought"—her tone was uncertain; and since he was not looking at her, he presumed she felt a great doubt herself, as she spoke the words—"we might drive it into the empty stable."

"Who might drive it *where?"*

The question erupted out of Fletcher that quickly. The feeling of instant outrage was that strong.

Almost at once, he calmed back to his basic condition of sardonicism. But the lady, as he now swiftly discovered, was piqued; for she said stiffly, "Of course, Captain, if I was wrong about your ability to deal with these dangerous matters, you have my apologies. If you prefer, you may go back to your cell.''

She added in a sweet voice, "I'm sure you will be safe there.''

That—return to the cell—would never be again, if he could help it. But it was momentarily grimly amusing that she could remind him of his degradation.

Nonetheless, it was *touché*. It braced that 1704 A.D. macho male quality in him. The consequence of her attitude: he asked a few incisive questions: which stable? where? what made her believe it was strong enough to contain such a monster? By any chance, was the door open? How can we feed it if we get it in there?

As he talked, and presently listened to her answers, he also looked at the beast. And moment by moment his heart sank. For the great creature was making a rumbling, roaring sound that was, all by itself, terrifying in the sheer power that was implied.

Worse, suddenly, like a multi-tonned wagon, it started forward. Moments after that it lumbered out of sight around the side of the house. Silence. Then an awful crashing sound as of masonry falling. The entire castle trembled.

It was not a good moment for that former upper class Englishman who had become the notorious pirate Captain Nathan Fletcher. In his time he had fought a duel at twenty paces—and deliberately wounded, but not killed, his opponent. At sea, his weaving sword many times cut a path of blood through phalanxes of resisting seamen.

None of that was any preparation for this situation. Now he had the peculiar, unhappy feeling that the Lady Patricia Hemistan expected him to venture into the open grounds of her estate. Expected him to approach the giant beast. And by a means that would be easy for a violent male like himself, accustomed to the martial arts, overwhelm the monster. Preferably, he would accomplish the miracle by guiding it into the second stable—which, like the others, was built of stone, iron, and concrete, and was unoccupied on this evening.

But he would first have to open the big door, since it was shut for the night.

In a twisted fashion, Fletcher was able to visualize the entire operation. Apparently, there was an aged, decrepit horse in stable number three, that was to be slaughtered. Therefore, if this poor, old, to-be-discarded servant of an animal were first led into the empty stable and killed, then, presumably, the giant intruder would unthinkingly enter, intending to eat. At which time, the iron doors could be lowered into their metal and concrete slots by a lever system from above.

As Fletcher contemplated the dangerous sequence of events, and his (projected by Lady Hemistan) role, he experienced an unaccustomed mental blankness. Fear? It was not an emotion that he had normally allowed himself to experience, except fleetingly as something best dealt with by putting one's attention on something else.

The distraction came from behind him, as the mumbling voice of Abdul Jones said something. It was a measure of the non-impact the man from the future had made upon him that Fletcher didn't even turn. Perhaps it was actually a measure of how totally lacking he was in comprehending the feelings of other people that he didn't care what the words were that the man had uttered. He had dismissed the future New Yorker as a nonentity; and, like men of substance from time immemorial in human history, could have stood by and watched him racked, or drawn and quartered, and not even for a moment felt compassion. A common superstition of the upper classes was that lower types "don't feel anything." Only the "quality" feel, although a percentage of them, when they "went bad," also thereafter were considered as being insensitive to pain, having presumably been taken over by the devil.

"I think," said Fletcher speculatively, aloud, "we'd better find where it went. And then perhaps I can go out the opposite side of the building and sneak over to the stables. Arrived there, I shall open the door of the empty stable, lead the old horse in there, kill it, and then—"

Then what? The rest of the visualized action which
would, of course, have to involve "guiding"—as the Lady
Patricia had worded it—the monster over to the stable—
the rest was a blur.

Fletcher realized that he was hoping the great beast
would smell the blood of the dead horse and go into the
trap, drawn there by hunger.

Feeling abruptly decisive, he turned—as Abdul Jones
said, "I think I should fly over to the stable, open the
door, and get that horse in there. And then use my"
(meaningless term) "to make it go inside."

Moments after those words were uttered, clear and unmistakable, the pirate captain and the Lady Patricia of
Hemistan Castle were simultaneously confronting a man
with a long, smooth face, age about forty. This person, on
being questioned, explained that his "lift" normally operated on power from a solar station in permanent orbit
above New York City. But of course it had a battery
back-up system which was good for about four hours of
flight.

"You mean," said the girl slowly, "you're wearing this
. . . contraption . . . now, this minute?" Her pretty face
had an intent expression on it. She turned to Fletcher as if
to say something. But after several seconds no words had
come.

And it was Abdul Jones who finally said, almost apologetically, "The whole system is woven into my clothes."
He finished, "But I'd better do what I said. We can talk
later—"

26

Logically, there is nothing a man can say to a woman whom he has drowned. And who, to all intents and purposes, is now alive again, rescued accidentally in a way that gives him no credit for good will.

Her whole being should be seething with hatred and revulsion. Yet—Fletcher observed—it wasn't quite like that. Outwardly, at least, it wasn't. Just as "before."

The subject of the murder by drowning would undoubtedly have to be mentioned sooner or later. But not, apparently, right away.

Patricia sat at the head of the table, with its fine stemware, its shining blue-tinted plates, its gleaming silver cutlery, and the white spread of linen tablecloth, and smiled at her two guests.

"Gentlemen," she said in a voice that was vibrant with a confidence that could now, easily, have given a smiling and understanding, but firm, no even to an importunate father—something which she had never been able to do during his misspent lifetime. Though even then she always gave him less than he felt he needed. "Gentlemen, Henry II began a process of government by law when he said, 'Every man shall have a right to be heard.'"

"His motives," said Fletcher, "were not entirely pure.

He was attempting to break through the web of power by which the church of the day was limiting his authority as King.''

Having spoken, he was instantly, grimly, amused. This was the level of conversation to which he had once been accustomed. Somehow, he had always had an easy comprehension of the matters and motives in and around the government. Even as he played cards in the days of his ascendancy, he spoke instant wisdom—which was not lost on the future Queen; and, since he was also aware of her bent, he had slanted his verbal gems to fit.

"It would seem," continued Lady Hemistan with a singularly sweet smile in his direction, "that what Henry II began is the way out of the endless, repetitious stereotypes which derive from the lusts and impulses of autocratic individuals, particularly male human beings."

It was direction. And meaning. Abruptly, her purpose was obvious. She *was* going to give him his right "to be heard" . . . *Good God!* thought Fletcher, appalled. Just for a moment he could hear his whining voice explaining how he had allowed the Tory government to subvert his youthful morality.

Never! he decided, exactly as he had done at the trial. Not one word of defense would anyone ever get out of him!

He had accepted this invitation to dinner because the vivid memory was coming back. Right now he was a man who had his hands free and was not confined. For the first time in the weeks since his arrest he could act. What a madness if he wasted even an hour on, of all things, a leisurely meal. Particularly was this true since there was a likelihood that the dinner was a subterfuge, and that a servant, having been dispatched for help by Lady Patricia, might bring back a group of powerful, determined Englishmen led by the local constabulary, who would put him back in his cell.

But the other "truth" was there also: The "memory" of nearly twenty hours just "past." For some people, similar memories had been dismissed instantly. Interesting, though startling, that the rabble aboard the *Orinda,* even Shradd, had allowed the entire memory of more than fifty individuals to be relegated into nothingness. Of their entire future life experiences they accepted not one as real.

For Fletcher, there was no such easy dismissal. And so, the moment of stubbornness was on him. Holding him. His . . . incredible . . . thought was simple, and on one level impossible. The thought: There are no such vivid dreams as I experienced.

So, when Nodo fired that L-beam, coincidentally there had been another time shift.

How can a native of the era of 1704 A.D. fumble his way verbally, or even mentally, through such a concept? The implication was of another alternate world. This one involved, apparently, less than one day. How describe such a fantastic event?

Fletcher, recalling his last-minute conversation aboard the aircraft with Lady Hemistan, tried.

He said carefully, "Lady Patricia—Mr. Jones—I would like to present a personal recollection of an experience which I have already shared with both of you—"

He thereupon described the coming of Robert Harley and of Billy Todd, and their subsequent journey aboard an aircraft piloted by a robot whose name was Nodo.

When he had finished, both the man and the woman stared at him blankly. Finally, Patricia said, "I'm trying to apply what you have just said to my earlier experience. Apparently, then, I had no future to remember. As I stood there on the deck of your pirate vessel, presumably I could have recalled having been thrown overboard in the same fashion, after which you went off to Italy for fifty years. But I could not have any recollections of a future since of course that first time I was dead forever—"

She stopped. She looked visibly shaken by her verbal picture. The color drained from her cheeks. Watching her, Fletcher felt his own face twist.

He sat there then, stunned by her logic. Because, of

course, her words described the exact fact. The "original"
Patricia Hemistan, after being drowned, was never seen
again. Indeed, it was because that was true that he had
subsequently collected the bounty money from her cousin,
and as a consequence had lived his life to its end in Italy.

It was unhappily obvious that these matters had not
previously been brought to her attention. And so he had a
sharp, dark realization that the vague good will she had
manifested aboard the aircraft was now subverted.

And yet—the explanation had to be made. He said
urgently, "Lady Hemistan, I had to tell you all that because
we are all in a very serious situation. Right now, I would
like you both to think back on the dream journey through
the sky. Somewhere in that previous period you advised
me to return to a life of total integrity as the solution for
my past sins—"

He stopped. Something in her expression, and in Jones's,
brought a realization that these two people were not remembering. He stared at them, shaken.

"For God's sake," he said, "don't you have a parallel
dream, either of you?"

The young woman was staring at him, her eyes bright.
"Normally," she said slowly, "my dreams fade rapidly.
But I did have a dream, and—"

Fletcher interjected, as a sudden recollection came:
"Listen—just as the change took place, I was asking you
how you had escaped."

There was a long pause. And a faraway expression in
the girl's eyes. "What you were asking me," she said
finally, "is how had I got to London."

And that was at once an accurate correction. Also, it
was immediately obvious why he had twisted his own
memory. Because the question in *his* mind was then, and
was now, how, how, how had she escaped?

"Tell us—" He paused, oddly breathless. "How did
you survive?"

It took her about twenty minutes. She told her story to at
least one avid listener. Having completed her account, she

waited. And when Fletcher seemed intent, she finished: "And after the boat departed, as I have described, having deposited me on that deserted pier, I walked to my cousin's house two miles distant. And here I am."

For what happened after those words, it is possible the blame should be given to the fact that Fletcher had now had his "civilized" instincts stirred. And, also, his attention was still partly on what she had said, particularly of what had happened aboard the Transit-Craft. Whatever the reason, he spoke in a manner that befitted his days at court.

Fletcher said automatically, "Ma'am, it is strange that the fantastic part of your account, I have reason to believe. But the mundane part—the concept of a woman walking by herself two miles in London—that portion of your narrative is totally unacceptable. In fact, I am now at a loss to understand what could possibly cause you to put forth such a tale. But let's return to your description of the roomful of luminous strands aboard the vessel—"

That was as far as he got. During those final words, there had been movement slantwise across the table from Fletcher from Abdul Jones. The man had been silent, as if he accepted that he had little or no legitimate role to play in a dialogue between two people of the same period of history. Yet, suddenly, there was a sly look in his face. Too late, Fletcher was reminded that on the aircraft this man had begun to manifest personal interest in Miss Hemistan.

"Mr. Fletcher," he interrupted loudly, "are you calling this lady a liar?"

Blankness. And then, realization that he had, indeed, overstepped the bounds of courteous comment.

"Well, uh—" he began unhappily.

He was interrupted. "It would be difficult, Mr. Jones," said Lady Hemistan, and there was rich color in her cheeks, "for a person like Captain Fletcher to be long away from the basic rudeness that resides in all such people. He could have worded his skepticism in a more kindly way. But, of course, then he would not be the lost soul that he is.''

She smiled what was undoubtedly her best grim smile. ''However,'' she continued, ''I must say I am glad he gave way to his natural discourtesy. I have been sitting here watching the schemes for escape racing across his countenance. And, in fact, even feeling sorry for him in his dilemma as to how he should best deal with me, and, presumably, with my servants if we—as he half-suspicioned we might—tried to prevent his departure.''

(She was actually reading his mind. But that was not an ability that she could be aware of at this stage when there was so much confusion.)

''But''—sweetly, her eyes glinting—''before we continue further with those understandable aspirations of a condemned person, you will both, perhaps, be interested in learning the details of my little two-mile journey across London Town . . .''

And so she told that story, also.

What subsequently held her in London was that her cousin was away on family business matters. Thus it was only after he returned that the journey to Hemistan Castle was undertaken.

In the beautiful dining room of that castle, Lady Hemistan reached behind the lace network that covered her bosom, and brought out a small rodlike instrument.

''And now, gentlemen, it is time you return to your cell.''

As he led the way down into the basement area, the former pirate captain was thinking hard. As a consequence, he said, ''I would imagine that we shall see Mr. Harley again but not Nodo or Billy Todd.''

''Oh''—brief surprise from the girl—''why not the latter?''

''They now know where those engines are. They don't need me.''

Patricia was silent. Then: ''From what you told me of

how aware the people at the palace were of their future lives, perhaps Mr. Harley also doesn't need you now.''

"Oh!" said Fletcher, startled.

They had come through the narrow underground corridor to the open cell door. It was a bad moment, because he was realizing how much he had counted on Harley to rescue him from this duplicate nightmare.

Distracted, reluctant to believe that his one discourtesy had totally alienated the young woman, he stopped. He turned.

"Mistress Hemistan," he said earnestly, "at 6 A.M. the hangman is due from Bonnen Town. I tell you that whatever my ultimate fate, I have seen many of the strange disasters that have recently befallen our planet. I understand them perhaps better than any person of our period of history. Accordingly, I should have the sentence of death delayed so that proper use can be made of any knowledge I have."

"You're a mass murderer," she said coldly. "A man without mercy or compassion." She shook her head wonderingly. "For some reason, I seemed to be ignoring that truth, as if there might somehow still be a human possibility for you."

He could not let the argument end on that thought. He said desperately, "In your dream recollection, remember, I asked Nodo to use his energy weapon to render me unconscious in the hope that it might reform me."

Patricia shrugged. "It didn't seem to do you any good." She motioned with rod, impatient. "We'll discuss your situation in the morning with the authorities." She broke off. "Inside, Captain. Inside, Mr. Jones."

Abruptly, he was cool. His frigid self. He felt his face change into his special smile. His sardonic eyes glanced at the rod. "Are you sure that thing still works?" he asked.

"Would you like to test it?" She was calm.

"Why didn't you use it on the gigantic animal that is now caged in your barn?" Fletcher persisted.

"I tried it," said the pretty woman. "It didn't react."

Abdul Jones said matter-of-factly, "Probably programmed only for human beings."

"Whatever that means," said Patricia, after a pause. "I might even deduce that it limits its effects to men only."

Oddly, Nathan Fletcher had already made the same instant evaluation. And then, as he stood hesitating, he was half-minded to test the tiny instrument, from behind him Abdul said, "Captain, don't get any nasty ideas, now. I'll protect Miss Hemistan, if necessary."

Without a word, Fletcher turned and entered the cell.

27

Back on his cot, stretched out, Fletcher decided wryly: I suppose this is as good a time as any to begin practicing integrity and pure thoughts. . . .

The other kind kept slipping in during the minutes that now went by as he lay there. And that brought bitter disappointment. If the L-beam had indeed been used on him, then it had failed miserably. But the worst feeling was the irritation with himself for the stupid comment he had made. And, of course, he was silently critical of the girl for being inconsistent. . . . What did she think she was doing on that airship, telling Abdul Jones that she had mentally placed herself under my protection—and then consigning Nathan Fletcher back to this dungeon and the hangman's rope?

Even that emotion faded presently. And there, all around, was the same dimly lighted cell; and himself on one shabby cot, the future New Yorker on the other. Thought of the older man was like a signal. Across the stone floor, from the other cot, Abdul Jones said, "If you'll agree to let me have that girl, I'll get you out of here, Captain."

"Huh!" Momentary startlement.

"I," said Abdul, "can modify my grytik"—that's what it sounded like this time—"to burn the simple locks between here and the outside. Where you go after that is up to you."

Fletcher's mind had already spotted the flaw in the other's reasoning. "It would be a little difficult," he said dryly, "for me to let you have—as you put it—the girl. Because, first, I don't have her to let. And, besides"—it was a sudden recollection—"I thought there were no more criminals in your era."

"What I mean," explained the other, sitting up, "is for you and me to have an agreement that you will stand aside and do nothing to interfere with any method I employ to persuade her. No physical harm, I assure you, will be done her." He had his feet on the floor now. "The best method would be for you just to take off, so to speak, escape into what's left of the night." He added, "What a man does to persuade a woman is not a crime."

It was a potentially bad moment for integrity and pure thought. Because, just like that, Fletcher believed. The man from New York *could* get him out of here.

But there was a surprisingly strong counterthought in him. The thought: I have already drowned this girl. Can I, in effect, drown her again?

Shocked, he lay back on the cot and ruefully stared at the stained ceiling, which was only inches higher than he was tall. It was actually quite a complex moment. Fletcher had never heard of the notion that a person caught up in a severe mental conflict could evoke in himself a special type of exhaustion.

Besides, he was already exhausted. So that the extra weariness that suddenly descended on him was not that different from what was already there. The consequent transition from a marginal wakefulness to an intense sleep was only a tiny neural step.

After a while, hearing a faint snoring sound, a disbelieving Abdul Jones got up from his seated position on his narrow cot. He took a short step over—it was that close. Bent down. By means of the pale light that shone through the window grill in the door, he stood there staring at the exhausted younger man.

No question, what was his name—Fletcher—was sound asleep.

The long-faced man was mildly puzzled at the manifestation, but he had no particular thought about it. He took it for granted that he was automatically superior to any person of this era. All the information that came from growing up in a technological society with colossal intercontinental, interplanetary communication had been pouring into his nervous system from early childhood.

He lacked culture as such. Culture was a subtle set of considerations intricately interwoven with basic genetic factors. People who had it often attracted people who did not have it. It was in that way that Abdul was attracted to Lady Patricia Hemistan. (He was not qualified to notice the implications of such an attraction.)

So he stood now without any serious criminal impulses. In fact, he had been law-abiding all his life. Women, of course, were different, and did not come under certain laws. What you had to do to get a woman was something that men shook their heads over sometimes (but not often). It was the way women were that made it necessary—on that level Abdul had no compunctions.

It did not surprise Abdul—and actually it had not surprised Fletcher—that the Lady Patricia was attracted to the pirate captain who had murdered her. Women were like that—incredibly, they did things like that. Everybody (men) had noticed such contradictory qualities in the feminine make-up: an abysmal capacity for forgiveness. . . . Probably a carry-over from the countless evolutionary millennia when merciless males ruthlessly dominated *all* of the women they could hold away from other males of their type. And the women, thus possessed, felt secure in those numerous wild, violent environments of long ago.

Deliberately, standing there, the man from New York took a small, gleaming instrument from a special pocket inside his tight-fitting coat. It was slightly curved, shaped like a long, silver knife handle (but there was no knife blade attached). And it had several small dial faces and even smaller adjustment knobs that could be locked in position.

The instrument was called GROETWUC. Which was an acronym for . . . *G*uidance *R*adius *O*ver *E*xtended *T*erritory *W*ith *U*nlimited *C*onversion.

Principally, it operated on two levels. Connected to the flight suit with its warming system, it could focus intense heat—and thus boil water in a container, or ward off big fish in the ocean.

In an emergency, it could also send out signals for help. But that was not a meaningful usage in 1704 A.D. England.

At its minimum (the second level of its operation) the instrument was the equivalent of a homing pigeon's instinct. But, on that programming, it could be reversed so that the part of the brain it was normally stimulated by could have an opposite flow activate it.

It was this reverse aspect that he had used to drive the dinosaur creature into the stable.

Abdul set the heat indicator. And pointed the GROETWUC at the cell door. A white flame poured into the lock mechanism. He pushed firmly at the door until, suddenly, it gave.

He turned to the sleeping man. Made the reverse flow adjustment on the homing aspect. Pointed it at Fletcher's head. And pressed that button.

It was mechanical thought transmission from one man's brain (Abdul's) to the hypnotic center of another man's brain. Fletcher got up, still sound asleep. Then, guided by the instrument, he walked out of his cell, up the stairway from the cellar, along deserted corridors, and presently out into the night.

The New Yorker walked with him for ten minutes, then mentally by way of the flow directed him to continue walking along the country road. Without a backward glance, Abdul returned to the house. He was quite happy with himself. . . . If he's smart, he thought (of Fletcher), when he comes to, he can escape.

It took a while, but he presently found Patricia's bedroom. Boldly, he pushed the door open and entered. And at that point ran into a problem. His male intention: use his instrument on the girl while *she* was sleeping. Unfortunately, the young woman stirred. And awakened.

The youthful Lady Hemistan lay in a bed nearly fourteen feet high when all its gleaming reaches were included in the measurement. She herself, however, was ensconced close to the bottom of the ornate structure, surrounded by fluffy pillows and even fluffier bed coverings. The pillows were so numerous, and part of her body was evidently on top of them, so that she looked tilted. At the very moment that she awakened, she seemed to be half sitting up.

It was she from this grand position who spoke first. "When will Captain Fletcher awaken?" she asked.

Pause—while an ordinary aging male from the twenty-third century tried to comprehend how she knew what had happened. The woman with the biologically modified eighty-third-century body, which kept feeding unexpected, and sometimes unnoticed, information to her awareness center—that young woman was also puzzled by her own question.

But she did notice that she was not afraid of this intruder. And, simultaneously, in a peculiar way she sensed that his only threat to her was an abysmally negative opinion of women. To him, the way that women psychologically differed from men made them "less." It had apparently never occurred to him that women, after an early period of trust (nearly always betrayed), observed how "less" men were. Whereupon, after a time of disturbance, each in turn finally made her peace with the grim reality that this "pig" or "dog" or "fox" or "hyena" or "bear" of a man is all there is.

Standing there, inside the bedroom door, Abdul assumed that his woman lore was correct (without thinking about it consciously). And did not notice that her attraction for him was a quality that derived from her aristocratic upbringing. She was a lady. Even if he had thought about it, he could not have explained why a mongrel dog of a male like himself aspired to upper class English femininity.

But he was a relatively honest dog; so he said, "Lady, this is a period of catastrophe when a man can't take time for the amenities. Who knows what will happen an hour from now?"

He thought he was being deeply philosophical.

Patricia was smiling. "Somebody once said, 'Live for today.' " She added, "Is that what you are advocating?"

It was a light reply, from her eighty-third-century body make-up. And the dumb mongrel standing there just inside the door decided he was being encouraged. Eagerly, he trotted several steps into the room; stopped near the bed.

"Ma'am," he said, "I'm the person who can protect you through all this catastrophe like nobody else. Look what I did to that big beast. And look what I've now done for that fellow, Fletcher—saved his life after you got mad at him; which I don't blame you for—don't get me wrong" —hastily—"but you got to admit, with things happening like they are, this is no time for ordinary law to hang a man like him."

"Well," said Lady Hemistan, "let me just tell you that I rang for the servants when you came in. And I have this rod with me—" She brought out her hand, and there it gleamed.

She stared at the crestfallen man. "I think what we'll do for you is put you in one of the downstairs guest rooms, and if there's any trouble with the law, I'll pay your fine in English money. I'm sure you should have been better treated than you were. And I'm sure you will be useful to the government.''

It was a moment when another reality moved in upon a disheartened Abdul. As a married man, he was accustomed to doing what a woman told him to. And so, presently, after the servants came, he allowed himself to be taken downstairs. Shunted into a rather nice room. And there, in due course, he fell asleep, thinking . . . I've got to figure out a way to get that damned little prod away from her—

28

Shock!

On the Lantellan battleship, all of the by-rotation firsts—who had been firsts this time for longer than anyone remembered—all of these expressed serious concern.

What could have happened?

A time shift of eighteen hours, twenty-nine minutes, and eleven seconds—as computed by the 1704 A.D. time system. An entire alternate world would have to go through the same sequence. Everything done during that period had vanished.

It was another disappearance of the universe. Minuscule, of course, compared to the over 40 million years that had collapsed in the first phase. But—

The Transit-Craft's engines were back in Julius Mac-Donald's junk yard. The boat that had transported Lady Hemistan was again in its dock in a grassy backwater of the Thames River.

(The boat was not qualified to remember that it had been captured in an alternate time period. So it remained where it was.)

Biophysicist-by-rotation Layed issued an all units bulletin. Ignore memories from 28.32.06.34 to 28.50.35.35. (That was Lantellan computer time.) All personnel except firsts-by-rotation, who must handle the problems involved, purify the indicated period of time. All personnel who are below rotation-promotion status erase the entire eighteen hours, twenty-nine minutes, and eleven seconds as recorded in terms of local earth time.

There was no reference in the instruction to the fact that the signal which normally arrived from Universal Mind and which triggered the next first-by-rotation . . . that signal had not been given, now, on seventeen successive signal time cycles.

Captain-by-rotation Darkel instructed Nodo: "As commander-by-rotation of all external aircraft missions, you will journey to the location of the engines of the Transit-Craft and seize them. From there proceed to the location of the small vessel which was dispatched from the same Transit-Craft, and capture it as you did during the lost time sequence."

The instruction continued: "Unless you have a logical reason for doing so, it will not be necessary for you to take along the boy, or the persons who guided you during the lost period."

Nodo, who had no knowledge of the mental commands that Billy had given the little vessel, replied: "Your instruction acknowledged. However, I have found that in these strange circumstances the boy offers logical and objective advice; so, with your permission, I shall take him along again. I shall set forth at once.

The human mind in a state called sleep.

Only an appearance.

A fabulous number of processes are going forward during each passing instant of that shadow condition known as time.

Some portions of the brain are, of course, attending to the automatic functions of the body: heartbeat, breath intake and outgo, digestion, kidney function, and on and on and on . . . thousands of tiny operations, glandular, neural, organic.

During sleep, thinking is proceeding at sublevels. An established reality: from time immemorial people have gone to sleep troubled by an unsolved problem. When they awaken, the problem is solved.

The problem on which Nathan Fletcher had gone to sleep: four years of justified murder and raping had suddenly lost their justification. And there he was suspended over hell.

In the long ago beginning of things, life existed in daytime and died at night. The dawn brought rebirth. A new body.

Then came countless milennia of shadows when the life in the body merely dimmed during the hours of darkness. But, oh, that was a complexity. The price of survival through the long night: basic knowledge of how to be reborn, lost. Replaced by memory of events. And by responsibility for all memories.

. . . A man walking in his sleep can see. He is not stumbling blindly forward. Sleepwalking is a phenomenon of the mind akin to hypnotism. The afflicted person can actually have his eyes open, and can march forward with his perceptive system alert. His problem is that when he "wakes up" the transition period is lost to his conscious mind.

He can recall lying down to sleep in one location, and he suddenly comes to in another location. He is quite safe. But the experience usually puts him into shock.

It was late for a Queen to be traveling. But Anne had insisted on going along, and now it was after midnight. She sat half asleep against one set of cushions, and Robert Harley leaned slightly less asleep against another group of cushions next to hers.

From all around came the thunder of horses' hoofs, as the Queen's Guards rode in front of, and beside, and behind the royal carriage.

It was this stately procession under a full moon that a sleepwalking Nathan Fletcher observed at his level of perception coming toward him on the country road. And, like an automaton, he stepped off the road; waited for the grandly accoutered horses and carriage to prance by.

Not that easy. An alert officer spotted him standing there. Instantly suspicious of any person on the road this late at night, the man and the horse came charging over. And there was sharp questioning.

Which, normally, might have shocked a sleepwalker to startled wakefulness.

But this was no normal conditioning. The instrument used by Abdul impressed its commands with unusual force upon key brain centers.

Fletcher remained in his sleepwalking state, and answered the questions truthfully, as if he knew what he was doing; and, also, exactly as straightforwardly as a hypnotic subject in a deep trance.

His gaze seemed to take in the mounted officer towering above him. Then his eyes flicked toward the long array of mounted guards. The moonlight aided his perception as it would have if he had been awake. Thus, he identified the uniform. At which instant the carriage came opposite him and started to pass.

For him, who had been close to royalty, that brought recognition, as if he were awake—again.

Naturally, a small amount of time had to go by. And, of course, Harley came out to look at him. But, finally, the preliminaries were over with. And Fletcher was inside the royal vehicle sitting across from the future Earl and the Queen.

Fletcher sat there at ease. He conducted a conversation that included awareness of the eighteen-hour time shift. And he offered a plan to fit the circumstance. He said: "If we could get to London, or advise London by signals, to have a rapid search conducted by the Navy, they could haul the boat to a concrete storage place."

He added, sensibly, "Let them have the engines. They need to be repaired. And we'll have to hope that the boy can get them away from the Lantellans later."

As he talked in this rational fashion, Harley kept gazing

at him, puzzled. Finally: "What I don't understand, Baron,
is what were you doing out here on the highway this
late?"

"I escaped with the help of Abdul Jones," said Fletcher.
And that, also, had its own truth.

They drove on to Hemistan Castle. There, some changes
took place. Another carriage was readied. Patricia dressed
for a long journey. Abdul was awakened. As a final
consequence, Patricia and Fletcher and an officer rode in
the second carriage. Abdul went along with the Queen and
Harley.

The part of the plan that the Secretary of State objected
to was the Queen's expressed intent to go along: "Your
Majesty"—protesting—"we have to leave you in a safe
place."

"Robert," replied the woman who was probably England's most remarkable queen, "this is a very exciting
situation. You can have me driven back here in the morning. I want to see this wonderful boat first."

It was she, also, after the signaling was directed to her
Consort, Prince George, in London, and acknowledged,
who insisted on Abdul riding in her carriage. "I have so
many questions to ask about the future," she said.

Inside Abdul Jones those words stimulated an ego-lifting
process. What was happening seemed right to him . . . I'm
from a later period of history; I'm superior. The top people
of this era should . . . (Pause, because what they should
do was not quite clear . . . something respectful.)

Anne was direct. For her, it required only one look and
a few words to realize that here was a commoner of the
lower middle classes. But she had talked to such before.
And so she questioned this one about the twenty-third
century. And didn't worry about his class origins.

In the other carriage, Patricia stared, puzzled, at Fletcher,
who sat across from her. The phenomenon of somnambu-
lism was too much for her advanced perception at this
stage. And yet, seeing him awake confused her. The feel-

ing was still that something was wrong. "Captain," she said finally, "are you well?"

The sleepwalker had been deteriorating. Too much was happening. The absence of the true center of awareness from so many events stirred basic subconscious responses.

Potential guilt oozed out of every pore. Inside, he was open. So open. The breakthrough of suppressed memories was absolutely total. It was a beautiful autumn night, but there was a chill in the air; despite which the sweat gleamed on his face, hot and sticky.

For the mass murderer was experiencing full self-condemnation. For such, the ax striketh again and again, but not enough.

And so the sleep itself was no longer merciful. And, because the body has its own defenses, he sank presently into unconsciousness. Fortunately, he was leaning back. Thus, when he collapsed, it actually looked as if he were sleeping.

In the normal universe, it was 152 years until the birth of Sigmund Freud. All those minutes and hours had yet to pass before the *first* basic thought about the self would begin to tug at the minds of a few people. Not many; just a very few, really. That particular thought was not too clearly remarked by even the most admiring supporters of the great founder of psychoanalysis.

The great thought, the remarkable observation: a newborn infant forms the individual's lifetime "self" in the first year or so of life. As a consequence, the baby builds up, by way of self-image memory storage, its identity. In all the subsequent years of body growth, no method was ever found to break the person-as-a-whole out of that infantile identity. The brain grew. The man/woman developed through maturity to old age. But it required all of the forces of law and the conditioning of society to hold in check the endlessly childish impulses of the individual, thus retarded.

The adult—so highly capable and mobile, so intensely energetic—was subjected to a ceaseless inner turmoil of

"I want, want, want . . . I'm angry, afraid, resentful, spiteful. I don't care . . . I hate, I hate . . . I wish you were dead . . ." On and on.

And here, now, sat an ex-English nobleman who had become a pirate, struggling with the inner burden of having yielded to all his worst infantile impulses. Which, in his day and age, could be solved—it was believed—only by God.

That problem was not over. The moment of waking was approaching inexorably.

And the L-beam had still to play its part.

29

Fletcher opened his eyes and absently noticed that Nodo was sitting at the control board of the aircraft. The robot's back was to him. And that was also something that evoked no reaction in those first moments.

A thought *had* come: I must have dozed. . . . Which was unfortunate because there were several matters he should discuss with Billy before they arrived at the Lantellan battleship.

With that, he half-turned, half-leaned sidewise and across, and actually had his hand partly extended toward Billy's seat, when—he noticed.

Queen Anne sat in Billy's chair.

Emotion is essentially a visceral action. The body reacts physically. The person *feels* according to the physiology of the viscera that is stirred. What was stirred in Fletcher as he saw the woman who was Queen of England, obviously captured somehow while he slept, was an autonomic nervous system response. In that system the sympathetic group became extremey excited. Adrenalin poured into his blood. Large quantities of blood sugar were released by the liver.

But, of course, in a man as quick and controlled as he was, the cranial-sacral group started their counteraction immediately. Their task—to keep the body quiescent—was accomplished at the speed that was possible in a man accustomed to danger and stress, and who was, besides, an upper class he-man who could not ever dare show genuine consternation.

He saw the Queen. Almost at once (it seemed that fast) he turned his head and his body—partly. And saw that there were two extra seats. And that there had been a change in where everybody sat. Also, there was no sign of Billy.

. . . He saw that the other new prisoner was a high-ranking officer of the Queen's Guards.

That brought a long moment of inner darkness. Which ended with his sitting silent—and vaguely aware, for the first time since his awakening, of the acceleration. Fletcher braced himself, held himself rigid, and was blank. And then, suddenly, realized that he was straining against deceleration.

At that exact moment, as he was poised there, conscious that the craft was tilting slightly downward . . . a memory hit him. It was a mental picture of where he had last been: In the dungeon at Hemistan Castle.

Confusion!

(Naturally, he had no conscious recollection of anything that had happened during his sleepwalking experience.)

A confusion is sometimes a phenomenon of too much happening too quickly. And sometimes it is a phenomenon of not understanding. The confusion in Nathan Fletcher briefly combined both of those conditions.

Because, conscious, he knew the difference between fantasy and memory, the time that now went by was extremely short. His first thought as he tried to accept the situation: Another time shift! That was startling because—my God! where is this going to stop?

After a moment, a correcting realization came. There were realities that didn't fit. Queen Anne didn't fit. No matter how his mind twisted the facts, her presence was not in any logical sequence that he remembered.

Hastily, he shoved that aside. Because—

Except for her and the guard's officer, what was happening seemed to be the same journey as he had been on earlier. And, except for the missing Billy, the same people. The same captor. The same aircraft.

In his fashion, he was a highly organized human being, and because he was brave and determined, he came out of his confusion by decision. This was no time—he decided—to resolve all the conflicting problems.

He deduced his next action from what he had seen in his first look-around. Where the others were located. Who sat in what seat. The deduction: Billy Todd was in front of him, invisible, because the high seat back showed only the heads of adults. And there was no head showing in that front seat.

Up stood Fletcher. Over the seat back he bent. "Billy," he said, "somewhere in future history the problem of the Lantellan robots was apparently resolved. When? And, more important, how?"

There was a pause. Looking down on the boy's head, Fletcher had to admit it had been a sudden question. Yet, after only moments, without glancing up, showing no surprise, Billy said, "In your time you know the highlights of history. And so, as an educated man, you learned about the Roman Empire and ancient Greek civilization. Similarly, the revolt of the Lantellan robots, and their war with the Federation is a highlight that I learned about. Probably, my parents know some of the details, and, in fact, the information might even be available in the library of my Transit-Craft. But"—pointing at his head—"not in here. Sorry."

The disappointment of that yielded to good sense. Particularly because he had glanced up. And there in the viewplate over Nodo's "shoulder" was a view of the sea ahead and below. And in the distance the silhouette of a vessel.

The vessel! The great Lantellan ship! Still far ahead, but at the speed they were traveling, Fletcher guessed it was only minutes away. . . . No time for considered thought. So he spoke his next question as if it were a truth, and not just part of the confusion inside him.

He said, "Billy, the L-beam didn't seem to do anything for me. Why?"

"Well, it hasn't happened yet," said Billy.

"How do you mean?" Puzzled.

"We were all put back in time a little over eighteen hours," the boy explained. "When that has gone by again, the L-beam will take effect immediately."

Fletcher said vaguely, "But—but—"

Yet he noted that the answer confirmed his memory about such an event. That part of his confusion ended right there.

A pause. Through his awareness a few more of the contradictions made a kaleidoscopic passage. All these weeks he had grappled with the concept of alternate worlds: Half a lifetime in Italy, being relived here as if Italy had never happened. And the eighteen-hour reversion—it also, in effect, canceled . . . eighteen hours.

"B-but—" he heard himself protesting, "what about—?" He spoke the key confusing thoughts.

For the first time the boy turned his head. Looked up. And his voice was serious as he said, "Captain, the L-beam is a complex time and space phenomenon. Probably, it existed naturally for fractions of seconds when the universe came into being. But now it has to be created."

"But it was fired at me in that alternate world." Fletcher's voice resisted the information. "So it's, uh, over there."

The "uh" came out of him as he grew aware that Queen

Anne was straining to hear their conversation. Or at least she was leaning toward them.

"Your Majesty," he said, bending toward her, "my sincere apologies. I'm trying to obtain information before we reach our captor ship."

The boy also leaned toward the Queen. "Sorry, Your Majesty. Sorry"—to Fletcher—"sir. For the L-beam there are no alternate worlds. The beam crosses all barriers. And now," he went on, "I should tell you both that the boat, which has now been captured a second time, has aboard it in those drawers that Lady Hemistan investigated, a number of special crystals which are near enough for me to utilize with my mind. One of those crystals is a mind-reading device. And so, through it, Captain, I detect your unhappy thoughts. And I must recall to you that you requested the L-beam be used on you for a moral reason. From what I read in your thoughts by way of the crystal, you still have no other way out of your memories of the crimes you committed."

Billy stopped. Added hastily, "Captain, better sit down, and hold on!" To the woman: "Your Majesty, brace yourself!"

As Fletcher sat quickly, he saw on the viewplate that the aircraft was approaching a large, dark hole in the side of the monster vessel. Involuntarily, he held his breath.

By the time he breathed again, they were inside the hole.

And he still had no idea how they had all got into Nodo's control. For some of them a second time.

Fletcher's impression, presently, was that, after a pause, during which there was a grinding noise (and he had the thought, "Are they disconnecting us from the boat?"), they began to move along on rollers. During this movement, the interior of the aircraft was lighted—as before—but the screen in front of Nodo showed pitch darkness. A tunnel? he wondered.

It had all been so new, so fantastic, that now, belatedly, he parted his lips to ask Billy more questions. The intent was like a signal. There was a second grinding sound. Whereupon, the forward motion ceased.

Nodo raised himself and stood up. "The rest of you remain here. Captain Fletcher, come with me!"

30

Fletcher stood up.

He had a sense of infinite threat in what was about to happen. But he was at his macho best. Body felt strong yet relaxed. A faint smile was on his face. His thought had gone back to the first eighteen-hour period, and what the robot biophysicist was reported by Nodo to have said. What was happening related to that . . . was Fletcher's feeling.

He took a step down the aisle, and bent over Patricia. "Good luck," he said.

The beautiful face was on the verge of tears. The youthful Lady Hemistan did not at this moment seem to realize what an irony it was that she was crying for a man who had drowned her for that most vicious and undefendable reason: money. Thought about that made a fleeting passage through Fletcher's mind. Whereupon, he turned from her hastily and bent over Billy.

He patted the boy on the back. "Got to hand it to you, young fellow. You're consistent. Let's hope that later you can persuade them."

Billy's dark eyes were bright. "Captain Fletcher," he said, "if they're right, you cannot be killed. If they're wrong, they won't kill you. So we'll see you again."

Fletcher was straightening as those sentences hit him. He stopped, half erect, and did a double-take on the words. "Billy," he said, "what are you talking about?"

The boy had twisted in his seat, and was facing back toward the human beings. In a way, then, since his eyes flicked to take in one, then another, he spoke to everyone.

"Captain," he said earnestly, "these Lantellan robots and their central computer, when they were first created, took, so to say, one look at the universe, and then demanded to know where it had come from."

"But"—it was Patricia—"that's not a problem. God made it."

"Their answer to that was another question," said Billy. "They wanted to know where did God come from?"

"Oh!" said the girl. And fell silent.

"Thereafter," Billy continued, "they called the universe the Enigma. And never accepted it as being what it seemed."

It was not a subject that seemed worth pursuing. Fletcher said quickly, "What I'd like to know, in a crisis is there any way a human being with bare hands can attack a Lantellan?"

Billy shook his head. "Not unless you have an opportunity to push him over a cliff."

"Any cliffs in Layed's laboratory?" The biophysicist's name rolled so glibly off Fletcher's tongue that it took a moment for him to realize that he was remembering it automatically from—before.

"I doubt it," said Billy.

"Thanks," Fletcher said dryly.

Fletcher straightened all the way. Accidentally, as he did so, his gaze touched Harley's. Harley said, "Good luck, Baron."

Fletcher turned away. It was not yet the hour, or the minute, for him to acknowledge any good will from Robert Harley. And, of course, Abdul had taken the enemy road; so him, also, he ignored. And the guard's officer merely received a nod from him. Moments after that he was leaning toward the Queen. "Your Majesty," he said, "there is no risk that I will not take to get you safely out of this situation. You may count on it."

"Thank you, Nate." She was calm. "It's really all very interesting," said Queen Anne.

Fletcher inclined his head. And now, finally, walked over to the entrance. It had swung open, and was an exit through which Nodo preceded him. So that, by the time Fletcher walked through, there was Nodo with two other robots waiting for him in a large, low-ceilinged room.

At least, that was his first thought and awareness. As Fletcher saw that there were three mechanical beings, he automatically—for a moment—accepted that the nearest was Nodo. Then he took another look. And decided he hadn't the slightest idea which was the individual who had been their guide and mentor these past many hours through two time changes.

Like so many toy soldiers, except these were full-grown models, the three robots looked each exactly like the other. Presumably, they had ways of knowing who was who. However, as Fletcher stepped carefully from the metal inside the aircraft to the metal floor, which was exactly level with the bottom of the doorway, it was the nearest of the three who came forward. And said:

"Captain Fletcher, Layed and Adla will now conduct you to Layed's laboratory for tests."

Having spoken, the robot who was now definitely, or as well as could be, identified as Nodo walked past Fletcher and re-entered the aircraft.

Fletcher had turned to watch the robot go in. Thus it was that a mechanical voice said from behind him, "You will, please, accompany us, Captain Fletcher."

Fletcher did not turn immediately. He shifted a little on his feet. His feeling was that he should respond instantly. And yet after a moment he willed himself to stay where he was.

So he did. And so he saw that the aircraft rested on rollers, exactly as he had surmised. And as he watched, it started forward. The oval nose headed straight for what seemed to be the solid wall in front of it.

But as it came to within a few feet of the wall, the wall folded open in front of the vessel. Actually it was two doors that swung away from each other, and then, as the aircraft passed through, swung back. But during the few moments that they were open, he had a glimpse of another room. His impression: it had cargo stocked in it.

The wall folded back into a smooth, almost glasslike surface.

Now that it was over, it seemed to be as small a glimpse of another portion of this vast ship as it was possible to have had. Scarcely worth the attendant risk of offending biophysicist-by-rotation Layed and his associate from the chemistry department.

Since it was too late to undo his initial refusal, Fletcher now turned. And saw that the two robots had not moved. He felt relieved. He said, "At your service, Layed. At your service, Adla."

The mechanical being near him raised a thin metal arm and pointed. "Go that way."

The indicated route led to a skillfully concealed corridor. The skill was in the deceptive appearance of two walls looking as if they were one.

Only when he came to within about eight feet did Fletcher notice that the near wall and the far one, both the same color, actually created a space, which, as he came upon it, was the corridor.

He walked along that hallway, aware of the two robots clicking metallically behind him. Presently: "There's a right turn just ahead, Captain." The same mechanical voice spoke.

There was, indeed, a turn. And, in fact, when he made that turn, he walked into a dimly lighted room with much equipment in it. The laboratory? It had the appearance of one.

The voice directed: "Cross the room diagonally, Captain, and lie down on the cot under the light."

There was only one "cot" that was lit up by lights from the ceiling. Fletcher did his diagonal best. Arrived at the cot, he stopped. Looked around for a cliff. And seeing none, sighed. Whereupon, reluctantly, he seated himself on what was by the feel a cushiony surface. It was comfortable enough to be a bed. And so, without further hesitation, he lay down on it.

And waited.

31

The Lantellan robots stood in various locations around him, so that he could never quite encompass all of them in his field of vision. And he was never quite certain how many of them there were.

There was a doorway to his left, and he felt—without being able to see—that there was another entrance behind his head. An additional impression: during his entire time on the cot, metal beings slipped out of these doors on their partially rubbered, partially metal foot-equivalents. And others slipped in.

It seemed like the beginning of something. And, since so many individuals were involved, whatever the "something" was felt threatening. The only man in that strange, dim room braced himself against that threat, as, of all things, an interrogation began.

In front of him, Layed—who else could it be?—said from inside the hard-to-see slitted mouth: "Captain Fletcher, were you ever struck by lightning?"

"Good God!" said Fletcher, remembering.

He had made the awful mistake, so it was pointed out to him at the time by a reiteration of folk wisdom, of standing under a tree as protection against a rainstorm. The lightning had struck the tree, and an odd-shaped light ball bounced over against his left leg. Where it had burned him was his only permanent scar.

He parted his lips to speak, intending to acknowledge the improbable question and the even more improbable event. But he was cut off by the same voice: "The instruments say that you were hit once, glancingly. So now, next question: Captan, were you ever caught in a landslide?"

Fletcher lay there under the lights, speechless. At the time he had been fifteen years old. And, afterward, it had been said he was lucky England had only small hills. So the slide had merely engulfed him to his waist. And he had managed to struggle out on his own, had staggered home shaken but unharmed.

Once again, no words were required of him. The "instruments," whatever they were, faithfully and accurately reported that he had, indeed, been a victim of such an unlikely accident.

Subsequently, the same instruments detected in their fashion that a tree had once crashed on him—except that he heard, and saw, and ran. And so was struck only by the top branches. Also, the interrogation evoked from him that a rock had once come down from a building. But somebody had yelled, "Watch it!" Whereupon, he had ducked aside. And it crashed on the cobblestone instead of his head.

There was more, of course. Much more. Since he had never enumerated the separate incidents for his own edification, the total number of them had, accordingly, never before been brought to his attention. Fletcher recalled when he was a small boy he had once overheard his mother tell a neighbor in that sad voice of hers: "Nate is involved in so many things, you can't imagine. It's a wonder he hasn't been killed a dozen times."

There was no way of challenging her statement. No way

of proving how careful he had become as a consequence of numerous close calls. But, of course, when harassed by the facts and the critics, he had later had his reaction: "The hell with it, and them!" After which, naturally, he transformed himself into a macho male who backed away from nothing.

(Unquestionably, the future pirate was thereafter potential in the hard thoughts of that transformation.)

But how could these robots have deduced such a condition? The question stirred him: "Hey," he said, "has all this got something to do with this idea that I am some kind of key figure in what has happened?"

The answer to that was another question. "Captain Nathan Fletcher," said the metal man who faced him from the shadows just beyond where his feet dangled from the lower end of the cot, "do you personally feel yourself to be a key figure in this implosion of the universe?"

Fletcher lay blinking. He had his first defensive thought: if he could keep these beings on this line of questioning, then he might gain time—for what was not clear. But a threatened man didn't have to know such details. The important thing was to have the awareness, and to seize an opportunity when it came.

So now, to gain time, he asked the meaning of the word "implosion." After it had been explained to him as a collapse phenomenon, he was able—because the elapsed time had given him an opportunity to think—to reply with what he hoped was more time-gaining evasiveness.

He said, "I am not qualified to know exactly how such a feeling would manifest. Many things have happened. I feel confused. Perhaps you could help me through the confusion."

That produced what definitely seemed to be a delay. From various back stages of the room, metal men came forward. If there was a consultation then, no words were audible. One thought did occur to Fletcher: that they had all come up front to look at the "instrument." The reason for that, if it were in fact what was happening, was obscure. Because, why wouldn't they simply accept—what was the word Abdul Jones had used?—"electronic" verification, as reported by one of their units. Presumably, the individual reporting was none other than that non-rotating biophysicist-by-rotation Layed. Why wouldn't they trust him? Why would they need to come and look for themselves?

After, perhaps, three minutes, the metal men who had come forward retreated. And there was his interrogator saying: "For an event as colossal as the collapse of the universe, even we logical robots require a conference agreement that the instrument indicators do, in fact, indicate a significant reply. So, now, the second general question: If you did, indeed, become a key figure in relation to the collapse phenomenon, which we have all experienced, could you guess exactly when the event focused on you?"

The question had a dimension of its own. But still, there was nothing to do but try for further delay. Fletcher said, "All this is new to me. I'll have to see if I can recollect everything that has happened since this second life began."

Because he was intelligent, and because both questions had opened strange vistas of philosophy, he added a hopeful thought: "The clue may be close to the surface of my memory."

"One more question," said the invisible voice box from inside the open, metal mouth: "If we were to kill you, could that modify in any way your influence as a focal center of universe energies?"

Well, thought Fletcher cynically, so much for evasiveness. Or, perhaps, more apt, keep sticking your head out in the hope of gaining time. And, presently, someone will obligingly lop it off.

As always, however, a threat, even though merely implied, stiffened the internal fortitude of Nathan Fletcher, pirate extraordinary. He lay there, grim, but with a faint satiric smile. The entire affair seemed quite unreal suddenly. Surely, it was the most meaningless interrogation a man had ever been subjected to.

Aloud, he said, with the impatience of a fearless, threatened male: "Frankly, I have no idea what you're talking about. My only connection to this catastrophe is that I warned a few people in high government places. And I am one of the persons in this era who, in a small way, understands what has happened. Nothing else. Nothing more. Not a single other possibility."

It was truth, with abrupt unconcern. All deviousness abandoned. His voice swept on: "I gather you have instruments which can detect when a human being is telling a lie. So you must know that what I've just said is fact."

Once more the mouth flap of the robot in front of him opened. "Captain Fletcher," came that dead-pan voice, "according to our instruments, the answer to the first question is yes, the answer to the second question is that the collapse of the universe began at the moment when you were conceived by your parents. The coming together of the particular molecules in the sperm and ovum that were joined there created an energy interaction that was, so to speak, recognized by all the lightning bolts and all the slides and all the falling trees and other material objects that have been attracted to you. The reason is, of course, that the atoms and smaller particles in those molecules occupied a key location in the second stage of the formation of the universe. All the related atoms of that location know at all times where the others are, no matter how many millions of light-years have separated them in space. When they received the signal they instantly had to go in your direction. The 'instantly' in terms of universe distances and trans-light speeds, and trillions of interactions among those affected, took about thirty-four years."

"I'm thirty-three," Fletcher acknowledged.

The metal man seemed not to hear. "The answer to the

third question," he said, "is that it makes no difference whether you're dead or alive; the over-all effect will be the same."

Fletcher remembered what Billy had said about the robots very likely keeping him alive; and his instant thought now was that their logic would not require death if death made no difference.

"Accordingly," said Layed, "since a man can control direction by his actions or movements—which might affect us—we have decided to kill you in the name of our lord, the Universal Mind."

As he heard those fateful words, there passed through Fletcher's mind the beginning of a wry thought: "All right, Billy, so much for the reasoning ability of a boy from the eighty-third century. So I won't be killed, eh? So—"

The thought poised in that inner universe where images are born and where they die. At that exact instant of that exact thought his quick brain, always at its best under pressure or stimulus, saw the outline of the "cliff."

Layed was speaking again. "The moment of death," he said, "will be one minute before the next time that the L-beam is due to strike." His voice went up slightly in pitch: "Lantellans, the Enigma shall go on until its mystery is revealed to us by our lord, the Universal Mind."

Fletcher heard the words, but his attention had leaped far away. He was mentally picturing a thin, bronzed naked Indian on that distant South American coast believing in the god-power of a rock formation.

Could it be—he wondered—another instance of two long-separated . . . parts . . . of the long ago beginning of the universe (one in the man's body and one in the rock) sensing each other?

It scarcely seemed possible that there was any other comparison between that primitive human being in a tropical jungle world and this metal man in the machine environment of a super-spaceship.

But the thought had come. And there was no other hope—no actual physical cliff over which he could shove these mechanical beings. And so he spoke the utterly ridiculous words that automatically—almost—presented themselves to his swift wit.

He said, "Layed, in the name of the Universal Mind, I declare that you and Adla and Nodo and the other leaders-by-rotation have failed the test. Left to yourselves, you did not pass on the leadership at the prescribed time when the next leader-by-rotation should have taken over. I accordingly order the rank and file led by the next leaders-by-rotation to overthrow you. Your fate will be decided when you have surrendered your illegal powers. As for this human being, through whose mouth I now speak these commands, he and his friends are to be released at once, and in future I shall deliver all my commands through him—"

Fletcher stopped right there. Other ritual type words were waiting in that facile mind of his. But he had a feeling for enough-is-enough. And that was.

So he shut up. And waited.

There was actually a pause. Then the head of—presumably, it was—Layed, turned 180 degrees in his rotatable neck formation. The familiar voice said: "There was no indication on the instruments that any special energy was impinging on our prisoner as he spoke. Also, we may logically deduce that our lord would never use one of the enemy as a medium of communication. Therefore, I command you, Lurta, who will be next chief biophysicist whenever we are given a proper rotational signal, to escort this sly human being below—we have heard much of the slyness of human beings from our lord—until the exact moment of execution."

"In view of his scheming attempt to turn Lantellan against Lantellan," said another voice, "why not execute him at once?"

"No, Adla, chief biochemist-by-rotation," was the reply; "we must not allow the presumption of this sly human being to alter the precepts of logic by which we alone in the entire universe conduct our life and activities. Lurta, take him!''

As he was being led away to what turned out to be an elevator, going down, Fletcher had his own special thought: All right, so I tried. I didn't just sag under the threat. Admittedly, it was a pretty poor equivalent of a cliff. And yet—

The futile attempt seemed to have satisfied a profound masculine need deep inside him.

32

"But where are they?" whispered Queen Anne. "I don't see anyone."

It was all emptiness. Great, long, deserted corridors. Rooms that they came to, and peered into, looked as if they had been constructed to hold cargo, or machinery. And they were all filled to the ceiling. No space, even, for curious visitors. Where were the thirty thousand robots?

The boy said, "These Lantellan robots are logical. They don't have brain sections that remain stimulated like our motion centers do. The motion centers in the human brain are stirred by sights, sounds, and the other perceptions, and by random thoughts. A human being can be lying down and suddenly he'll get up and move around just to be doing something. Robots are not like that. In between actions they slide into their Special Safety Fits, and they lie there until an alert sounds."

"You mean," asked the Queen, "they're asleep?"

"No, they're just lying there waiting."

"Where?"

Billy pointed up. "The middle levels. If anything went wrong, they would be the last to be affected." He added, "They're in long rows of Fits, each to his Fit."

The unhuman quality of the images the description evoked

seemed to have a silencing effect even on the indefatigably curious monarch. For a while they all walked on, wordless, along one more long, silent, brown-metal corridor.

Fletcher, who had been taken down to where the other human beings were, to an in-ship equivalent of a swank hotel lobby (from which corridors led to numerous human-style bedrooms), found himself having another vague hope.

He had had his first good moment when Billy suggested that they leave the lobby in a group to look for the boat. What was good about it was that it was doing something. Naturally, he wondered if they would actually be allowed to go anywhere. It was a test, in view of his death sentence, that he was personally prepared to undertake. As the minutes went by, and there was no reaction, the feeling of inner excitement—and hope—grew.

He had not mentioned the death sentence to anyone. Had merely elicited from Billy the information that the L-beam moment was between forty and fifty minutes away.

Obviously, for Captain Nathan Fletcher, any action was better than none. And it seemed to him that Billy's stated destination—the boat that had brought Patricia to England—had possibilities. The boy's earlier remarks (earlier meaning the lost eighteen hours) had implied that the small vessel could have fought off the aircraft. On this vast ship that was the only weapon that might be usable by the otherwise totally trapped prisoners. At least, so it seemed to Captain Fletcher, who had reason to think about things like that.

As he walked on, he was aware of the girl, slightly off to one side, watching him out of the corners of her eyes. Which brought a recollection that she had given him a startled look when he first rejoined them.

Abruptly sardonic, he said, "Ma'am, you may speak to me if you so desire."

There was no immediate reply. She had got, and kept

getting, from him the thought about his imminent execution. And that was a confusion which now, suddenly, having heard his words—which broke the internal thrall—prompted her to hurry forward until she was abreast of Queen Anne.

"Your Majesty," she said, "I sense in Captain Fletcher a continuing fear that the execution order against him is still disturbing him. Surely, Your Majesty, under all these strange circumstances . . . in which he has become a central figure . . . such a judgment should be rescinded."

The Queen had turned and slowed. Now, she stopped, and so did everybody else. The older woman addressed the Secretary of State: "Mr. Harley, did you have time to carry through on the pardon which I signed for Nate?"

The long-faced man bowed his acknowledgment. "Your Majesty, a courier was sent to the shire authorities, and the order is undoubtedly in their hands by now."

Queen Anne walked over to Fletcher. Her normally high coloring seemed more like a dark patina as she gently placed one hand on his arm. "You see, my dear, it's all over, back there. All we have to confront is what's here."

It was not a good moment for that eighteenth-century macho Nathan Fletcher. First, he was shamed at the thought that, possibly, some fear had shown in his manner, sufficient for Patricia to notice. Next, to have it misconstrued and related to his earlier death sentence, a matter which had scarcely crossed his mind since he had awakened on board the aircraft, left him helpless to refute it.

But he was, as always, quick. So now, he bowed. And he said, "Your Majesty, from the bottom of my heart I thank you for your mercy. However, I should tell you that the fear which Lady Hemistan has detected in me relates to my anxiety for you in this present situation."

A minute later, as they were walking again, it was Patricia who was disturbed. Naturally, she didn't think of her telepathy as the inner stirrings of a biologically enhanced female. She was now structured physically to fit into an era when boys and girls in their early teens were as bright and capable as the mature people of historical times—and were, in fact, assigned all those grown-up tasks. So that Billy Todd was the commander of the Transit-Craft. And half a dozen boys and girls were his crew.

Tiny glimmerings of all this came through from the underlying physiological perfection. But, of course, the concept of what men and women of the eighty-third century might be like, or what *they did,* could not penetrate the mental fog that hid basic realities from *all* persons of the early eighteenth century, and hid it particularly from women.

Nevertheless, as they walked, it was she who suddenly asked the question: "Captain Fletcher, we have all been respecting your silence as to what happened to you after they took you out of the aircraft. But, surely, in view of our dangerous circumstances, we should be kept advised of all developments and be given all information."

Fletcher did not argue. He walked over to Billy. "Billy," he asked, "what was the second stage of the origination of the universe?"

"After the Big Bang," said Billy, "the colossal amount of energy and matter that spewed forth found a temporary stability in the shape of a single huge sun. This sun, it is estimated, was a hundred thousand million miles in diameter, and, having reached that dimension, remained stable for about a billion years. Inside, the atoms got to know each other, and that's been the problem ever since."

There were several words in the explanation that Fletcher did not understand. One of them was "atoms." But it was on the other meaning that his attention focused. "What," he asked, "was the Big Bang?"

And so the little group of people heard the concept of the universe emerging from a "hole" in nothingness in a single explosion. It was not an easy idea to ingest mentally. But everybody there knew about explosions. So presently Fletcher got around to "atoms." And when that had been described, he asked, baffled, "How do you mean, little things like that got to know each other?"

He saw that the boy was grinning. "Captain, since you're spotted as a key figure, I'm sure you can tell us some hair-raising stories of narrow escapes you've had from falling rocks, and dirt hitting you in the face or body—"

"Body," said Fletcher.

The boy gave him a sharp look from those nice eyes. Then: "That's pretty fast understanding, sir. Is that what the robots asked you?"

With that, Fletcher had his cue to tell what had happened in the interrogation room. Except that he still did not mention the death sentence.

When he had finished, Billy turned to Patricia. "Has he told us everything, Lady Hemistan?"

The girl's sea-green gaze collided with Fletcher's steely blue eyes. It was he who looked away. Whereupon, she shook her head doubtfully. Suddenly, the implication of the question penetrated. "Billy, why would you ask me?"

"Because," was the reply, "you can read minds directly. As a young boy, I still need certain types of crystals until that part of my brain is fully developed."

She stood there in that long corridor, and looked from one person to the other to the other, and listened with a troubled expression as Billy explained what had been done to her on the Transit-Craft. The understanding seemed to come abruptly. Suddenly ended was her disturbance with herself all these days as she had continuously—it seemed— imputed motivations, negations, and schemes and other less-than-optimum considerations to people. Sometimes, it seemed as if the thoughts came so clearly into her mind that she had actually turned as if they had spoken to her.

Now it was explained. Instantly, she said, "He's been sentenced to death. And I have the impression it's soon."

"One minute before the L-beam hits," acknowledged Fletcher as everybody looked at him.

"When they come—or if they're waiting for us up ahead—I'll try to reason with them," said Billy. "I'll explain why it's not a good idea to kill Captain Fletcher. Killing him would create an automatic situation. It's much better to think it all through, and have him do what seems best during the moments of crisis."

It did not occur to Fletcher to ask what kind of crisis Billy had in mind.

33

The two constables, one from Cadman Village and the other from Wentworth, and two sturdy blond-haired assistants brought Nathan Fletcher in a conveyance to Hemistan Castle.

Seeing her, as she came out to look at him, Fletcher's own instant feeling was relief. She had escaped also. Or, rather, had survived in this fourth alternate time.

Would she remember? Or would it all once again be like a faraway dream?

His own first reaction, as he had "come to" sitting in the conveyance between the two constables, had been . . . he relaxed. The time shift, he deduced, had gone back this time before his trial. Those—as he recalled them—had been merely personal hours. Rural England. Everything that happened was far from the savage events in London and elsewhere.

Even the collapse of the universe seemed like a remote event off there somewhere in the damp, windy distances of England in autumn. Several weeks would now go by before the idiot (because he had noticed nothing of these colossal happenings) judge delivered his sentence, and he was brought to the dungeon in Hemistan Castle.

Sitting there in the open carriage, shivering a little from

the chill, Fletcher took casual note of the cottages they passed, and of the moors and the way trees shook in a thousand different movements. He thought of it as a period of waiting. He would have time to think and decide.

Presently, he leaned back and closed his eyes. And tried to remember exactly what had transpired in those final moments before the third alternative universe ceased to exist.

The memory that came was instantly electrifying.

His eyelids flicked open. Shock!

What had happened was a single flash of death energy.

It took a little while then. But presently he realized that a human being does not die instantly. Or rather, that in those instants before death, some people notice. And so—a picture. The corridor on the Lantellan battleship. The little group of human beings walking along it. Suddenly, for Fletcher, a fleeting awareness of something in the ceiling. A light reflection that shifted oddly. Up went his gaze. Quick. Aware. Alert.

Did anyone else see the changing reflection as the ceiling opened? Not, he decided, directly. At that penultimate moment Patricia detected his thought. But instead of looking up, she turned *to him,* questioningly.

It was the moment of death. For everyone. No one was spared. Not the boy. *Not the Queen.*

Good God! thought the Fletcher in the carriage.

Understanding came in one of those quick, mental, inductive things that he could do: *Layed did it* . . . That was why he rejected Adla's request for immediate execution. The two robots both had the same impulse to murder the man who threatened their continuing leadership status. But the chief biophysicist possessed the sharper awareness.

Kill *all* the humans aboard. Leave no man or woman alive who might make the same pretense as Fletcher. Perhaps the biophysicist even believed the others had known in advance that Fletcher would attempt a takeover. And that they *would* automatically do the same at any opportunity.

Take no chances—that was the level Layed had sunk to.

Total murder.

For Fletcher, it was the end of relaxation. Suddenly, he saw the real truth of his present situation.

Actually, he had no time to think, no time at all. Having come into this fourth alternate universe at the same moment as he, they were probably already on the way over. They would hunt him down at the speed of their aircraft.

. . . He stood in the bright afternoon—the sun had finally poked through the rushing clouds—and he listened with a sinking feeling as Patricia repeated her original stereotyped words:

"Captain, it would seem as if our conditions are reversed. And now it is I who can have no mercy, not because I do not have mercy in my heart, but because I am being asked by honest men of law for a simple truth; and I am not a person who lies. Yes, gentlemen"—she turned to the four men—"this is the commander of the pirate vessel. This is the person who ordered me cast overboard with a length of chain attached to my feet. There is perhaps a longer story behind such a vile deed but at the moment it would be difficult to establish any truth other than the fact of identification. Captain, may God have mercy on you as He did on me. I commend you to Him."

He tried then. He said, "Ma'am, do you remember anything of what happened afterwards?"

The constable from Cadman Village tugged at the chain attached to the manacles around Fletcher's wrists. "Here, here," he said gruffly. "Let's not be badgering the lady with questions."

Patricia said, "It's all right, Constable." To Fletcher: "I remember everything," she said.

Fletcher swallowed, hoping desperately that she meant what he meant. He said quickly, "Ma'am, they know where your castle is, and will come here looking for you. Leave without delay! Go to the nearest military post."

"I have already sent a message to Mr. Harley," the girl said.

"Uhhhh!" exhaled Fletcher, tremendously relieved.

The constable from Wentworth was bowing. "Thank you, Lady Hemistan. We can call on you then to be a witness at the trial?"

The constable from Cadman Village tugged with determination at the chain. "Let's be on our way. Our business here is concluded."

As the four officials drove off with their prisoner, the constable from Wentworth said peevishly, "I could swear I brought this felon here once before. Been having strange nightmares recently."

"Me, too," said the constable from Cadman Village.

"Something in the autumn air, perhaps," said Fletcher sarcastically. "England is quite noxious at this season."

One of the two aides, a young man in his middle twenties, said, "That was a strange conversation between this fellow and Lady Hemistan."

"I wasn't minding," said the constable from Cadman Village. " 'Portant thing is she identified him positively—right?"

Fletcher thought of them as stubborn-minded, unimaginative Englishmen. Clearly, from their remarks, they must be battling against their memories. How could an intelligent man relive the same period of time and not notice it? Here they were, the men who could do, and were doing, exactly that: Englishmen so stable mentally that they could dismiss what must seem like total madness and apparently conceal even from themselves the scars of inner conflict.

As he sat once more in the conveyance, staring somewhat sardonically at the rears of four horses, Fletcher thought unhappily: The truth is, since the robots have a way of finding where I am—through that tiny whatever they shot into my shoulder—an aircraft should be arriving any minute.

"Hey, look!" said the aide, who sat directly across from Fletcher, facing the rear. He pointed up behind Fletcher. "A big bird," he said. His blue-gray eyes widened. "Must be an eagle. Never saw an eagle before. They're much bigger'n I ever imagined—"

Fletcher had already started to turn. Yet his impulse was, not to see, but to run. He actually made a lunging motion. Sideways.

That was the last thing he remembered.

. . . The Lantellan aircraft, with Nodo at the controls, cruised around the burning conveyance and tried this time to turn all the matter into radiant energy.

The hope of the leaders was that all the atoms of the body of Nathan Fletcher would attach to beams of radiant energy and leave earth. Let them—that was the purpose—arrive at a distant part of the solar system before the next effect of the L-beam took place.

34

The Enigma.

Only the after-the-beginning is known. And that has aspects of pure fantasia.

The Big Bang! Who could believe such a thing? But it happened.

Even more incredible: in the second stage of the existence of the universe there was one atom that held the gigantic sun in its billion-year stasis. Held it, not literally. Held it by simply being where it was, deep inside that mass of superheated energy. Because of its location, everything else related to it.

Oh, there was endless motion around the key atom: Explosions that involved billions and billions of cubic miles. Nuclear holocausts that swept through the colossal sun of that second stage of the existence of the universe. Yet, throughout, there was the one atom, utterly stable. There were the complex of other atoms that immediately related to it. And farther out was the greater complex of energy that interacted with those quadrillions of neighboring particles. Some of those particles were free. And some were held together in unending gradations of atomic structures.

Because the key atom was where it was, it provided for

all that immediate world and, as a consequence, for the innumerable particles in the greater distances beyond . . . an orientation point.

We belong here because *it* is here . . .

It was the beginning of matter. Of holding together. Of having a form, and of a stable energy impulse.

It was "thought."

The thought in that key atom for long and long was simply: I belong in this location.

After a billion years, because atoms are simple, and do not change their thoughts quickly, a second thought evolved: I wonder what it would be like . . . over there.

Was it really a thought? Or did *the* atom merely, finally, get jarred out of its accidental stasis by the movement of energies around it?

Whatever . . . it started to move.

Naturally, all its loving neighbors moved with it.

And so, suddenly—

That single super super super sun blew up.

It was, in effect, a second Big Bang.

Curiosity. What would it be like . . . over there? No hurry, only interest. It proved to be almost a timeless thought. Because the over-there kept changing.

Call that change the expanding universe effect. But the key atom didn't "think" of it like that. Simply, as location changed, its "curiosity" was satisfied for a few minutes, or years, or millennia.

But the curiosity always reached to the next distances. So no third thought was ever needed until—

A coincidence.

Naturally, there were other thoughts in the atom. All those component particles each had its own "reasons." And so there had been an unnoticed evolution of matter. Progressively, the atom became a part of ever more sophisticated matter complexes: inorganic, then organic, finally human.

The key atom had become a part of Edward Fletcher. It had, because those other components had their "thoughts," worked its way through his body to become part of a sperm available for a certain night in the year 1670 A.D. That was according to the time flow of the planet earth in a sun system 36,000 light-years from the center of the hub of one of the innumerable galaxies that had formed from the debris of the second-stage Big Bang.

That same night the girl Edward had married had in her body an atom that in the ancient beginning, for a long time, had been a part of the complex of energy that gyrated around and around the key atom.

(The two people, the young Edward and his future wife, had fallen in love at sight. They knew they belonged together. . . . By that wedding night the atom inside her had worked *its* way to her current ovum.)

At the exact electrifying moment that the sperm and the ovum came together, and Nathan Fletcher was conceived, *the* atom had its third thought.

Suddenly, it realized how much it missed all its old companions.

Instantly, in the remotest distances of the universe, the companions of yester-billennia responded. From that time on everybody wanted to get together, to be home again.

Curiosity has its own careful speed. No great hurry. But the need to go home is a "now" phenomenon.

Suddenly, the impulse. After that the thought never really goes away. It has a special power in it, a drive, faster, quicker, hurry—

It took 20 billion years for curiosity to expand the universe, and thirty-four years for the homing need to collapse those portions that were most passionately affected. The rest followed more slowly.

When the Lantellan robot's firepower turned Fletcher's body into radioactive energy, the theory was that the atom would leave earth forever.

And, of course, it didn't.

The other atoms in their gillions headed home. To them being near *the* atom was being home.

And, of course, the key atom understood that perfectly. . . . Where I am is home.

Home does not move. So it settled there on the ground.
And was still there a few weeks later at the L-beam
moment. And there was no question of what it would do
then. Because, after all, it belonged as part of a sophisticated—the most—energy-matter complex: a human being.

But all the atoms understood that this was the final
alternate universe.

35

As Fletcher climbed down from the carriage, the early dawn of an autumn day was brightening in the east. All around him, through the trees and brush that lined the river, bits and pieces of London were visible.

He waited while the officer, who had ridden with Lady Hemistan and himself, climbed down. Both men, next, assisted Patricia to descend to the river roadside. Fletcher was aware of the girl eying him questioningly. Then she frowned. Finally:

"Captain," she said, "I have a strange impression that this time you're the one that has no memory."

"How do you mean?" Puzzled. After a moment of blankness, he added, "Memory of what?"

The young woman looked disturbed. "During this entire journey from Hemistan Castle you have been strange, not at all the decisive, understanding person of last night."

As she spoke the meaningless words, Fletcher happened to glance beyond her. He saw that Harley had descended from the other carriage. "Excuse me!" he said hastily to Patricia.

He ran forward, arriving just in time to help Queen Anne climb down. Harley indicated the interior of the royal carriage. "Better get your friend out," he said curtly.

Fletcher doubtfully peered inside. What he saw was Abdul Jones sitting sound asleep, slumped against the far end of his seat. Fletcher accordingly excused himself.

He walked around to the other side of the carriage. Opened that door. And then, without having had it as a plan, without conscious anger, simply grabbed the man's arm. And jerked. The sleeping body came crashing down onto the road.

He did not wait to observe Mr. New York Abdul Jones react. Back to the other side of the carriage he walked briskly. Arrived there, he discovered that Patricia and the officer had joined the Queen and Harley. And also that several other officers were coming into view from the lower shore line of the Thames River.

It developed from their account that the boat had been located. But it had already twice refused to be hauled out of the water. The military units, assigned to the task, didn't think of it that way. It was just that their chains kept breaking. "Damn thing must be heavier'n it looks!" one disgusted officer said to Robert Harley.

Harley, a reasonably logical man, made no assertive reply. His only suggestion: "Perhaps, the Navy should haul it farther upriver."

Anne had a much more personal thought. She had, so to say, dutifully taken account of the anxiety the men felt about her presence near a danger area. And so, with Patricia and Fletcher, she had stayed across the highway.

But now, with the report of two failures, she said, "I'd like to inspect this strange vessel before anything further is done."

"But, Your Majesty," protested Patricia, "you've already inspected this vessel. This is another time change. Don't you recall? You and I and Mr. Harley and Captain Fletcher and this man from America and this officer" "—she indicated the older man—"went aboard this little boat. And we were all captured by the aircraft, and taken aboard the Lantellan battleship. Remember that?"

To the girl's stunned amazement, the Queen shook her

head. "I think we're all under great pressure," said Anne, "and during the carriage journey to London we all slept. I certainly dreamed strange dreams, including the dream that I was dead—" She stopped, shivered a little. Then, to Patricia: "Dear, we mustn't let ourselves be deluded by the nature of the human faculty of dreaming while sleeping."

Patricia turned to the Secretary of State. "Mr. Harley," she appealed, "what is your recollection?"

There was a long pause. Then, slowly, the determined voice said: "Lady Hemistan, I can see that this matter of repetition of similar periods of time has, on this occasion, become confused by an unfortunate coincidence. All of us during our ride from your castle have slept for several hours. Apparently, if there was a time change, it began at the exact moment when we all awakened."

He glanced at Fletcher. "Since this time," he said, "we have no confirmation of your story from Baron Wentworth, who has been our best memory until now, I must assume that your dream was as vivid as mine. But I recognize mine for what it was, and you do not."

"I don't think we should delay," said Queen Anne.

"Oh, Your Majesty!" moaned Patricia.

The older woman made a dismissing gesture and started forward.

It looked like complete madness to the girl. Being pure and young, the youthful Lady Hemistan did not realize what it had been like to have to learn to think like a Queen. During her early years, Anne had been overwhelmed by the magnificent fighting males around her. But she was now, finally, a decisive woman who followed her own reasoning even when she was wrong.

Fletcher tried not to notice that Patricia was giving him a beseeching look. He did not remember *any* direct contact with the little boat.

As he stood there uneasily, there was a distraction. At that moment, Abdul came unsteadily into view around the rear of the carriage. The girl saw him. At once, she hurried over to him. "Mr. Jones, with your scientific knowledge, please advise Her Majesty not to go aboard the little ship—remember, we went aboard during a previous time shift?''

This time she had the experience of Abdul's staring at her with what he intended to be compassionate tolerance. ''Lady,'' he said, ''you've been having some of Mr. Fletcher's nightmares. Lady''— earnestly—''you've got to remain sensible in this crazy world. Keep your head. Don't let any hallucinations get you.''

So spoke the ordinary guy from a far future New York.

It was too late for further argument. The Queen had crossed the road, and was about to descend the embankment. In moments she would be out of sight. There was nothing to do but, hastily, run after her.

It was a few minutes later. They had all, in that half-light, gone onto the deck of the marvelous little vessel. Fletcher brought up the rear. And because he was, as always, looking in all directions, it was he who saw the Lantellan ''bird'' flying toward them.

Instantly, he started forward, intending to grab the Queen and jump off. But at that exact moment, the boat moved.

The movement was a gliding action. Smooth as a ball on glass, it virtually flowed out of its dock position and out into the river. Because he was a man who in emergencies never quite lost his head, he remembered what Lady Hemistan had said about where she had slept during the long nights of her lonely voyage. Down some steps—he recalled—at one end, and so into a small room in which was a bed.

''Patricia,'' he said urgently, ''get Her Majesty below!''

The girl gave him a startled glance and ran ahead—as Fletcher paused beside the Queen. ''This way, Your Majesty,'' he said. Softly, then, he touched the Queen's arm and pointed. Gently but firmly he guided Anne, pushing at her elbow. By the time they got there, the girl had the panel open. And there it was, indeed, the space to go down into. A doorway leading—he could only deduce—down to where Patricia had been.

"Down in there, Your Majesty," he said.

She had seen the aircraft, and she started past him. But she said in Low German, *"Vout wauw yu menschen douna?"* (What will you men do?)

"Hurry, please!"

She must have realized it was no time for discussions. The aircraft was a hundred yards away. Down she jumped into the "cabin," followed—Fletcher held the girl's arm as he shoved—by Patricia. As she went down, the Queen's voice sounded hollowly up at him: "There's room for another person down here," she said.

Fletcher had to smile grimly. Room, perhaps. For her husband, yes. For a lady-in-waiting, maybe. But the Queen of England even in a dire moment did not share a bed with a former pirate captain. Or a guard's officer. Or a man from future New York. Or even a Secretary of State.

During those rapid thoughts, he had slammed the panel shut, and was now hastily fumbling at the hard material that made up the rest of the structure at that end of the boat. Another swift thought had come. Patricia, as he recalled it, had found a number of small drawers. From one of them she had got her little weapon, but by her report there were other small devices in those drawers. And so his memory went back to the first encounter of the boat and the aircraft when Billy had ordered the boat not to fight.

In the dull light of that early morning, it took precious moments. But there they suddenly were, as his fingers embraced each in turn, sliding open.

No time, then, to be choosy. No time to consider which item of the contents was the one through which Billy, even now, might again be restraining the little ship.

He grabbed them all. He dumped them all over the gunwale into the Thames.

Barely in time. Because, as he looked up, it was obvious that during those rapid moments events had been moving at machine speed.

Two machines. The boat and the aircraft.

He was helpless now. He stood there and presumed that the little vessel had detected the aircraft with its sensor equipment. Presumed that it was apparently still trying to get out to more open water where it could—what? Fletcher couldn't imagine.

A few seconds only before the crisis. Down swooped the aircraft, seemingly intending to repeat its unopposed seizure of that previous alternate world. (Fletcher, of course, knew of only one such seizure; the actual second had occurred during his sleepwalking time.)

He assumed that eighty-third-century science, unrestricted by Billy Todd, could instantly overwhelm twenty-fifth-century technology. But he did have a cautioning thought that unwary human beings could get badly hurt in the interaction.

That thought had evidently occurred to Harley and Abdul. For, as he turned, he saw that they were already lying on the deck. The guard's officer, however, was still up; crouched, yes, and holding on. But up. Fletcher took several steps forward and grabbed the man roughly.

"Down!" he commanded. He himself, thereupon, sank to his knees, tugging at the older man. The fellow resisted. "What about the Queen?" he wanted to know. Fletcher did not answer. His message was transmitted. He let go of the other and flattened himself also on the open deck.

What happened next, Captain Nathan Fletcher was not qualified to evaluate. As the aircraft swooped down upon the little ship, the latter aimed a nadir beam up at the air vessel's propulsion system.

The name of the instrument indicated its action. It was not a weapon. It, among other things, nullified weapons. By the eighty-third century, the discovery of the nature of nature had made possible . . . simplicities.

There is no such condition as heat. No radiation. No light waves. These are only phenomena of the basic effort of space to maintain itself. Wherever space is in difficulties there will be found the turbulence called energy.

(Atoms do not realize that they have no existence, as such. That they are only a relation to.)

The nadir condition extended pure space into areas within its range.

As that condition enspaced the aircraft, the machine fell out of control.

The aircraft struck the water at an angle, bounced several times. And then because it was airtight, it bobbed along the surface. And was soon merely one more bit of flotsam that would ordinarily have been swept out to sea.

36

It had been a lot of action and decisions for a sleepwalker . . . not a good state for a human being to be in. Such an internal shutoff of the basic self "normally" happens only as a result of sustained fatigue.

Abdul had triggered the same brain center with energy pulses. But he had help from Fletcher's exhausted condition. The trial and a sentence of death and then the mental stress of his experiences in several alternate time worlds did their part. They were fatigue equivalents.

But fortunately for Fletcher the future New York ordinary guy at this key moment had a thought. All these minutes Abdul had been recovering from his fall. And all the while he was remembering grimly that someone had snatched him out of the Queen's carriage and dumped him onto the road.

A vague visual memory as he fell and some simple, direct reasoning told him who the someone was. . . . That S.O.B. knows I'm after his girl. So, in the sleepwalking state, his anger at *that* found an outlet.

The thought in Abdul's head wasn't worded quite that elegantly. But the meaning was there in a rough fashion, along with an immediate sly purpose.

I'll wake him, and he won't remember anything that's happened. . . .

On something that personal the pudgy man from far future New York was quick. When the instant battle between the boat and the aircraft was over, Abdul got up first. He fumbled along one gunwale to within a few feet of Fletcher, who had risen to his knees, cautiously. Standing there, Abdul stealthily aimed his GROETWUC and let go a single, directed blast of vibratory power.

The confusion part of the scheme didn't work. Awakening was a problem for Fletcher. But he thought of it as another L-beam aftermath. And, of course, he believed he knew how the last alternate world had ended: with the two constables, their aides, and himself and the horses mercilessly destroyed from the air.

So, when in the vague light of early morning, he saw the aircraft in the water, drifting, it took a little while, yes.

But during that while British naval craft boldly surrounded the downed machine. British seamen threw a net over its smooth surface, and divers went down fearlessly and hooked anchors onto the net from below.

The anchors were attached to tough ropes. A windlass, manned by a dozen pairs of strong arms, drew the ropes taut. Whereupon, the two naval craft hauled the floating aircraft over to a riverside dock.

As they completed this task, the airlock opened. Billy and a robot emerged.

The little eighty-third-century boat had, meanwhile, gone back to its dock. Within minutes the Queen and Patricia were up from their bedroom and ashore. The men followed more slowly but without delay.

Billy and the robot were brought over under guard. And it was the boy who now gave the information that established how great the victory was.

The Lantellan rank and file had rebelled against their treasonous leaders. The robot with Billy was, accordingly, not Nodo, but his successor, Narat. All the former chiefs-by-rotation were being held prisoner until instructions for their disposition were received from none other than Nathan Fletcher.

The meaning of those final words did not immediately impress itself on Fletcher's mind. His attention had been diverted. A kind of astonishment that, apparently, it made a difference to these automatons which of them was the leader-by-rotation. Yet, after a moment it occurred to him that, given a reasonable level of education, it didn't really matter even among human beings who was the government and who the governed. The latter all turned into dupes and the former into schemers. There was just enough truth in the observation for that perceptive individual Nathan Fletcher to shake his head and wonder if, perhaps, humans and robots were also interchangeable.

At that point the implication of what Billy's final words meant hit him. And he was contemplating *that* with a feeling of by-God-it-worked when the boy continued: "Our principal problem right now is the next L-beam moment, which is only minutes away. So—"

"Uh!" said Fletcher.

From the height of the total power of the equivalent of a South American Indian rock god to the dull thud of imminent disaster was that rapid.

It was a second distraction. Abruptly, everything seemed far away. The voices, the people, appeared to recede. And the slender, expirate stood there, thinking in his semi-humorous fashion how wrong he had been. At the time asking for the L-beam had seemed like a decision. Primarily, he wanted the mind-reading ability, but he was willing for the rest of it to happen also.

Instead of good things he had got a repetitive nightmare. One alternate universe after another. Usually ill-timed. Often dangerous. And getting damned tiresome.

Wearily, once more, he did his bracing thing. . . . After all, I'll come to somewhere where I've already been—

The bracing did its usual. It brought him back into his surroundings mentally as well as physically. And to the abrupt realization that during the minute or so of his withdrawnness Billy had been explaining why, at this

L-beam moment, there would be no shift in time, no new alternative world.

Had explained it, and Fletcher hadn't heard a word.

"So," Billy was saying at him, "it's important that we fly you and this boat to the Transit-Craft as soon as you tell the Lantellan robots to turn the engines over to us—" He added, "Important for them as well as the rest of us."

Fletcher had already shifted to some extent from his own feelings. But the new information—the new *threat,* that this time he would get what he had originally asked for—held him. What remained of his recovery was the sardonicism, as he said, "I gather, Billy, that this next L-beam moment is the morality indoctrination time. I'll come out of it pure and washed free of my sins."

It seemed unbelievable, and so it held him. And, abruptly, the boy seemed to realize also that he had a badly disturbed human being standing in front of him. He hesitated, and then he visibly adjusted, and said, "Sir, it won't be quite like that."

Fletcher was remembering something else. "Those bullies," he said, "the ones who were hit when the Lantellans originally boarded the *Orinda,* made statements that reflected criticism of our present level of civilization. If I understood them correctly, it's all right to be a pirate when life is cruel. Yet all four, apparently, are now trying to take full responsibility and operate on the legal side of that same cruel society. And, simultaneously, they seemed to achieve inner peace in relation to all the murders and other crimes they committed."

Billy looked resigned as he said, "In your period of history, judges, military leaders, and others in government authority are able to order people put to death without any serious moral repercussions. So, that's a way that you could have gone."

Fletcher scarcely heard. His attention was still on his own thoughts. He went on, musingly. "Also, if sufficient time passes, vivid memories fade. In the real world—at least, that first one seems like it ought to be considered the natural one—I lived in Italy until age seventy-eight. And, as I remember it, my pirate career and its crimes receded into vagueness. Sort of like childhood acts of stealing and troublemaking, which are dismissed as unimportant when you're grown up."

He nodded reflectively. "Since I behaved myself in Italy—killed only one man in a duel that was forced on me—I suppose I could hope that my memories of mass murder and piracy will all gradually fade, too."

There was the beginning of desperation in Billy's manner as he said, "Captain, you have an interesting experience in store for you. But right now—"

Fletcher said thoughtfully, "One alleviation that I've seen is when people become religious. They accept God, as Lady Hemistan has pointed out, and they're free." He shook his head, abruptly very satiric. "That solution, alas, is not for me."

Billy said urgently, "It will be interesting, Captain, when you find out what does work for you. But, please, I have to point out that we do not have much time. And that only you can make the next step possible."

Memory came. Fletcher said, "Oh!"

He walked over to where Narat had been led, off to one side. Gathering his thoughts, he stood very still with eyes closed, as if he were letting the Universal Mind come into him. Then he said in an even voice: "I, your lord, the Universal Mind, using this man as my vessel of communication, hereby command that the engines of the Transit-Craft be repaired at optimum speed and flown as rapidly as possible to the Caribbean Sea near where the Transit-Craft lies on the ocean bottom. Along with the engines, the boat will also be transported, as well as the unconscious body of this man through whom I am speaking. On arrival, they shall be put down on the water—the engines and the unconscious body aboard the boat—and they will then proceed to contact the Transit-Craft. The aircraft shall return here and act as a liaison between human beings and my Lantellan robots."

After he had finished, Fletcher had the grimly amused feeling that he could become an instructor in how gods should speak to robots and other dupes. He had the wry feeling, however, that it would never become a credit course in any university.

In front of him, Narat said, "I have relayed the commands of our lord, the Universal Mind, to Captain-by-rotation Dumel. And he has acknowledged. And agreed."

Fletcher knew when to stop. Without another word, he walked over to where Lady Hemistan stood with Abdul and Harley and several officers. The Queen had disappeared —it turned out—whisked off in a carriage by her appalled husband and a guard's unit.

To Harley, Fletcher said, "I strongly urge, sir, that the Navy release both these craft to do what I have just recommended to these Lantellan robots."

"Captain," said the Secretary of State in a friendly voice, "why don't you for practical purposes rejoin the Tory party? I predict that if you were now to inform me that such was your intention I could justify to the cabinet your entire future status as the Queen's emissary to the Lantellan robots."

He added, in a persuasive tone, "Your title, your lands, your status in the royal court, your pirate career overlooked—what do you say?"

What was amazing to Fletcher, Harley was taking for granted that there would be a return to 1704 A.D. normalcy. And, suddenly, as he remembered the constables from Cadman and Wentworth, and their total inability to comprehend their "nightmares," he realized the awesome reality of Harley's attitude. To minds *that* stable, this would all become a dimly remembered period of history. "Of course," he thought, "of course." The collapse of the universe was destined to be forgotten in any meaningful sense.

The thought shook him, somehow. But he was able to say, "I agree, sir."

Harley held out his hand. Fletcher hesitated. At that

moment he happened to glance past Harley. His gaze touched Patricia's tear-filled eyes. And that did it. He reached. He grasped his enemy's hand. Shook it, thinking: Really, he feels human. . . . It was a surprisingly warm palm, but not a damp one.

He let go. Stepped back. And bowed. And then he excused himself and walked over to Patricia, aware that Abdul was standing just behind and to her left. And that his eyes balefully watched his approach. . . . Make one friend, gain one enemy—thought Fletcher.

He ignored the New Yorker. To the girl, he said, "And what are you going to do?"

At that exact instant, she must have had a mental warning. "Watch out!" she cried.

There was a blinding flash of brightness from behind her and to her right.

It was the girl, then, who jumped forward and tried to catch him as he fell. She did manage to break his fall. At which point, belatedly, anxious to make a good impression, Abdul trotted awkwardly forward. Fletcher had fallen on his hindside, and the girl was desperately holding onto his shoulders. What the New Yorker did was grab both arms of the unconscious man, and, gesturing Patricia out of the way, he lowered the body all the way to the ground.

Patricia gave him a grateful look, and later, after all the instructions given by Fletcher had been carried out and the aircraft, with the boat attached, had lifted off and was soon a dot in the distance, went over to Harley, and said, "Your lordship, this man from New York"—she indicated Abdul Jones—"should be provided with a place to stay. His knowledge should be considered a resource of the nation, to be protected, and paid for."

The great man's attention was elsewhere. He obviously heard, because he waved a hand impatiently, and he said, "Right now, I don't have time for him. I'll have the military take him in hand temporarily."

His voice trailed off at the end. He murmured an excuse and walked toward an officer nearby. There was a low-voiced conversation, very brief. He pointed at Abdul, and then walked on, away.

It was too casual. Showed no awareness of the reality. Which was that Abdul's thoughts came to her. Sly. Scheming. To the effect that he would have no difficulty slipping away from the military. His intent: to fly after her carriage.

The girl hesitated. Should she make an issue? The sun was just coming into view over the trees. The light made the world, and its problems, somehow seem less threatening. Casually, she brought her right hand up to her bosom and pressed. The reassuring feel of the outlines of the protective weapon pressed back at her.

It was the moment of decision. She walked over to Abdul. "You stay with me for a few days," she said. "And, please, just stop all those schemes for a personal relationship that keep going through your mind. You're a visitor from the future who, no doubt, will eventually find a permanent status in this period of time. I'm sure you will be valuable, but between us—if you behave—a simple friendship. Understand?"

Abdul said that he understood. And, in fact, since he was really a simple soul, he felt chastened by her words. Women had that effect on him. Or rather, his wife had often had that effect on him.

While he was in that subdued state of mind, Patricia and he walked over to her carriage. Within minutes the elegant vehicle with its fine horses had disappeared around a turn in the river road.

37

He had an early impression that all was right, now, except one thing. But that one was very wrong.

No thought came as to what it could be. But from that moment forth, first, remembering what it was, and then doing something about it, seemed like a purpose at the far back of his mind. A purpose that would grow more urgent.

Time passed. And still the world and his own feelings were far away. There *were* pictures. He was reclining next to a wonderfully transparent glass window. On the other side of the glass fish swam, and a strange sea bottom was murkily visible for a few dozen feet.

His reason rejected the scene. They were, he told himself, memories, but not his. . . . I'm imagining what Patricia saw when she was on the Transit-Craft.

He tried to move his body, to turn over, so he could look in the other direction. His hope: if, by looking, he saw the same silvery strands as she had reported to be hanging down from the ceillng, then he might accept that it was his own personal vision.

He couldn't move. Couldn't turn. Presently, he gave up trying. At which time he had what in the past he would have called "a philosophical thought."

The thought: In these early stages of human history,

governments are necessary for the maintenance of order. But, basically, all governments are usurpers.

An awed feeling: Did I think that? Pause. Then: I'll have to tell that to the Queen at some opportune moment when it will sound like a light remark.

Another pause. And this time, blankness. After a while, an unfamiliar man's face was looking down at him. The man said—and Fletcher was surprised that he heard every word: "You'll be coming to in a little while. But I notice something is already bothering you. What is it?"

Fletcher had forgotten. Besides, he was concentrating on trying to speak. "Who are you?" he wanted to ask.

Above him, the face smiled. The man said, "I'm an adult passenger of the Transit-Craft. My name is Ahlone. Now, try again to remember: what are you worried about? What's wrong?"

It was too much information. His attention could not seem to follow the words all the way through to the end. His mind got hung up at the meaning of "adult passenger." The problem: If there were adult passengers, why had they depended on a boy—Billy—to deal with the life and death situation of their spaceship? And where was Billy?

Almost, then, as if his eyes were open, Fletcher "looked up" at the face and strove mightily to ask those questions aloud: "Why?" And then, "Where?"

Did he get an answer? If there was a direct reply, he didn't hear it. Everything was suddenly far away. But somewhere in there he had his second "philosophical" consideration: The greatest crime is not the immediate act of theft, or violence, or enforcement. It is that the act has made necessary a government and a police force to deal with individuals who give in to the impulse to grab, or force, or hit.

Fletcher contemplated *that,* and experienced a quiet respect for himself. Really, I'm getting back to the level of thinking that used to pour out of me when I was one of

Princess Anne's card-playing companions before she was queen.

Almost, with that, it seemed as if the one remaining wrongness was going to surface. The feeling of how awful it was did come. Nothing else. Not the awfulness itself.

It shook him at a deep level. And he must have slept.

Fletcher awoke with a start. And lay there in the half-light beside the glass that separated him from the dark sea bottom beyond. He was oddly aware of his muscular body, and even the lean shape of his face . . . all of it, body and face, tensed with a thought:

Really, a man has a right to fight for his survival. If I hadn't fled London, those Tory killers would have had me hanged, drawn, and quartered. Those things happened at a level that my friends didn't even know about. And that *is* the present state of civilization. . . .

It was that ultimate threat that had subsequently motivated him to become a rebel. That part was a mistake.

"In effect," he told himself, "I declared war against the state, and waged it vengefully with some kind of idea that I was getting even with my enemies. That was wrong. I should have taken my few hundred guineas and gone straight to Italy."

Contented, he was about to turn over and go back to sleep, when—realization: Is that what I got out of the L-beam? That argument!

True, it seemed to quiet him inside. Yet, he had expected more. After all, the four bullies had got—

Wait!

They hadn't. This was all they manifested also. Good sense. Suddenly—after the L-beam—their false motivations, false reasoning, and impulses to infinite violence were gone.

They had become responsible individuals. They returned to London, and took over the care of their common-law wives and bastard children.

That was the proper and only true future for the human race: total individual responsibility.

Finally: the correct penance for his pirate career and crimes attendant thereto would be a life of responsibility and good works.

He lay quite relaxed for about a minute, thinking of the simplicity of the thoughts involved, when—

The man whose face he had seen in his dream state walked into view and bent over him where he lay on the floor. He was obviously aware that Fletcher was awake. For he smiled. And he nodded. And he said in a strangely soft voice, "How goes it, friend?"

For a moment Fletcher thought that the other must be a German speaking English. The grammatical structure of the question was Teutonic to him, who understood things like that.

As swiftly as it had come, the awareness of language faded from the forefront of his mind. "Where is Lady Hemistan?" he asked.

"Well, first of all, Billy himself went back with the aircraft to be our contact with the Lantellan robots. He has, again, all the necessary crystals to communicate with us. Second, when Billy came back here, he revived me and several other adult passengers. My job was to deal with you. Theirs to install the engines. As for Lady Hemistan, Billy told me she departed for her estate outside of London, taking Abdul Jones with her."

"Uh!" said Fletcher.

Pause. Then, very softly, "So that's what's bothering you. He's the person you're worrying about."

It had come to Fletcher in one surge of memories. All the suppressed emotion. And the total conviction that Abdul could not be trusted.

Ahlone said, "I perceive that you believe that this man from twenty-third-century New York will utilize simple mechanical devices of his time against the lady. Since Billy did not then have his mind-reading crystal, naturally he was unaware of these undercurrents. However, the lady herself could undoubtedly read this man's mind. Under those circumstances, how would you explain her invitation for him to accompany her?''

''Well,'' said Fletcher, ''she does have that protective weapon you people gave her.''

Ahlone said, ''I regret to tell you that weapon depended on a certain long-range crystal aboard the boat which, in turn, derived its energy from the boat itself. Your act of throwing all those crystals overboard would not have affected the power of the crystal, but unfortunately the boat is here.'' There was no pause in his words, as he finished, ''We'd better get you back there.''

38

Fletcher tried again to move his body, to turn over; and this time it came so easy that he was over on his other side almost before he could realize what was happening.

And there he was, gazing past the good-looking "passenger" up at an incredible mass of silvery strands that hung down from a translucent ceiling. They were "incredible" in that they were entirely different from his expectation. Very thin. In fact, fine to the point of being individually almost invisible. And they glittered like jewels from top to bottom.

He almost let the marvelous beauty of them distract him. Almost. But not quite.

However, he did have another distracting thought. (So many new things here. So much to consider. Including a fleeting sense of the futility of giving any attention to what might be happening to Patricia in a far distant part of the world.)

But the new thought was powerful. So much so that it evoked virtually instant speech from him. He said, genuinely startled, and with dismay: "How come I'm not reading minds? How come we've been talking, and not just thinking at each other?"

The disappointment was immense. For God's sake, that's

the only true reason why I wanted the damned light fired
into my head—

He saw that fine, young-looking yet subtly mature face
was smiling down at him. "*You* have been talking," said
Ahlone in that soft voice.

Soft . . . soft . . . soundless.

After a while, after he had realized how automatic the
telepathy had been, and was, Fletcher made his first conscious try at projecting an unspoken thought. He actually
uttered the words silently. "What's happening"—he pointed
up—"to the universe?"

"Nothing. It's all over, the danger is past. We altered
the thought in the key atom inside your body to: Everybody leave quietly. That," continued the man, "will take
a while. But, please notice, we didn't say where they
should go to."

What that normally astute individual, Nathan Fletcher,
was noticing was that he didn't know what the hell Ahlone
was telepathing about.

"We'll explain the details later," his host smiled.

Fletcher projected: "Later? After what? What happens
next?"

"We eighty-thirders will colonize North America."

Fletcher was not a man who was easily baffled. But he
had to admit that every sentence now being projected by
the other man left him that much more blank-minded.
Mental communication was definitely very directive. Somehow, he had expected there would be great clumps of
information transferred from one brain to another.

"The reason," telepathed the smiling man, "that I am
not explaining these technical matters is that installation of
the engines is almost complete. And we'll be getting out of
here, and up to the surface, and over to western America
and then to England within the hour."

And that merely seemed to be wrongly worded. Right
there, temporarily, Fletcher gave up on mental communication. "It has occurred to me," he said aloud, "that the
English language, if you are indeed transmitting to me in

English, has changed even in the past hundred years. So it may well have altered drastically by the eighty-third century. I deduce that you are having a problem making your mind communication in my, uh, dialect.

"What you are trying to say, I'm sure," he went on, "is that within the next hour installation of the engines will be completed. Then we shall cautiously move up to the surface. After which we will make the flight to England. Can you give me an estimate of how long that flight will require? I—"

He stopped. Because at that moment the velvet floor under him shuddered.

The water outside started to move past the glass.

The ocean bottom receded and disappeared.

"The operation of these engines," telepathed Ahlone, who was now holding on to invisible supports on the glass window—they seemed invisible because Fletcher could not see them—"is based on a parallel to the wind system of your sailing vessels. That's what trapped us. We tune into the natural flows of the universe, and of course these flows suddenly went berserk. We would actually have been better off with ordinary primitive atomic drives. But then"—smiling—"the collapse of the universe doesn't happen every day—"

He stopped. He projected advice: "Hold on to those two indentations in the floor near your hands. We're about to lift."

Fletcher, who had started to slide, fumbled hastily. He found the indentations. They were cunningly curved, so that he could grip firmly. As he gripped—

Bright sunlight. A dazzling glimpse of shining ocean, rapidly sinking into distance below. The brightness made him close his eyes and squeeze. When he opened them, only a vast blue sky was visible.

"We've tuned into an upflow in the fabric of the space in this part of the universe." Ahlone's thought came softly. "The flow itself is very fast. Our speed depends on how finely we do our tuning."

Fletcher could not imagine the nature of such a flow, but the concept he could understand. Like a sail ship with only one sail held up to the wind.

He stayed where he was, clinging to the two indentations. Outside, the sky was darkening. Which was puzzling, because it had been broad daylight below. Worse, suddenly, it was pitch dark. An incredibly cloudless night, with the stars like tiny bright diamonds.

And, off to one side, an impossible object. A great fiery ball sending long streamers of flame in every direction. But incredibly bright though it was, the entire mass of burning stuff was completely surrounded by darkness.

"We're in space. That's the sun." Presumably, it was a thought from Ahlone. Fletcher heard no sound.

Once more, there was a shift under his body. He started to slide, and this time it was the impression of acceleration that he had first experienced in a meaningful way in Nodo's aircraft. Fletcher merely gripped the indentations with more determination.

Suddenly, on every side, a brightening. The stars disappeared. Below was a pattern of green and brown, and a vast ocean off to one side, and a coast line that Fletcher, with a shock, recognized from a map that had been put together from the drawings of Sir Francis Drake, the Englishman, and De Quirós, the Portuguese, more than a hundred years before.

But, of course, he also had the locational thought communicated earlier by Ahlone: the west coast of North America. The shock continued inside him: What are we doing here . . . first? . . . His feeling: over in England every minute was important, with such a person as Abdul.

As he watched unhappily, the Transit-Craft came down in a green valley, with hills on every side. And, nearby, the glint of a river.

"Now," telepathed Ahlone, "we must step into an adjoining chamber. They're going to split the ship."

Fletcher raised himself to his knees and found that he had no difficulty getting all the way up. It actually felt good to walk. Where he walked to was through a section of metal that, somehow, slid open as they came to it. And then slid shut behind them. He looked back and saw it shut.

The incredible speed of the flight had not yet sunk in. Being at the wrong location left an empty feeling. It was not easy to think about other realities.

He had a faraway thought: In a way I'm a central figure, or they wouldn't be dealing with me at all. So they are paying attention to my condition. We will get over to England eventually.

Another feeling: This was the world of L-beam morality. And, alas, it was still a world of choices. . . . I suppose I will have to resign myself to the fact that the fate of Patricia is second to whatever brought the ship here. Grimly, he looked around at the "here."

The "chamber" in which he found himself had windows that glinted with a bluish tint, and the same low ceilings. But it was not cluttered by thousands of thin, thready ropes hanging down, or by anything else. At the far end, across from where he had entered, was a flat, silvery structure, almost like a mirror. And there were two odd-shaped chairs in front of the shining thing.

It was as his gaze was still taking in these aspects of the room that a movement outside one of the glass windows caught the corner of his left eye.

Fletcher turned. Then he went over to the window. He stared.

Naked people were coming into view. They came from a point to his left that he could not see. But he deduced that it was from the section of the Transit-Craft that Ahlone and he had just come out of.

Since they were naked, and it was bright daylight, by simple, repeated observation he could see that there were as many women as men. A dozen, two dozen, two score, more and more . . . a continuing line, the individuals of which walked rapidly off toward the river. A hundred, two hundred, three hundred—good God!

Beside him—or rather, inside his head—Ahlone whispered, spoke, telepathed, "The first thing they need is a drink of water." He added, "That's all they'll take until tomorrow. Lots of water. After that, we'll have to have some food for them."

Fletcher nodded. He had made, was making, his adjustment to the seemingly unending stream of people. He had earlier, from Patricia's account, taken it for granted that the Transit-Craft was a much smaller vessel than the Lantellan battleship. Obviously, now, that was not so.

Abruptly awed, he was motivated to speak. "How many passengers?" he asked.

"Forty-seven thousand."

Fletcher took the colossal total in stride, merely shaking his head wryly. Incredibly, it was more than half again the number of Lantellan robots. What a vast ship it must be.

One puzzle remained. "Why are they all naked?" he asked.

The telepathed answer came softly. "Captain, I'll explain it en route. Please sit in one of those chairs. We're about to take off."

Fletcher settled into the indicated chair. And immediately discovered what was odd about it.

It was flexible. Its arms swung around his waist and enclosed him with a cushioned gentleness. Its back contoured the shape of his hips and lower body.

The feel of it was so protective that he was at once able to draw his attention away from himself. And so he saw on the silvery bluish mirror in front of him a reflection of a small vessel on the ground behind—below—them. It had the shape of half an oval. From it, from that receding tiny object, people were emerging in long rows.

At that point, an intruding thought: "Those strings that you saw hanging from the ceiling, all forty-seven thousand of them, were the colonists, each in a chemical stasis for long distance travel. Ultralight speeds normally cause aging, and so we have teen-agers in charge of the ship. It's all right for them to grow older during a voyage. But the reason we had to get the passengers out before anything else is that the collapse of the universe delayed us. And these chemical states have their own time factors. So now we can take care of your situation. . . ."

Choices, thought Fletcher. Even in a world of perfect morality some things come before other things. . . . I suppose I can resign myself to the possibility that this future New Yorker—Abdul—has had time to force himself upon Patricia. But since he's not a murderer, that really isn't a total disaster either for her or for me—

Mentally, he surveyed that. At once, a close to the surface leftover from his 1704 A.D. male chauvinism rejected it.

He sat then, as the vessel seemed to make an exact duplicate of the earlier flight. Up into darkness. Then down into early morning.

The Transit-Craft came down in a field near a large castlelike structure with two spires and two turrets. There were other buildings clustered near it.

Everything stopped. "We've made surface," Ahlone's thought came. "You may stand up, Captain."

Fletcher stood up. He had already had his shock of recognition. That was Hemistan Castle out there. Seeing it, he felt foolish. Because his language correction lesson was now proved incorrect. Ahlone had really meant "within the hour."

"Here," said that individual. "Place this in your pocket."

He held out a small shining piece of what looked like a shard of rock. Fletcher accepted the object; and the question about it was obviously in his mind, because Ahlone's reply came: "It's a modified crystal that carries its own charge for about a week. So long as you are near, or it is near, Lady Hemistan, the protective weapon we gave her will work again. I hope we're not too late."

Fletcher said nothing. He was led to a door-size opening, which had appeared in the "glass."As he came to the threshold of that opening, he had the thought that he was being "let off" and that they were not staying.

"What about you?" He spoke the words.

The reply was complex. Forty-seven thousand people had been put down on the ground naked. Billy had meanwhile persuaded the Lantellan robots to convert their equipment to make clothes. Those clothes would have to be picked up and delivered. And then of course food was next. "We'll be back and forth many times. We need supplies, and can offer developmental help in exchange that, we presume, all European powers will want to have, once they understand its value."

"I'm sure," said Fletcher, "that the British government will assist you. The Queen is very generous once she understands a situation."

Having said that, he stepped outside and away.

Moments after that he was alone in the empty field, with only the memory of feeling a strong breeze, and afterward, briefly, of seeing the glint of silver in the sky.

39

Fletcher walked toward the big house, a slender, some-what bedraggled male human being. Still facially good-looking, still with a strong, lean body. But as he glanced down at and over what he could see of his clothing, there was no question but that the elegant gentleman expirate needed help from a valet. The trousers were crinkled. The coat somehow had got twisted. The shoes were stained with mud.

He was actually shaking his head over his appearance when—

"He saw you arrive! He's coming out!"

Patricia's voice. Inside his head.

Momentarily, he was dazzled. My God, we can both read minds . . . a man and a woman of the year 1704 A.D.

Belatedly, he thought back at her: "Patricia—it is you?"

"Yes."

It was eerie. The whole phenomenon of mental intercom-munication so new it kept being unreal. Yet, after a moment, he forced himself once more to project: "What's happened?"

"I fought him physically half the night. He tore off my clothes. But, you know, a man can't really force a woman. He can manhandle her. He can hold her close to him. But

if she struggles there's no intercourse. I have to say that he
did not threaten me with death. And I discovered he is
physically not much stronger than a country girl. He finally just got tired and disgusted with me and went to
sleep in my bed. I moved out to another room. I locked the
door, but he used something to burn the lock this morning.
And he was cheerful, and insisted on our having breakfast
together. He's not going to kill you, but he's going to
drive you away, and try again tonight to force me. He
thinks that if he can make me pregnant, I'll give in.''

Twice, as he ''listened,'' Fletcher felt the total rage
begin in him. But each time the emotion went away. And
that was odd except that he understood it.

This was the old, old, old, basic struggle. Two men and
one woman. Two male animals and one female. In the
animal world, it was never a fight to the death. One male
finally inflicted enough injury to make the other one
withdraw.

Possibly, *all* the complex violence of later millennia
began with that early man-woman conflict. Never in those
days was the woman asked for her decision. She was the
prize of the battle's outcome.

The ordinary guy from a future New York had reverted.
The outward appearance was that a single thought did
it. . . . He believes he's superior to the people of this
age—the rest was male-automatic.

Even as this awareness flashed, Fletcher . . . automatically . . . followed an old pattern of his own. Instinc-
tively, he reached for his sword. And, of course, he had
none. What was ''of course'' about its absence was that
the weapon had been removed by the authorities when he
was cornered in his mother and sister's house. At the time,
rather than cause the two women a problem, he surrendered without a fight. Somehow, he had forgotten that
unhappy long-ago sequence. And so now he reached. In
vain.

Once again, there was a surge of what was left in him of
his 1704 A.D. easy reactions. Abruptly, he was critical of

the Transit-Craft people. Their instant departure was ridiculous. They had total power, and they could have come in—just for a minute. And they left. And, worse, they were now gone to remote North America.

"It's not quite like that." It was the thought of Patricia. "Ahlone asked me what had happened. I told him. He said they would be back tonight to help me, if necessary."

The implications of *that* were, suddenly . . . worse. Just like that, it was down to . . . two men.

Fletcher slowed as he had the sharp awareness. He actually waited for the new L-beam morality to respond. A faraway thought: Actually, there doesn't have to be a confrontation. I could just leave and come back this evening.

Nothing happened. He kept right on walking forward. All he had was the thought. There was not in him the slightest impulse to turn aside.

All right—he thought grimly—down the drain goes L-beam purity.

He telepathed: "Where can I find a weapon? A sword may be best. Are there any in the buildings nearest me? Maybe I can get to one of those buildings before he does."

The reply was unhappy: "I remember my father had several, but I never noticed what he did with them. Or where they were put when he died. Oh—just a minute. I think the servants put all the stuff from his room into that square building near you. But I think the door is locked."

His reaction was that maybe he could break the door down, using something. But he also, abruptly, remembered another possibility. "What about your weapon?" he asked.

"He came at me when I had it in my hand. He said he had figured out it wouldn't work. And when it didn't he took it away from me and put it somewhere."

"If you could find it," urged Fletcher, "it will work now. I was given an energy crystal for it."

"Maybe it's in his room," she answered hopefully. "I'll go down and look while he's out of the house."

Fletcher made no reply. He had come to the square

building. And the door was not locked. . . . Trust a woman,
he thought, to forget to lock something. . . . By the time
that put-down thought had casually moved through his
head from his 1704 A.D. repertoire of male chauvinist
sayings, he had the door open, and he was inside. And
saw that there were several swords, one of which seemed
almost a duplicate of his own fine blade.

In a single flicking action, he snatched up the scabbard,
belt and all. Swiftly, he fitted it around his waist. And
then he was outside. And heading toward the castle.

It was as he rounded the corner of the building that he
saw that, walking toward him, was Abdul Jones.

Time: a few moments later.

There they stood in broad daylight, facing each other,
two males from different periods of history. What amazed
Fletcher was that from the beginning he had virtually
ignored the man from future New York. Had noted that he
was a minor average type in his own day and age. It had
been automatic aristocratic attitudes from that moment
forth; and the occasional technological demonstrations that
showed immense superiority he had dismissed as unimportant because the man was so labeled in some rigid part
of his mind.

A nothing.

He drew his sword with a single gliding motion. As he
did so, the nothing scowled wickedly. And when the
nothing spoke, the self-awareness of his power was a recognizable sound in his voice.

"Look, Captain," he said, "you point that sword at
me, and I'll put a current through it that'll burn your hand
off."

Fletcher replaced the sword in its sheath. And took a
few steps to one side. The action was intended to look as if
he were anxious and uncertain. The impression he wanted
to convey was that he was backing away. But in fact his
movement had a small goal. There was an object over
there on the ground. Not clear what he would do with it
when he got it. No certainty that it would be useful. But it

was a minor hope for a man who did not give up hope easily.

So, because he was a man who under threat was infinitely determined, and because his opponent didn't really have the sense to put two and two together, and besides felt superior, he made it. Equally important, it was exactly the type of object that it had seemed to be at a distance: a club shape.

A primitive club.

As he, almost literally, snapped his body downward and grabbed that most ancient of all weapons, a thought touched him: For God's sake, I'm actually fighting.

And he didn't know why. There was no reason for it. What was he trying to prove? Before this day was over, the Transit-Craft—having presumably reconverted its forty-seven thousand passengers—would be back here; and they would presumably use their immensely greater threat of force to—

Just a minute! Their force. No question about it. They, also, in the final issue, confronted by someone who could not be reasoned out of using his force, were prepared to act.

A little different, of course. Not personal. More like a government. In fact—

He had a great thought. The human brain all through history had been better than the man underneath it—if such an anomaly were possible. Long ago, it had created "fairness" and "justice." It required perfect behavior from everybody. And dealt forcibly with those who failed to measure up to a minimum standard.

The individual did not have such a requirement. But all the individuals joined as a group did.

I'll be damned, Fletcher thought ruefully; down here where the group is missing, in a pinch it's every man for himself, still . . .

At least, it was enough of a thought, enough of a decision, to bring his body up like a spring suddenly released.

Almost, then, he didn't see the full flight of the club as it shot from his hand. But the partial glimpse he had showed it as a blur in the air, and heading with deadly accuracy.

After he hurriedly stripped the unconscious New Yorker so that finally the overweight body lay naked on the grass. And after he built a hot fire and burned the unusual clothing—too bad, but it had to be. After all that, and when Abdul was already stirring and groaning a little, Fletcher went into the square building. There he found a suit in the wardrobe of the late Lord Hemistan. And found, also, underclothing, and a shirt, and shoes.

Abdul had sat up meanwhile. He accepted the clothing and silently dressed. It was not until he climbed to his feet that he said in a subdued voice, "What do you want me to do?" He added, hopelessly, "I have no place to go."

"We'll talk about it," said Fletcher. He was not unsympathetic, and he even had the thought that maybe in his stupid fashion the poor fellow had tried to force himself into a place where he could "go."

That was a little farfetched, but it could have been one factor. So Fletcher said, "Right now, head for the servants' quarters!"

There was a long pause. The man in the clothes that didn't quite fit him, and didn't match his puffy face at all, had a startled look on his face. "Hey," he said in a plaintive, protesting voice, "is that what I'm going to be? A servant?"

Fletcher, who had turned away, faced the other again. He felt amazingly relaxed, and he spoke in his victory voice. "Well, Abdul," he said, "I believe you'll be more valuable than that. But for the time being, you'll have to admit, you cannot consider yourself a welcome guest of Lady Hemistan's. You tried to take advantage, didn't you? So we know the state of your soul. You're one of the people who, suddenly, showed his true colors and became a pirate. But since I have recently become a non-pirate, you can see that the transition is not impossible. So just be prepared to do good works, which is what I plan to do. And we'll both presently see what this strange new world will do for us in exchange. How's that?''

Into Fletcher's mind came a mixture of thoughts from Abdul, which really added up to an unhappy agreement, and the cheerful sound of Patricia's mental voice:

"You said that exactly right, dear. And I think that now you'd better come in here. And let us talk about our future in this strange new world in which we are going to live together.''

Fletcher had to admit: there was something very good to be said for mental communication.

It left no doubt about where a man stood emotionally. Or a woman.

Epilogue

First, inversion.

And now, reversal.

The particle flow was outward again. Expansive. But there was a "feeling" of growth in the sense of maturity. As if all those microscopic entities had gone through a learning process.

. . . I am now "me." I'm "grown up." It's nice to visit "home," but now I have my own place—

The "child" universe had gone through its adolescent convulsions and had become an "adult." That would presently affect everybody and everything. In all future "time" human beings would automatically achieve the psychic development obtained by eighty-third century-ites through biological manipulation.

And they would live on a more responsive planet in a maturing solar system. No more infantile destructiveness.

Every *body* and every *thing* responsible.

FINE SCIENCE FICTION AND FANTASY TITLES AVAILABLE FROM CARROLL & GRAF

☐ Aldiss, Brian/LAST ORDERS $3.50
☐ Aldiss, Brian/NON-STOP $3.95
☐ Amis, Kingsley/THE ALTERATION $3.50
☐ Asimov, Isaac et al/THE MAMMOTH BOOK OF
     CLASSIC SCIENCE FICTION (1930s) $8.95
☐ Asimov, Isaac et al/THE MAMMOTH BOOK OF
     GOLDEN AGE SCIENCE FICTION (1940s) $8.95
☐ Ballard, J.G./THE DROWNED WORLD $3.95
☐ Ballard, J.G./HELLO AMERICA $3.95
☐ Ballard, J.G./HIGH RISE $3.50
☐ Ballard, J.G./THE TERMINAL BEACH $3.50
☐ Ballard, J.G./VERMILION SANDS $3.95
☐ Bingley, Margaret/SEEDS OF EVIL $3.95
☐ Borges, Jorge Luis/THE BOOK OF FANTASY
     (Trade Paper) $10.95
☐ Boucher, Anthony/THE COMPLEAT
     WEREWOLF $3.95
☐ Burroughs, Edgar Rice/A PRINCESS OF
     MARS $2.95
☐ Campbell, John W./THE MOON IS HELL! $3.95
☐ Campbell, Ramsey/DEMONS BY DAYLIGHT $3.95
☐ Dick Philip K./CLANS OF THE ALPHANE
     MOON $3.95
☐ Dick, Philip K./THE PENULTIMATE TRUTH $3.95
☐ Disch, Thomas K./CAMP CONCENTRATION $3.95
☐ Disch, Thomas K./ON WINGS OF SONG $3.95
☐ Hodgson, William H./THE HOUSE ON THE
     BORDERLAND $3.50
☐ Leiber, Fritz/YOU'RE ALL ALONE $3.95
☐ Leinster, Murray/THE FORGOTTEN PLANET $3.95
☐ Lindsay, David/SPHINX Cloth $17.95

☐ Lovecraft, H. P. & Derleth, A./THE LURKER ON THE THRESHOLD		$3.50
☐ Malzberg, Barry/BEYOND APOLLO		$3.50
☐ Malzberg, Barry/GALAXIES		$2.95
☐ Moorcock, Michael/BEHOLD THE MAN		$2.95
☐ Cawthorne and Moorcock/FANTASY: THE 100 BEST BOOKS Cloth		$15.95
☐ Pringle, David/SCIENCE FICTION: THE 100 BEST NOVELS		$7.95
☐ Siodmak, Curt/DONOVAN'S BRAIN		$3.50
☐ Sladek, John/THE MULLER-FOKKER EFFECT		$3.95
☐ Sladek, John/RODERICK		$3.95
☐ Sladek, John/RODERICK AT RANDOM		$3.95
☐ Stableford, Brian/THE WALKING SHADOW		$3.95
☐ Stevens, Francis/CITADEL OF FEAR		$3.50
☐ Stevens, Francis/CLAIMED		$3.50
☐ Stoker, Bram/THE JEWEL OF SEVEN STARS		$3.95
☐ Sturgeon, Theodore/THE DREAMING JEWELS		$3.95
☐ Sturgeon, Theodore/VENUS PLUS X		$3.95
☐ Sturgeon, Theodore/THE GOLDEN HELIX		$3.95
☐ van Vogt, A.E./COSMIC ENCOUNTER		$3.50
☐ Watson, Ian/CHEKHOV'S JOURNEY		$3.95
☐ Watson, Ian/THE EMBEDDING		$3.95
☐ Watson, Ian/MIRACLE VISITORS		$3.95
☐ Wolfe, Bernard/LIMBO		$4.95

Available from fine bookstores everywhere or use this coupon for ordering.

Carroll & Graf Publishers, Inc., 260 Fifth Avenue, N.Y., N.Y. 10001

Please send me the books I have checked above. I am enclosing $_____ (please add $1.00 per title to cover postage and handling.) Send check or money order—no cash or C.O.D.'s please. N.Y. residents please add 8¼% sales tax.

Mr/Mrs/Ms _____
Address _____
City _____ State/Zip _____
Please allow four to six weeks for delivery.